THE EYES of TANDOR

THE EYES of TANDOR

NANCY MANGINI

BookPress®
publishing • media

Any requests or questions for the author should be submitted to him directly at mangini.nancy@gmail.com.

Published in Des Moines, Iowa, by:

Bookpress Publishing
P.O. Box 71532
Des Moines, IA 50325
www.BookpressPublishing.com

Publisher's Cataloging-in-Publication Data

Names: Mangini, Nancy, author.
Title: The Eyes of Tandor / Nancy Mangini.
Description: Des Moines, IA: Bookpress Publishing, 2025.
Identifiers: LCCN: 2025909580 | ISBN: 978-1-960259-38-7
Subjects: LCSH Genetic engineering--Fiction. | Extraterrestrial beings--Fiction. | Life on other planets—Fiction. | Science fiction. | BISAC SCIENCE FICTION / General | FICTION / Science Fiction / Genetic Engineering
Classification: LCC PS3613 .A64 E94 2025 | DDC 813.6--dc23

First Edition

Printed in the United States of America

10 9 8 7 6 5 4 3 2 1

I dedicate this book to my paternal grandmother, Cleo B. Schoonover, one of the first American-born women to earn a Bachelor of Science degree in 1904 at Valparaiso University in Indiana and blaze a trail for future generations of women in my family to follow.

PREFACE

313 AD

Proclamation to the People of Rome
By Order of Emperor Constantine

Henceforth, all loyal citizens of the Empire shall follow the teachings of Orthodox Christianity. Any persons found to be practicing pagan worship or advocating apostate Christian views shall forfeit all their goods and rights of citizenship.

~

As the focused mental force of the Conclave withdrew from the quantum space inhabited by humans, Sern watched the civilization that the Tandoran Community of Keepers had "guided" toward adherence to the Plan for Order in All Things begin its inevitable descent into a thousand Earth-years of chaos and darkness.

1633 AD

Papal Edict by Pope Urban VIII

The Holy See hereby finds Galileo Galilei to be guilty of heresy in advocating for the heliocentric view of the heavens put forth by pagans in direct opposition to the Scriptures. He is therefore sentenced to be imprisoned for the rest of his life and to cease all such advocacy on pain of torture.

~

Although the Keepers had not planned to revisit the human universe so soon after the last adjustment, this particular sentient species was becoming more and more difficult to guide through the genetic manipulations that had proved so successful in other quantum realities, making more frequent intervention necessary. In the privacy and depth of its own young mind, however, Sern wondered if the Tandoran goal of controlling the evolution of others might someday lead to the destruction of its own species.

1

Today in Another Time and Place...

Sern didn't think six millennia was too young for a Tandoran to be taken seriously, even though the age of most other Keepers ranged from ten to several thousand millennia of recorded existence. After all, six millennia of service to the Plan had earned it an individual designation, short though it was, to reflect its junior status in the Community. Senior members of the Community bore more lengthy designations to reflect their positions of authority. Grendi, for example, had served the Plan for the better part of fifty millennia while Xfrenda, known informally as X, had been on the job for longer than any Tandoran could remember. As such, it was not only the most senior member of the Community of Keepers, but one of the original Founders of the Plan that all Tandorans now served, in one way or another.

Back in the time before remembering, X had discovered that Tandorans could alter the life paths of species inhabiting alternate timelines through manipulation of their genetic structures using the focused efforts of a mentally merged Community. With this discovery, it realized that Tandorans could "guide" how sentient life evolved whenever and wherever it was detected. After several millennia of study and discussion, X formed a coalition of Tandorans known as the Community of Keepers to codify the Plan for Order in All Things and began the work of harnessing sentience throughout the multiverse. Justifying its ambitions, X had convinced most Tandorans that only by controlling the development of emerging civilizations could Tandor ensure the continuation of its own superior existence.

As the last surviving member of the Plan Founders (all the others had ultimately, if mysteriously, faded from existence), X enjoyed a position of unquestioned authority on its world, so that when it commanded something be done, nearly every Tandoran, and especially members of the Community of Keepers, saw that it was done.

Every member, that is, until Sern.

Not that outright disobedience was ever an option. Sern would have been eliminated from existence immediately by its fellow Keepers had they suspected what it was thinking. But thinking was not doing, so Sern continued to flow in concert with the Community, mostly unnoticed being one of the most junior members of the group, but harboring thoughts and urges that would have shocked its companions and brought destruction upon itself had they come to light.

When a Conclave of the Keepers gathered periodically to mingle essences and observe the progress being made in the alternate universes and timelines being guided by the Community, Sern communed silently with its fellows as expected, while allowing its very private thoughts to stay hidden deep within its small, semi-solid being.

As usual, when X revealed its public mind, a common understanding emerged among the Keepers that the various species of sentient beings being guided by their efforts were acting just as they should. Except, of course, for the species calling itself *human*, which seemed to require more guidance than all other species under Tandoran control, combined!

Tandorans knew these creatures as *humonids*, solid-form beings with the kind of aggressive tendencies that could lead to their own destruction along with the destruction of other species in their quantum universe. The humonids' evolutionary timeline ran closely parallel to, if somewhat behind, that of the Tandorans and was thus watched very carefully by the Keepers as humonids had been known to veer from the Plan often enough to require concentrated efforts to bring them back under control.

But where X and the rest of the Community found satisfaction in the carefully crafted, predictable evolutionary outcomes of their charges in parallel realities and timelines, Sern sensed an underlying wrongness.

Take the humonids. By suppressing propagation of a genetic code sequence that enabled the species to produce the brain chemicals that helped them recognize value in challenge and change, the Keepers had "guided" identified leaders of the growing population to shrink from the unknown. Thus, many prominent humonids had sought only the familiar and foreseeable, turning the species back toward the preordained future dictated by the Plan—a point of pride for X and the Keepers.

But Sern saw the unfolding of events in the humonid timeline as something that should not be. Instead of triumph, it sensed that this victory made its own universe somehow smaller and less than it could be. Being young, however, and utterly alone in its view of things, Sern kept all these thoughts locked away.

"ONCE AGAIN," X intoned, "THE HUMONIDS REQUIRE REINFORCEMENT AND ADJUSTING."

"Where should we focus our merge?" sang Grendi, resonating its reply with the Tandoran leader's pronouncement.

"FIND THOSE WHO SEEK POWER IN THEIR PRIMITIVE SOCIETY. STRENGTHEN THE GENES PRODUCING FEARFULNESS WHEN CONFRONTED WITH AN UNKNOWN."

As the mental merge implemented the genetic adjustments dictated by X, the Tandoran leader decided to attempt actual thought transference, something no other Keeper had the mental muscle or authority to accomplish.

"I NOW IMPLANT VISIONS OF THE TECHNOLOGIES HUMONIDS ARE AUTHORIZED TO DISCOVER—TECHNOLOGIES THAT WILL DISTRACT AND ISOLATE THEM FROM EACH OTHER WITHIN THEIR OWN COMMUNITIES," X sang triumphantly, satisfied that the ideas it broadcast among the altered beings would soon take form and result in the programmed actions it envisioned for the troublesome species.

"...but why?" whispered a small, thin note among the Keepers who were otherwise in complete concert, and the mental music came to a sudden halt, replaced with a thunderous silence.

"WHO BREAKS THE HARMONY?" roared X.

But only silence replied.

"WHO QUESTIONS THE PLAN?"

The terrible stillness that echoed in the minds of the Community soon became unbearable. Finally, Grendi offered a desperate thought to break into the mental void that had descended on the Conclave.

"Perhaps there is one among us who does not fully understand the state of perfection in which we dwell, never having been outside of that state. Perhaps that one needs further education and a time apart to better appreciate who it is and what it is meant to do," the elder Keeper offered.

Murmured assents drummed among the assembled, but all

waited for final judgment from X, whatever terrible form that judgment might take.

After what felt like an eternity of uncertainty, X addressed the Conclave.

"IF ONE SUCH TANDORAN EXISTS WITHIN THE COMMUNITY OF KEEPERS, AS GRENDI SUGGESTS, IT MUST BE REMOVED AND RE-EDUCATED. IF THIS DOES NOT QUIET ITS QUESTIONING, IT MUST BE ELIMINATED. NOW, IDENTIFY THIS QUESTIONER! WHO CHALLENGES THE PLAN?"

But no Keeper came forward or offered to name the offender as no Tandoran had ever considered the possibility that such a rogue individual could exist in the well-ordered machine that was Tandoran society.

With unresolved discord hanging in the air, the Conclave dissolved as individual Keepers assumed their more solid states. For the first time since the Founders had instituted the Plan, the Community found itself in a disturbing state of disharmony.

X was furious.

Grendi and its peers were terrified, of X's fury and of the strange uncertainty that clouded their minds.

Sern shrank back into the throng of junior Keepers, careful to shield the sense of guilty pleasure it felt at finally having been heard.

2

Today...

When the constant buzzing of her phone finally pulled Tess Bailey out of the only deep sleep she'd had for days, the screen showed it was 2:15 a.m. As she fumbled for the device vibrating on the nightstand, Tess turned over on her side to see who could be calling her at this hour, knowing it could only be one person—Eric Chow.

"Good God, Eric," she growled, stabbing the Answer icon on the screen and bringing the phone to her ear. "What the hell is it now? Who died?"

"Tess! Tess! I know it's late, or maybe it's early, but I had to tell you as soon as I was sure! And I'm sure! And you're not going to believe it, but it's true! Honest!"

When his frantic declaration was greeted with silence, Eric dropped his normally high, thin voice to a conspiratorial low pitch.

"Are you alone?"

Another silence.

"Damn it, Tess! I need to know if anyone else is there!"

Pressing the fingers of her other hand to her throbbing temple, Tess sighed. "No, Eric. No one else is here. Just me and my aching head. Christ! Wait a minute."

Tossing the phone on the bed, Tess reached for the glass of water by the bedside, gulped down the pills she kept at the ready to head off surges of her chronic headache, and picked up the phone again. "Now what's this all about, Eric? What's true?"

"It's the genomic studies I told you about. The ones I started with your tissue samples. The ones they told me to drop. The ones they said would get me fired, blackballed from the university. But I kept looking anyway. And I found it. I really did! But now, I don't know what to do with it. I only know that if they find out what I did, I'm toast, and you might be locked up like a lab rat!"

Eric normally talked fast. Hyper, some people called him. Although usually preoccupied with some all-absorbing scientific mystery that made conversation an afterthought, tonight he was practically babbling.

Tess closed her eyes, trying to focus on what the researcher was telling her while her drugs were kicking in. Tissue samples? What was he saying? "Eric, calm down," pleaded Tess, hoping he would at least lower his voice until the pain behind her eyes subsided. "Are you talking about the tissue samples they took at UCSF last year?"

"Yes, yes! And you've got to believe me, Tess! We're both in danger!"

"Of course, I believe you, Eric," Tess moaned as her now-pounding headache reached epic proportions. "But can't it wait until tomorrow? I'm absolutely fragged!"

"No! You have to know now, and only you. Otherwise, they'll kill it!"

"Kill what, Eric? What are you talking about? Who'll kill what?"

"I can't say more on the phone. We have to meet. Do you know any place that's off the grid?"

Sighing, Tess remembered that her chapter of the Sierra Club had won a designation of Urban Sanctuary for the Baylands salt marshes along the shoreline in the South Bay to protect migratory birds on their annual flights to and from nesting grounds and offer some respite for locals who needed to get away from the noise of the plugged-in society in Silicon Valley.

"Okay, fine. Let's meet at the entrance to the Baylands, next to Moffett Field. I'll be there in about an hour."

"Thank you, Tess. You won't regret it!"

***

For many of her thirty-four years, Tess had experienced an increasing number of health problems. Chronic stomach pain, joint swelling, headaches, low-grade fevers, and a level of fatigue that someone her age was not supposed to have. When she finally decided to confront the symptoms, she was referred to the top research hospital in the area, the University of California at San Francisco's Mission Bay, where she had suffered through a dizzying array of painful, invasive testing procedures and encountered a low-level researcher named Eric Chow.

Although the test results were inconclusive, they had fascinated Chow. After running several unauthorized DNA scans on her tissues and finding that she lacked a gene necessary to make an enzyme that would safely metabolize the drug cocktail ordered for her by Dr. Pucinelli, the head honcho at the University, Chow, had called Tess to warn her that she might not live through Pucinelli's planned therapy. Eager to thank him in person for saving her from a potentially fatal medical mistake, Tess had asked the man to meet her for coffee in Palo Alto, halfway between her home in the Silicon Valley and Eric's workplace in San Francisco.

Arriving at The Coffee Spot in the Town and Country Shopping Center, Tess felt like she was stepping back into the last century's hipster era when espresso was still considered vaguely subversive. Farm implements hanging on the oak-paneled walls between black-and-white photos of student radicals from the 60s completed the impression of a place where people gathered to talk rebellion.

As she stood in the doorway, Tess spied an Asian man sitting at a small table at the back of the darkened room. When he waved at her, gesturing for her to join him, she assumed it was the Eric Chow she had spoken with on the phone. Although they'd never met in person, Tess felt the young man's appearance matched his voice perfectly—young, thin, jumpy, and uncomfortable in social situations. In other words, the type of scientist Tess was used to working with at NASA as a technical writer who could make any complex concept understandable.

As Tess pulled out a small chair across from him, Eric felt more relaxed than he had been while waiting for her. Coffee dates had never been his thing, or any date for that matter, but this woman seemed to bring a calm tolerance for his kind of social outcast that put him at an unaccustomed ease.

Tess was shorter than he'd pictured her on the telephone, about five-four, slightly built, with close-cropped red hair. Her strong jaw, piercing eyes, and determined manner made her presence in any room a memorable experience. Tess Bailey was a woman who could not be ignored.

"Thank you for coming," said Eric.

"No, thank *you*," said Tess as she hooked her purse on the back of her chair and leaned across the table on her elbows. "If it hadn't been for you, I'd probably be dead by now."

"Actually, that's what I wanted to talk about, if you don't mind. Your DNA, that is."

"What about my DNA?"

Eric paused as the teenage waitress approached their table to ask Tess what she wanted to order.

"Coffee, black," said Tess.

When the waitress retreated, Tess repeated her question with a smile, but significantly more intensity.

Caught in her gaze, Eric replied with an intensity of his own. "I've never seen anything like it. And neither has the human genome database."

"What do you mean?"

"I mean that besides the fact you don't have a common gene that makes certain protective enzymes…"

"Yes, I know, you told me."

"… you seem to have a very uncommon gene that I can't explain. Yet."

"Uncommon, how?"

"Unique. A gene that I've never seen before. Nor has the UCSF Human Genome database, which is the largest one in the world. Right now, I don't know what this gene does or what it's for. But I'd like your permission to try to find out," said the researcher, clearly excited by the prospect of tackling a new scientific mystery.

Tess thought for a moment, examining the twenty-something scientist across the table from her. Although he apparently forgot to eat so often that his clothes hung loosely from his shoulders, he seemed sincere, and she did owe him.

"Well, I'm all for pure science, no matter who conducts it. You know I write technical papers for NASA researchers, don't you?"

"Yes, it's in your medical records at UCSF."

Somewhat unnerved that this man had such intimate knowledge

of her medical and personal history, Tess hesitated, and then replied, "Fine. All I ask is that if you find something, you keep me in the loop. Before you go public with it."

"Absolutely," Eric said, sensing a kindred spirit in the pursuit of knowledge. "And I promise, I won't bother you again unless I have something concrete to report. Not even for coffee!"

And that was how they'd left it until Eric called in the middle of the night, consumed with excitement and fear, begging her to believe that he'd discovered something that could endanger both their lives.

***

The marshy salt flats at the southern end of San Francisco Bay were just barely visible as the heavy black of a moonless night sky began to give way to the gray of morning fog. As Tess pulled onto the dirt patch used for parking at the entrance to the marshland, she spied the darkened form of another car parked behind a clump of tall sedge grass.

She killed the engine and sat for a moment, breathing deeply. This cloak-and-dagger routine was unnerving and ran contrary to her up-front, tell-it-like-it-is nature. But Eric had implied that their safety could depend on being able to disappear for a while, so here she was, headache and all, ready to step out into the bone-chilling ground fog to face whatever had spooked Eric so thoroughly.

When someone tapped on her car's back window, Tess twisted and saw Eric bundled up in an oversized ski jacket, gesturing for her to get out and follow him. Tess pulled on her own coat and climbed out of the old Prius, locked it, and followed the diminutive scientist down the narrow path into the marshes.

After a mile or so, she called to him to stop, pointing to a rotting picnic table uphill from the path. Eric turned to follow, finally sitting next to her on the table's ragged bench.

"Okay, Sherlock," Tess began. "What's this all about? Why the big mystery, and why did I leave my warm bed to meet you in this backwater place?"

"Like I said on the phone, it's because of what I found out about the gene you have—the one that isn't in the database."

"I got that much from your call. Now explain it—please!" Tess demanded, somewhat surprised to find that the cold morning air actually eased her headache. She'd have to remember that since pain in various forms was her constant companions these days.

Looking out across the marsh into the expanse of blue-gray water, Eric began speaking quietly. "I believe that your unique gene, your mutation if you will, might change brain chemistry. It could allow your body to manufacture neurotransmitters in combinations and concentrations that shouldn't be possible—at least according to accepted scientific thought. Tell me, do you ever 'blank out' in the middle of a discussion? Go to a place in your head where you see things differently, understand things differently, *know* different things than everyone else?"

Tess considered his question. Yes, of course she did that. It was how she had come up with the tech start-up ideas that nobody else had considered. But it wasn't a unique trait; there were lots of start-up ideas thriving in Silicon Valley—just not hers.

"Let's say I do," Tess replied cautiously. "Is that a bad thing? It isn't like I have seizures or anything. It's just a way of seeing things."

"Exactly. It's a way of seeing things not only as they are, but as they could be. I call it *innovative vision*, IV for short, and so far as I know, you have the only genome hard-coded to turn it on."

"But wait a minute," said Tess, raising her hand to stop this line of reasoning from going any further. "People get innovative ideas all the time. Some of them even start successful companies and become very rich. Ever hear of Google or Apple, for Christ's sake? You can't tell me none of the guys who started those companies have this IV you're talking about. Look at how well they're doing! Look at how their ideas have changed the world. Maybe not for the better, I grant you, but changed it nonetheless. My brain chemistry can't be all that unique, gene or no gene."

"That was my first thought, too, so I hacked into some of the medical databases at UCSF to get a look at the DNA of the founders of some of those companies."

"You what?"

"Don't look so shocked. It's not that hard. Everyone's been to a doctor who ordered blood tests at some point in time. And despite what the government tells you about your right to privacy, it's all sitting on the grid, available to anyone who can get around the security. I can, and computer science isn't even my field! Anyway, although the genomes I compared to yours all had some underlying similarities, nobody had your specific gene."

"Fine. So like I said, having or not having my gene didn't affect their ability to exhibit this innovative vision, right?"

"Maybe," Eric admitted, "but the underlying similarities in their genomes said more to me than their lack of your mutant gene."

"Don't call it that. It makes me sound like a character in a CGI movie for kids," Tess grumbled. She was tired and hungry and cold, and although initially intrigued, she was beginning to lose patience with this nervous little man.

"Anyway," Eric went on, "each of the adult genomes I analyzed had what appeared to be an altered structure from their adolescent or pediatric sequences. And I can't be sure because I was looking at large blocks of time between the samples sent to labs, but the alterations appeared to take place right around the time each 'founder' got their great idea. Before the alteration, they all seemed to be following normal career paths in their chosen fields. They were high achievers, yes, but not innovators."

Tess looked at him as if he'd just grown a pair of horns. "Eric, you don't really mean to suggest that somebody 'hacked' into their DNA and tweaked it, do you? Because to my knowledge, that isn't possible—yet. Even with CRISPR, we're only just starting to look at the technology needed to eliminate inherited diseases. There's no way anyone could be doing what you're suggesting. No way!"

Eric looked down at the soggy earth and heaved a sigh.

"Maybe not yet, but it's coming, Tess. It's all tied up in ethical debates and patent fights right now, but we know the Chinese have been using it to tinker around with human germ cells. Who's to say they, or some other bunch of biohackers, haven't been messing with our best and brightest?"

Tess stood, not wanting to argue with him anymore. "Okay, Eric. Let's say someone or something 'fixed' these guys to be great innovators. Why should I care? The more the merrier, I say."

"Yes, but founder genomes aren't the only ones I've been tracking."

"What do you mean?" asked Tess, almost afraid of what was coming next although she was beginning to get a hint about where this conversation was heading.

"I've looked at famous, and some infamous people: power brokers, politicians, bankers, academic 'stars.' Most, if not all, have evidence of alterations taking place just before they made a big, public move like taking an action that altered the course of an industry or passing a law that buried some promising line of research, or held up financing that would have supported certain new ideas while funding other, questionable ones. And it's starting to look like a pattern!"

"Oh, great." said Tess, rubbing her temples again. "I'm out here in the wee hours of the morning, freezing my rear off with someone promoting his own personal biotech conspiracy theory. Just great."

"Listen, Eric. I appreciate what you did for me last year, more than you know, but this whole genetic manipulation thing is starting to creep me out. Let's just drop it, okay? I'll buy us a hot breakfast at Denny's, and we can part as friends."

"No. Listen to me, Tess. Don't you ever wonder why everything that's happening in the world lately seems to point us toward intellectual stagnation? Don't you ever wonder why the rich and powerful bad guys keep coming out on top?"

"No, Eric. I don't. It's just the way things are, the way the world has always been. Sometimes fools like me and my friends at NASA tilt at humanity's windmills, but after a while, we either die or get tired and quit. Now I'm tired, and I think we should both walk away and pretend this conversation never happened."

As she turned to go, Eric called out after her.

"I think it's your mutant gene that protects you from these alterations. And I think that whoever is doing this is going to notice you and find a way to take you out. And then they'll come after me for discovering the truth!"

Tess whirled around. "Really? You got me all the way out here to tell me that 'they're out to get us?' Aren't they classifying paranoia as a mental illness these days?"

"It isn't paranoia if you can prove the threat is real," Eric shouted. "Please, Tess, let me prove it to you. Then, if you still think I'm crazy, I'll disappear, and you'll never hear from me again."

As the morning fog began to thin and the sky lightened, Tess took a step backward to look at Eric and consider the situation. Here she was, conferring with a scientist whose skills she had reason to respect, telling him that his latest theory was nonsense and that he should just drop it. How many times had her friends and colleagues at NASA been treated like that before they sought out her help to explain their breakthrough findings? Just because she hadn't been able to help them break into the rarified world of VC backing or start-up funding didn't mean their discoveries weren't valid. She just hadn't figured out how to get them to the next level.

"Okay," Tess conceded. "You just used a word I can wrap my head around. Proof. If there's one thing I know about, it's scientific proof. But I warn you, I'm a tough audience. If I spot any holes in your assumptions or methodology that could influence your conclusions, I'll be out the door so fast you won't even see me leave!"

Eric blew out the breath he didn't know he was holding as his shoulders relaxed and his body shrunk back inside his ski jacket. "Thank you, Tess. Thank you. I won't let you down. I promise!"

It would take Eric several weeks to pull all his research notes together into a set of documents Tess could evaluate, so they both went back to their everyday lives. But as Tess returned to the mundane work of editing journal articles for NASA researchers to cover her living expenses while formulating new business plans for innovative start-up ideas, the theories that Eric had floated about why so many of her ventures were met with unexplainable roadblocks resonated with a new clarity.

3

But Why?

As the gathering of Keepers disbanded, the several thousand Tandorans who had ascended into the Community returned to their dwellings and the normal activities of their lives.

When Sern appeared at the entrance to its dwelling pod, its companions stopped the daily tasks to which they'd been assigned to regard it with unspoken questions.

What had happened?

Why had the Conclave ended so soon?

What did it mean to the functioning and status of their pod?

Sern turned away, unwilling to communicate with its lifemates for fear of revealing its thoughts, and thus its guilt.

But its agemates Pert and Lelt pressed forward, followed by the pod elders, Mernd and Delft.

"Respond, Sern," its pod demanded. "Help us understand."

Sern heaved a great sigh as it turned to commune with its group.

"In the midst of the great Conclave, an unidentified Keeper questioned the wisdom of the Plan."

Horror, gasps, and groans were elicited from its pod members.

"It broke the Harmony," Sern explained, "and the Conclave was dissolved until the Questioner can be identified."

"But what will become of that one?" asked Lelt, rapidly shifting between solid and liquid states to express its anxiety. "Will it be punished?"

"Of course," roared Mernd, showing its outrage by shifting to a rigidly solid form. "As it should be! Questioning brings chaos! We all know that. It's why such behavior is forbidden!"

Lelt wilted at the thought of what terrible consequences could be visited upon the questioning Keeper. Lelt never wanted anyone to suffer or be in pain.

Delft then assumed its position as the head of Sern's pod, using its solid presence to impose an unassailable authority.

"All right, Sern. What comes next? What is to be done—by us or to us—in light of this discord among the Keepers?"

"I do not know," Sern said truthfully. "No Keeper can remember it happening before, so there is no behavior pattern to follow. Perhaps the Most Wise Elders of the Community will come together to decide what is to come. Until then, I think we should go back to our lives and await their decision."

Pert, Lelt, and Mernd all bowed, accepting Sern's suggestion and returned to the semi-solid states of normal Tandoran individuals. But Delft hesitated. It had always had reservations about Sern's acceptance into the Community of Keepers at such a young age. And now, after less than a dozen Conclaves since Sern had joined, the Keepers were in disarray for the first time in memory.

"We shall see," pronounced Delft, regarding Sern with great

scrutiny. "We shall just have to see."

And with that, Sern's family returned to the tasks that each was created to perform to sustain the life of the pod and maintain their place within Tandoran society.

But as Sern turned its attention back to making hajra, the molecular soup consumed in great quantities by everyday Tandorans, it felt the burden of Delft's still solid form bearing down on it like a gathering storm.

Sern knew that Delft had never entirely approved of it, always having believed there was something amiss in the young Tandoran's nature. Whereas Lelt and Pert had been chosen from incubation for their sympathetic and pliable natures, Sern had been brought into the pod for its mental potential—a characteristic known to be more difficult to harness but possibly more valuable to the group. It was that mental ability that had identified Sern to the Keepers as a candidate for admission into the Community. When Sern had been accepted into that august body at such a young age, Delft had indeed enjoyed widespread approval for having nurtured a Keeper in its pod.

But there had been a cost. Not having the same level of mental acuity as its junior, Delft harbored a mistrust of Sern's judgment that all pod members felt, especially Sern. But without evidence of Sern's missteps, all Delft could do was stay vigilant, watching its podmate's every move.

Sern had become accustomed to Delft's suspicion of its motives and actions, but its podmates had not. Especially Lelt, who felt it had to protect Sern from Delft's disapproval and with whom Sern felt a special kinship.

"Ah, Sern," murmured Lelt when it was certain Delft was no longer within the pod circle. "It wasn't you, was it? Tell me it wasn't you! I couldn't bear for you to be blamed for this terrible deed!"

"I won't be blamed," Sern proclaimed with a confidence it did not feel. "But I also do not understand what was so terrible about the deed. Aren't we chosen for the Community because of our mental abilities? Aren't the capacities to question, analyze and understand some of those abilities?"

When it saw the look of horror taking over Lelt at the mere thought that, Sern, too, could be a questioner, it moved to sooth its lifemate with further affirmations of innocence and personal safety. After all, Lelt had been designed to care for its podmates, not enter into high-risk debates.

At the end of the work cycle, Sern nestled close to Lelt to further comfort and calm its mate. Perhaps it would all work out. Perhaps it could keep its inner questions hidden from the Community.

But with Delft's unrelenting scrutiny and its own growing sense of wrongness in the way things were, Sern doubted the peace could be kept for too much longer.

~

As it went about its task of gathering the materials to make the pod's daily requirement of hajra, a single thought continued to plague Sern—a thought that could get it erased from existence if anyone suspected it. But once posed, the thought would not leave its consciousness.

Why, he thought very quietly, *was the Tandoran Plan for Order in All Things universally believed to be superior to every other reality the universe had to offer?*

When its unusually analytical mind kept returning to the same answer—*because that is what X tells us to believe*—Sern could not get beyond the inevitable next question: *but why?*

And when the answers to that question began to emerge, each more disturbing than the last, the young Tandoran was left with the horrible feeling that it was alone in the universe, staring at a black hole of ignorance and arrogance that could engulf not only Tandorans, but all sentient life.

What if X was wrong?

What if the Keeper's careful manipulation of sentient development in other life forms was resulting not in beneficial guidance but in genocidal obstruction?

What if the very randomness in evolutionary development so feared by the Keepers was the thing that had enabled life to emerge and evolve in the first place?

What if the genetic attributes being manipulated out of existence in other sentient species by the focused minds of the Community were, in fact, the keys to those species' survival?

Then its internal dialog brought it back to its first, horrible question.

If all this is so, why are we told to believe otherwise?

Nearly fainting with the shock of thinking that X and the Founders had been, and continued to be, not only wrong, but possibly evil, Sern finally asked itself the most devastating question of all.

What could I possibly do about it?

~

As Sern and the rest of Tandoran society awaited news from the Most Wise Elders of the Keeper Community, that group discovered that it had no idea what should be done about the breach of harmony that had broken the conclave.

"Perhaps a cleansing of the entire Community is in order," suggested Grendi. "A one-by-one examination of each and every member to reauthorize its fitness to be a Keeper."

Murmurs of agreement arose from the gathering of Elder Keepers.

"But who should conduct such an examination and what should be tested?" asked Flexd, a Keeper known for its scrupulous adherence to the Plan, if not its intellectual prowess. "Who, besides X, is qualified to ferret out this questioner?"

"And how long would such a cleansing take?" asked Brendl, a Keeper who had advocated for more aggressive genetic manipulation of sentient species than the generally conservative Keepers sanctioned. "There are thousands of Keepers in the Community. Examining them all could take hundreds of cycles! How will we serve the Plan in the meantime? Do we allow the multiverse to evolve with no guidance while we clean our house?"

"IT WILL TAKE AS LONG AS IT TAKES," declared X in a tone that brooked no further discussion. "I WILL CONDUCT THE EXAMINATIONS. AND AS I DO, THE MOST WISE ELDERS WILL KEEP ME APPRISED OF THE EVOLUTIONARY PROGRESS OF EVERY SPECIES WE ARE GUIDING. IF AN EMERGENCY INTERVENTION IS NEEDED, I AND ALL THOSE WHO HAVE BEEN SUCCESSFULLY EXAMINED, WILL CONCLAVE TOGETHER."

"But X," intoned Grendi on behalf of the other Elders, "such diminished numbers will have less effect in other quantum universes. We know that as our Community grew, so did our power over the species we guide. How can we maintain that guidance if our power is lessened?"

"WE SHALL HAVE TO TRUST THAT THE RIGHTNESS OF THE PLAN WILL PREVAIL AND THAT THIS TIME OF QUESTIONING WILL SOON BE PUT TO AN END."

Subdued, the gathering of Most Wise Elders accepted X's pronouncement without question, but felt an edge of fear creep into their minds on the off chance that they themselves might be examined and found wanting by the unassailable authority of Plan Founder Xfrenda.

~

News of the Examinations spread throughout Tandoran society like a plague. Although only members of the Community of Keepers were officially notified of their need to be Examined, every Tandoran secretly feared it would be implicated somehow by the now-infamous, if anonymous, Questioner in the chaos that had resulted from the broken conclave.

Lelt, in Sern's pod, was especially fearful.

"Oh, what will become of us if X finds you unworthy?" it groaned to Sern. "What will become of you?"

"What, indeed," demanded Delft as though it knew of Sern's transgressive thoughts.

"As I said," Sern assured his lifemates, "no one knows what will happen because it has never happened before. When my time for Examination comes, I will do my best, as I have always done, to bring honor and status to this pod. Until that time, we must continue to serve the Plan as we have always done, with diligence and faith."

"Brave words," said Delft. "See that you remember them when X digs into that special mind of yours!"

Lelt groaned again. "Oh Sern! Will it hurt? What will X do to 'examine' you and the other Keepers?"

"Unknown," Sern responded, beginning to show signs of irritation for the fear and distrust it sensed. "But until it happens, I do not want to hear anything more about it from anyone here, including you, Delft, for I have given you no cause to suspect me of anything but working to the best of my ability for this family!"

As their forms solidified, Sern and Delft faced off in opposition to each other. Finally, after what seemed to be an eternity to the other podmates, Delft's form melted away into the adjoining workroom.

"Now let us all return to the hajra," said Sern with a new confidence in his pod-status, a confidence his inner questioning absolutely did not share.

~

Slowly, one by one, X undertook the monumental task of probing the minds of each member of its Community of Keepers. Given its age, however, combined with the level of its anger, every probe required nearly a half-cycle to complete.

Examinations typically began with The Summons, which told the subject to report to X's Domain—the largest and most substantial structure on Tandor. Upon arrival, the subject was brought before X for Engagement, a process requiring a physical, and ultimately, mental link. Once established, the link provided X with a means of probing deeply into the mental architecture of the subject.

Initially, X's probes sought information about the subject's attitudes toward the Plan and willingness to question established authority. At first, finding acceptable levels of reverence and mental compliance was enough to satisfy X that the subject before it was not the notorious Questioner. Of course, upon release from the link, both subject and examiner required a significant period of rest to recuperate from the ordeal, after which the subject was allowed to return to Tandoran society, and X sent out the next Summons.

When the Keepers discovered that several of their number appeared unable to fully recover from their experience, the damaged subjects were quietly dispatched to join a lower-status work pod that did not require mental acuity from its members.

Cycle after cycle, stories of this fallout from "the X Examinations" spread throughout Tandoran society. Tales abounded of formerly respected Elders enduring mental tortures that left them so injured they could only perform work reserved for those judged defective from incubation.

Thus, when the Summons came, lifemates of subjects mourned their loved ones as though catastrophe was not just possible, but inevitable. Soon, a general pall descended upon Tandoran society that reflected the sense of doom awaiting each and every pod. Normal societal functioning slowed as a growing sense of danger permeated all corners of the planet.

And although X always seemed to recover fully after each examination, owing to its superior strength of mind and will, it did not escape unscathed from the experience.

After several dozen probes, X began to develop a taste for mental voyeurism previously unknown to Tandoran adepts. At first, it indulged itself in quick peeks into the pleasure centers of its subjects to see what memories it might share, not having the time or inclination to create pleasurable memories of its own. Soon, it expanded its mental journeys to look into the dark corners that held thoughts of fear and loathing. Strangely enough, these images became even more compelling than the pleasurable ones.

As X continued its march though the mental mazes of the Keepers, it appeared to evolve into what could only be called an aberration for its species, becoming physically larger, more complex, more powerful, and more dangerous than any being Tandor had ever known.

4

Later That Year…

As Tess Bailey drove down Silicon Valley's Sand Hill Road, past the carefully groomed commercial landscapes fronting high-tech heavy-weights like Hewlett Packard, Lockheed Martin, SAP, and a seemingly endless array of law offices on the way to the bayfront highway that would take her south to Moffett Field, she kept replaying the latest encounter with the venture capital community in her mind.

"Think of a world where energy no longer depends on consumption of matter," she'd begun as the screen in the all-glass conference room flashed images of blue skies, smokeless factories, and crystal-clear seas. "Not carbon, not atoms of any kind, not anything we have to find and burn. Think of energy being available just by tapping into a closed system that already exists in physics and that could be perpetually sustained. Think of how that might change the world—and the fortunes of anyone with the foresight to see it coming."

When the six silver-haired men sitting around the conference table shifted in their chairs, clearly bored with the presentation, Tess decided to jump forward in her pitch and cut to the chase.

"Today, my partner and I are proposing to build a prototype of an energy generating system based on chemical phase change that would be inexpensive, nonpolluting, and ninety-nine percent efficient in terms of output," she stated, noting that two of the men were now at least looking in her direction.

"If properly funded in early stage development," she continued, "we could bring it online in five years and put the fossil fuel industry out of business within ten. When that happens, ground floor investors would suddenly find themselves to be the new Musks and Zuckerbergs in the Valley."

In the silence that followed, Mark Taber, a man that Tess knew all too well, turned his chair to face her directly and ask the question she knew was coming.

"Who owns the intellectual property on this, Tess?" As principal partner in the world-famous Venture Capital Coalition, Taber was used to having power and to wielding it. Either directly or indirectly, he had been involved in killing several of the ventures Tess had tried to start over the past ten years, some right at the point of launch. This time, however, she hoped that going at him right at the beginning with the sheer genius of the concept might have a chance to bring him on board.

"Right now, my partner, Dr. Richard Stonger, and NASA have equal standing on the patent application."

Taber's shoulder's relaxed and he sank confidently into his plush office chair.

"Well then, I guess it's a nonstarter, isn't it."

Turning to face his colleagues, Taber explained himself.

"Gentlemen, we all know those jarheads at NASA legal will

never negotiate a license agreement that could become a viable business plan in time to make a market window."

As the murmured assent in the room died down, Taber swiveled back to address Tess with a patronizing smirk.

"Bailey, in all the years you've been bringing me these proposals, have you ever been able to spring IP out of that bureaucratic dead end? Ever?"

Tess dropped her eyes, acknowledging his point.

"So why do you keep wasting my time, and yours? You're a smart gal, Tess. You've got brains and a boatload of business talent. Why keep swimming upstream? Why not come on board with some of the winners we've already got in the pipeline and make yourself some real money for a change?"

Exhaling as she put her laptop back in its case, Tess took a moment to form her answer—both for Taber's sake and her own.

"Because I want my brains and talent to have made a difference in the world for the time that I've got here. Selling the next hot video game or the new feature on a wearable piece of tech is not my idea of meaningful work.

Because I'm convinced that if someone with your standing in the business world really got behind one of these ideas, you could knock it loose from those 'jarheads'. After all, even they have bosses, and the bosses of their bosses get their paychecks from the US Congress, where I know you've purchased a great deal of influence, if you choose to use it."

"Now why would I cash in my political chips on a long shot that has more chance of failing than succeeding?" asked Taber with a condescending chuckle. "If I did that every time a bright idea crossed my desk, my batting average would be quite a bit lower in the start-up game. I bet on ideas that are headed for home plate. Not dreams that would take too much effort to get up to bat!"

As she ran her fingers through her short red hair, Tess took a deep breath and let out an audible sigh, resigning herself to being turned away once again.

"Fine. Gentlemen, to use Mark's annoying sports metaphor, I know my stats are in the cellar right now, but it's not because the ideas I've brought to you wouldn't have been successful if you'd decided to back them."

"Then why so many nonstarters?" Taber challenged.

"When I figure that out, Mark, you'll be one of the people I hope will be kicking himself for not getting 'on my team' when they had the chance!"

Exiting the double-wide stainless steel doors enclosing the economic center of power that fueled Silicon Valley, Tess asked herself that same question. Lately, however, her mind drifted toward the theory Eric Chow had proffered months ago—that someone or something was purposefully standing in her way.

Even taking misogyny, bureaucratic inertia, and economic downturns into account, the simple law of averages made her near-perfect record of failure not only improbable, but more and more disturbing.

***

When she arrived at the guard gate at the entrance to NASA Ames Research Center at Moffett Field in Mountain View, Tess absently reached for the hard badge that would get her through the layers of security at the former Naval Base, precautions that seemed irrelevant since the US had given up on its ambitions in space many years earlier.

Once a vibrant, bustling center for the development of the science and technologies that would take humans to other planets, Ames Research Center had fallen on the same hard times as all the other

NASA installations. Budget cuts that came with the formal ending of the manned space program in the first decade of the 21st century had relegated both the people and the projects they pursued to the scrapheap of national priorities. With no scheduled human Moon or Mars landings to work toward, NASA had disappeared from the public consciousness for the better part of a generation. Until now, few people under the age of forty even knew that it still existed as something outside the realm of historical docudramas like *Apollo 13* or classic science fiction films like *The Martian.*

Tess sighed with the familiar feeling of despair she always had as she drove past the crumbling metal skeletons of massive buildings like the huge wind tunnels used to test full-sized aircraft that were once alive with activity and were now abandoned to rust and decay.

Old, she thought, *but not dead. Not yet.*

Tess pulled into a parking space next to the small, one-story wooden building that housed what remained of the Physics and Energy Science Division. Trudging up the short flight of metal stairs, she tugged open the heavy entrance door to the sound of metal scraping on metal and entered the dark enclave of all that was left of Dr. Richard Stonger's domain—four laboratory benches, several aging computers, a variety of dusty, discarded equipment piled up against three walls, stacks of papers and binders scattered about, and a small room at the back corner of the lab where the once-famous scientist sat hunched over his desk, glaring at a glowing screen with a scowl on his deeply lined face.

"What the hell are you doing here," barked Stonger, startled by her approach. "I thought you were going to meet with the money guys today!"

"I did. It was a short meeting."

"And?" pressed the scientist with an intensity that belied his seventy-eight years.

Tess shook her head and pulled up the ancient aluminum kitchen chair with the cracking yellow naugahyde seat that Stonger kept in his office for guests. He didn't have many.

"Same as always. If NASA legal owns a piece of it, nobody's going near it."

"But didn't you tell them it would solve one of the toughest problems facing the planet today? And make them rich while we're doing it?" asked Stonger, rising to his feet as his voice rose in frustration.

"Of course, I did. But there's this unwritten law, it seems, between the finance guys and the bureaucrats to keep breakthrough ideas away from the public. It's like they're all reading from the same playbook, but it's one the rest of us aren't allowed to see. I don't know, Richard. I guess I'm just tired."

Tess absently rubbed her knees, sore from climbing up the stairs. For her, pain was a constant companion that moved around her torso, depending upon the stresses she encountered.

"You think you're tired, Tess? Wait until you're as old as me, when you can see your end coming and can't see any way to break through the walls they've built to keep you from getting anything done."

"What walls, Richard? What are you talking about?"

Since her conversation with Eric, Tess was becoming more attuned the possibility of unexplained barriers being set in her path.

Stonger began to pace as his inner sight guided him through the six decades he'd spent at NASA, beginning with the years spent interning with leaders in the emerging field of aerospace engineering and now seeming to end on the backlot of scientific obsolescence.

"When we came here to put someone on the Moon, we all worked together, sometimes around the clock, trying out new ideas that seemed crazy at the time because they'd never been tried, so we tried them. And we failed. And we kept on trying till we got it done. Back then, NASA didn't even have a legal department. There were no lines of authority, no pencil-pushers who got paid to say 'no' to anything that was new. Just bunches and bunches of smart, fired-up guys—sorry Tess, but not many women were in it back then. Nobody thought about patents. Nobody thought about making a buck off of what we were doing. We got paid to do what we loved—explore the unknown using math and physics and turn what we found into technologies that got us a little closer to the stars."

Embarrassed at his own outburst, Stonger stopped ranting long enough to see that Tess was looking at him as though seeing him for the first time.

"Sorry," he said, sitting down again. "You shouldn't let me get started. But you're the only one left who can understand the science we do here and still see over the walls they've built around it."

"Tell me more about those walls, Richard. Who do you think's putting them up?"

"The names keep changing, but the titles are always the same. Finance guys. Legal guys. Even HQ guys, although I'm told the new head honcho in DC is a decent enough sort if he'd stop listening to the bureaucrats who tell him nothing can be done anymore. Of course nothing can get done if they keep slapping the word 'Classified' on every advance we make. Don't they know that national security depends on us getting better in the sciences? And that getting better depends on sharing what we know, not hiding behind communications blackouts? Walls, I call them, just plain walls."

Tess nodded silently. During her years at Ames, she had contracted with the Agency to help dozens of scientists write legible professional papers about their work, even though the resulting documents were often hidden from the public by government or military censors. The joy in her work, however, was not the technical papers she produced, as well crafted as they were, but the special insight it gave her into the frontiers of every scientific and technical discipline—from astronomy to nanotechnology to supercomputers and beyond. And she saw it all, all the time, as disparate pieces of information dancing a wild gavotte in her brain.

At times, the dancers paused long enough to form patterns of meaning that took on sudden clarity and shape. It was then that she worked even more closely with her NASA colleagues to hone their discoveries to a point where her flashes of insight crystallized into start-up concepts—concepts that could, if supported and encouraged, become innovations.

"If it's so clear to us that this work should be getting out to help humanity, why do you think the higher ups are holding it back? Building walls, as you say? Are you seeing something that I've missed?"

Stonger let his balding head drop into his hands. "I don't know why, Tess. I only know it's happening. I can't tell you how many projects have been started and abandoned, and not for scientific or engineering reasons. It's like someone, somewhere is determined to stop every one of us who started down this road with high hopes and clear visions of what the world could become. And they're winning, damn it! We're getting old, all of us, and the older we get, the higher those walls get."

Dropping his chin to his chest, the old scientist slumped into his rickety chair and sighed.

"I know this sounds crazy, Richard," said Tess, leaning over to put a gentle hand on his shoulder. "But I may have an idea about why those walls are going up. Right now, though, it's just a theory."

As Tess shared Eric's preliminary findings with the aging physicist, his old eyes opened and shone with the intensity he'd previously reserved for the "ah-ha!" moments in his long career. When she was finished, Stonger began to believe that there might just be hope after all.

5

Came the Dawn

Even at 9 p.m., it was still light when Eric began the drive from San Francisco down the Peninsula to meet Tess at her small studio apartment in Mountain View. With daylight savings and the steadily warming climate, early September in California was growing as dry as the Middle East with every passing year. For once, though, Eric was glad for the unseasonably mild conditions as it meant he could leave the top down on his rusting blue, two-door Geo Tracer to make more room for the boxes of printouts, rolls of maps, and long whiteboard he was bringing to show Tess the validity of his claims.

It had taken nearly six months to gather it all together. He'd double and triple-checked his results and was finally able to put the data into an order that someone other than himself might be able to understand.

By the time he pulled up in front of the warren of nondescript, modular high-rise units that passed for affordable housing in the Bay

Area, it was full dark and Tess was waiting for him at the curb.

"I was beginning to think you wouldn't make it," said Tess, pulling on a sweater against the night air. "Are you still sure you want to do this?"

"Absolutely," said Eric as he climbed out of the overstuffed car. "I've emptied my lab and told UCSF I was taking some personal time. Since I've never taken any before, they were glad to get it off the books."

"What, no family to go home to? No wife? No kids?"

"No. Too much to do. Too many answers to find and not enough people asking the right questions."

"Come on, Eric. Not even a girlfriend?"

"Geez, Tess! Why do you care about my social life? If I remember right, you were sleeping alone when I called last March. Anyone new in your life since then?"

Irritated at how close Eric's remark hit home, Tess grabbed an armful of mailing tubes and turned toward the front door of the complex. "Fine. Forget it. Follow me. It's in the back on the second floor—number 202."

Working together, they slowly emptied Eric's car, filling Tess's cramped living quarters in the process. Used to San Francisco neighborhoods where anything parked on the street could be stripped of parts within twenty minutes, Eric expressed concern that someone might steal his car if he parked it in the guest lot a half block away.

"Don't worry," Tess said with a chuckle. "This is Silicon Valley. Unless it's electric, imported, or self-driving, nobody notices your car, especially if it has duct tape holding up the windows."

Not quite insulted for his choice of transportation as he had never actually given it much thought—it ran, it was easy to park, and it was cheap when he'd bought it from a grad student leaving the country—Eric parked his car and returned to set up his equipment and materials.

Propping up the five-foot-wide whiteboard on Tess's sofa bed, Eric taped a color printout of a detailed double helix in the center.

"Okay. Here's your DNA scan two and a half years ago when I found your IV gene, the one I think lets your body pump out neurotransmitters that make your brain chemistry special, to say the least. Let's call that point in time 'ground zero.'"

"Right. That was the scan that saved me from good old Dr. Puccinelli's one-way ticket to the mausoleum. By the way, thanks again for that."

"No problem. Now here are before-and-after scans of the DNA of some of the founders of successful local start-ups."

One by one, Eric taped similar printouts in a "before" row above Tess's ground zero image, then taped name-matched printouts in an "after" row below it.

"You'll recognize the names, Tess. These are guys who seemed to pluck a disruptive technology right out of the air, and suddenly the whole world was lining up to give them money."

"Don't I know it," she grumbled. "And their 'big things' never held a candle to some of the ideas I've pitched."

"Like I told you in the marshes, I think I know why. The DNA from tissue samples taken before these guys hit it big, when they were children or teenagers, all look fairly normal with certain differences you'd expect to find in non-related humans."

"Wait a minute. How do you know what a 'normal' DNA scan is supposed to look like when the genomic science to make that call hadn't been developed when those samples were taken?"

"Tess," Eric sighed impatiently. "Don't tell me you've never heard of cryostorage! They've been popping these puppies into little freezie tubes at UCSF for future research since before either of us were born. It's all legal because patients give them permission to do it in that stack of forms they make you sign when you check into the hospital. Remember?"

Tess remembered quite clearly how she felt at being treated like just another lab rat when she'd gone to see Puccinelli for the first time. Although she normally studied everything she signed in painstaking detail, the morning she came in she'd been hurried along, given a pen, and told the forms had to be signed right away as the doctor was on his way to a conference and couldn't afford any delays. So she'd signed them like everyone else and promptly forgot about the sheets of thin yellow carbon copies they'd handed her with her next appointment card. She supposed the permission language was somewhere on those copies, but like everyone else, she'd lost track of them over time.

"Point taken. But that means UCSF must have hundreds of thousands of freezie tubes stored somewhere, right? Where? And who else besides you digs into them?"

"Closer to two million at last count. And why do you think they needed that great big new facility in Mission Bay? They built it to install the newest medical hardware, like underground imaging bays, supercomputer rooms, and a very large cold storage facility for cadavers and—wait for it—more than two million freezie tubes of DNA samples from the largest cross section of humanity ever collected. No, it's not common knowledge. And yes, other researchers sometimes grab a freezie tube or two, but so far, I'm the only one who's sorted and studied the samples by life outcomes. So, we clear? Can I go on?"

Eric's attitude, like his personality, was at times, both smug and annoying. Ever since his tiger parents had insisted he play with microscopes at age three instead of blocks or trucks, he'd been labeled a bioscience prodigy, a title that had earned him a full scholarship at age fifteen to UCSF to study genomics and bioinformatics. But the PhD he'd earned at twenty-one hadn't taught him how to interact with people or curb his intellectual honesty when confronted with the star-powered egos driving the biotech world in search of fame and venture capital funding. For Eric, if the lab data didn't fit the marketing claims, he said so, right out loud to anyone and everyone.

When his grant funding predictably ran out, he took a job running medical tests in the UCSF labs to pay rent, but mostly to maintain access to the gene banks and supercomputers he believed could hold the answers to the genetic mysteries that had become a personal obsession, one of which was Tess Bailey's unique DNA.

"Go on, Eric," Tess replied patiently, recognizing his bravado as cover for feelings of inadequacy in social situations. It was a common trait among the very brilliant and the very single-minded.

"So compare the 'normal' before scans with your ground zero DNA. What do you see?"

"I see that my DNA has a section in the double helix that doesn't appear to be included in the other scans, right about here," said Tess, pointing to the area in her DNA that appeared to be structured differently from the same area in the other printouts.

"Yep, that's the place. Now look at that area on the "after" scans of these guys and tell me what you see."

Looking closely at the suspect area on the 'after' scans, Tess saw that a piece of DNA had apparently been added to the founders' structures, a piece that appeared to be the isometric opposite of her IV gene.

"Huh! It almost looks like a mirror image of my section, but backward and inside out. But where did it come from? Do these people know that their DNA's been changed?"

"I doubt that anyone, besides me, and now you, knows about it. Except, of course, for whoever or whatever did the changing. Like you said, the genomic science needed to evaluate DNA codes hasn't been understood until recently. So how would anyone have known where to look or even what to look for?"

Tess took a deep breath and sat down on one of her two folding chairs. The mild painkillers she'd taken to help her focus on whatever Eric was going to tell her were wearing off, leaving joints and various other body parts beginning to pound with a familiar ache.

Pushing her pain aside for the moment, Tess attacked the issues Eric raised by resorting to the kind of step-by-step questioning she used with NASA scientists when presented with data she couldn't explain.

"Okay, Eric. Let's back up for a moment. We may be comparing apples to oranges here unless the timelines of the DNA samples sync up between me and these other folks. Do you have a freezie tube of my DNA from back when I was their age, relatively? Without that data point as a benchmark, this gene hacking theory really can't be validated."

Once again, Eric met her challenge with a self-satisfied grin, an annoying habit Tess was having trouble ignoring as her general pain level rose.

"Of course I do. Remember those allergy tests your mom made you take when you were starting grammar school and you couldn't stop sneezing around the chalkboard? Blood tests and skin scrapes, right?"

Tess nodded, vaguely remembering the incident.

Bending down to dive into the cardboard boxes on the floor, Eric shuffled through papers as he talked.

"Turns out you were allergic to the teacher's perfume, but even back then, all those samples were shipped to UCSF for cryostorage, like everyone else's were. Ah! Here it is! The DNA scan of five-year-old Tess," said Eric, triumphantly rising to paste the printout directly above Tess's ground-zero scan in the young Founders row. With a blue marking pen, he highlighted the same gene structure in both her scans.

"As you can see, you weren't hacked. You've got the same hard-wiring you had when you were born."

Staring at the printouts, Tess took a few minutes to digest what

Eric was telling her, then launched into her next set of questions.

"Let's say, for the moment, that I believe you, Eric. These guys were altered in some way and I wasn't. If this is evidence of a conspiracy to genetically manipulate people, why them and not me? And if you say it's because I was beneath their notice because I'm female, you can take your data and march out that door right now!"

Eric put the marking pen down on the sofa, pulled up the other folding chair and sat down next to Tess. When he was seated, he took a breath and began softly, losing the arrogance he'd demonstrated when telling her about his discovery.

"No, I don't think it's a gender-based thing. I think it's because they can't get to you—not that they don't want to. I think your IV gene makes you immune, somehow, to whatever's been done—and is still being done for all we know—to those other people. And if that's true, the only way to control you is to contain you by manipulating other, non-IV humans into blocking you when you get close to making a significant difference in the world."

Tess blinked. *Can it be true?*

"Think, Tess. Of the new technologies we've adopted in the past fifty years, how many have actually improved the quality of our lives? Look at factory farming. We got more food, but we also got more chemicals in that food that probably harm us in a way non-technological family farms never would."

"How about cell phones?" asked Tess, desperate to challenge Eric's troubling hypothesis.

"Right. Cell phones have given us instantaneous communications and all the high-priced toys that go with it. But do they bring us closer together or do they help us self-isolate by feeding addictive tendencies with flashy screens instead of promoting in-the-flesh contact? Seriously, Tess, name a single advance that's been an unqualified benefit to our species. Just one."

"Space travel," Tess said with conviction. "It fired our imaginations and started an explosion of innovative work!"

"Right, and what happened to that when it began to gather steam in the 70s and 80s?"

"Well, yeah, after the moon landings, Congress pulled the funding from NASA, but we got the Space Shuttle and built the International Space Station—most of it, anyway."

"And then what? What happened to all that promising progress, Tess?"

"Okay. Politicians and bureaucrats killed it off, but the discoveries made during that time are still around, waiting to be given to the world! I know! I've been trying to do that for the last ten years! They're all still there, really!"

"Then why doesn't the world know about them? Why are they still under wraps?"

"Maybe it's me. Maybe I'm the wrong person to get them out there," sighed Tess, knowing it wasn't true but unwilling to accept the alternative.

"Or maybe you are exactly the right person and whoever is doing this knows it. Maybe, by keeping you contained, they have the best chance of blocking the kind of progress that would be threatening to them."

"Threatening, how? All I want to do is help the human race get better! How can that threaten anyone?"

Eric sat in silence for a few moments, looking at the floor. When he raised his eyes to look directly into Tess's worried face, he answered calmly.

"Maybe a human race that keeps getting better poses a threat to a nonhuman race."

And then it was Tess's turn to sit in silence.

6

The Club

Helen Miranski was nearing retirement, at least that's what her bosses at ARM Aerospace kept telling her. Apparently, it didn't matter to them that she had been one of the original developers of the supercomputer code that ran nearly every complex flight simulation at NASA and the Department of Defense. And it certainly didn't matter to them that she had devoted most of her working life to keeping ARM at the forefront of the space flight industry by working harder, faster, and more productively than the engineers in other companies competing for ARM's government contracts.

What mattered to her bosses at ARM was her age, her salary level, and most of all, her gender.

At sixty-four, with more than thirty years of experience, Helen was eligible for the same pay rates as G20 employees in the federal government, nearly $250,000 per year. Of course, she didn't get that, the company did. But ARM still had to pass on enough under California employment law that her payout rankled the top brass. And paying it out to a woman made it even worse.

Helen knew full well that nobody hired anyone in their sixties for anything anymore, unless it was for those CEO or Board Chair positions that were handed around to the boys' clubs from ivy league business schools. Now and then a Stanford or Cal Berkeley grad was tapped for a marquee position, but only after they'd made a name for themselves in the national media somehow.

In the field of computer science, age and experience were job-killers. In the Valley, the current mantra was "twenty is the new forty, and thirty is just about done!"

Never mind that Helen could code rings around the young programmers being courted by high-tech companies throughout the world. Never mind that she had successfully managed billion-dollar projects while fact-checking everyone's work to ensure the reality of success and not just the appearance of it.

She looked a bit like most hiring managers' mothers, or even grandmothers, so it was no use believing that her upcoming retirement was "a doorway to new opportunities" like the company HR director kept telling her. She knew that it was, in fact, a doorway to oblivion.

Miranski was used to making a measurable, positive difference in every endeavor she undertook, from grad school studies to women's rights political actions to international aerospace initiatives. Now, she knew fear for the first time in a very long time—the fear of irrelevance.

Before that happened, though, Helen decided to reach out to other veterans of the space age at NASA Ames to see how they were handling retirement.

What she found was not encouraging.

Most contractor employees she'd worked with had long since

been pushed out by their companies in favor of younger, cheaper workers. Those who remained were either drones who never made full use of their skills but also never made waves or those who were facing the same retirement cliff looming in front of Helen.

Although the civil servants employed directly by NASA appeared to be faring better financially, they, too, were being professionally marginalized by the massive federal bureaucracy.

Scientists who had accepted the early retirement incentives dangled in front of them by the Agency had exited their labs and their lives' work without a backward look or a forwarding address, often leaving warehouses full of binders and notebooks containing experimental data from research on projects that the government had either cancelled or underfunded to the point of extinction. Those who remained past the time their superiors at NASA HQ would have liked often found their pay rates, along with their access to test facilities and computer resources, substantially reduced. And if that wasn't enough to encourage their departure, offices they'd occupied for decades were reassigned to new hires who had little or no understanding of the basic mathematics and scientific principles that underpinned the technological tools they'd been trained to use. Relegated to inhabiting shared, low-level offices or temporary buildings that had been long abandoned by Facilities, these die-hards still came to work every day in the vain hope that someone would wake up someday to realize how shortsighted current space policy had become and reach out for their hard-won expertise.

Chief among these survivors was Helen's old friend, Richard Stonger. And although she had no plans to follow his example and become a lab mole in the Ames junkyard, she was curious about how he'd managed to keep his gate pass all these years and stay technically employed.

When a telephone call to his extension on the base went

unanswered, she knew better than to leave a message as Stonger was notorious for never returning phone calls, responding to texts, or answering emails. So that left only one option—make her way out to the tumbled-down wooden building they called temporary housing on base to see if she could buy Richard a cup of coffee and pick his still-active brain about what to do next.

***

"Finally had a bellyful, did you?" asked the aging physicist when Helen came to him for advice. "Told you not to pour out your life for those corporate peacocks."

"Seems to me you haven't done much better pouring out yours for government bureaucrats, have you?"

Helen sipped at her cold coffee, waiting for the sermon she knew was coming. Richard's rants were rarely brief, and she knew she'd opened the door to one of his favorite topics.

"Yeah, you're right. They've all gone mind-blind and tone-deaf to what we started to do out here. But we've got a lot of company, you and I. At least a dozen scientists and engineers that I know from just here at Ames have been shut out or shut down to, basically, shut them up. We're all too old, or too young, or too female, or too ethnic or too whatever to be allowed to get anything done. At least anything important."

Miranski sighed, feeling her depression deepening. If the legendary Dr. Stonger had given up, what hope was left for her?

"But I'm not done yet," said Stonger. "In fact, I may have an ace in the hole that's so far-fetched nobody but other rejects like us would think to use it."

Helen's head shot up, pinning Stonger with a piercing gaze.

"What? What are you talking about, Richard?"

"For now, I'm just going to call it the Club, at least till we get it going. About a week ago, a friend of mine, Tess Bailey, came to see me. You know Tess, the writer that fixes everyone's papers before they get sent in?"

Helen nodded. Of course she knew Tess Bailey. Everyone who worked at Ames knew about the woman who could make readable prose out of even the most jumbled lab notes. If her services were purchased to polish your work, you were sure to be published. It was known as "The Tess Touch."

"Well, she brought out a jumpy young fellow from UCSF bio something-or-other, spinning a tale that even I found hard to believe. But the more I heard and the more I thought about it, the more I think they might be on to something—something as exciting as the Apollo missions ever were, but a lot scarier."

"Scary how?"

"Before I tell you, I need your solemn promise that it will not leave this room, on paper or on your tongue. If it gets out before we get a handle on it, lives could be at stake, not the least of which would be mine—and possibly yours if you decide to sign up."

"Damn it, Richard. Sign up for what?"

At his silence, she sighed.

"All right. Fine. You have my promise. It's just between us. Now," Helen demanded with the unspoken authority that had made her a successful project manager, "*what* is so exciting, and *why* is it scary?"

Before answering, Stonger got up from behind his battered desk, walked to the hot plate that held what was left of the lukewarm coffee, and drained the glass pot into his old blue NASA mug.

"What if I told you that all the bad luck we've been having in the space program and in other areas of science wasn't actually luck at all? What if, every time someone with two brains in his head and a hunger in his heart came up with an idea that would lift us up as a species, that idea was blocked by someone or something that wanted to control how humanity developed?"

When he saw Helen rolling her eyes, he stopped and drilled her with his final question. "What if I could prove it, scientifically?"

That got her attention. Richard Stonger was not one to use the word "scientifically" lightly. If he said it, he meant it.

"You, Richard?" Helen asked, knowing his forte was physics, not politics. "How could you possibly prove such a hypothesis?"

"Okay," Stonger conceded, "not me personally, the young fellow who came here with Tess. He's a wunderkind in some kind of genetic research who's stumbled onto a set of facts that may actually be—what's the word those marketing guys use—game changing, only it's a game that nobody else knows we're playing."

"And what game is that?" asked Miranski with skepticism in her voice.

"Human evolution."

At Helen's stunned silence, the old scientist walked slowly back to the chair behind his desk, sat down, and continued.

"It seems that Tess and this young man have compiled what amounts to proof that our intellectual and societal progress is being manipulated, or at the very least directed, by some tampering with our DNA. How it's being done and by who are still unknowns, but they discovered it because, apparently, Tess is one of the few people whose genetic architecture is immune to this kind of tampering, which is why she's one of the few people who keeps trying to break through the walls they build around us here in research while most everyone else—mostly the higher-ups—seem to be building them, for one reason or another."

Before responding with the first of a thousand questions that were forming in her mind, Helen gazed at Stonger for a moment. Unlike the last time she had seen him, when he was wearing his advanced age like a heavy coat, he seemed to sit up straighter today.

Whatever outlandish theory was being proposed by Tess and her friend, it was having a tonic effect on the once formidable scientist she had watched wither under the twin burdens of increasing isolation and the professional marginalization visited on anyone who insisted on working into their seventies.

"You know genetics isn't my field, Richard. For the sake of argument, though, if this bio-researcher is right, why hasn't he been tampered with?"

"Tess thinks he's too far underground to be noticed by whoever's doing this. She thinks they're concentrating on gatekeepers like venture capitalists, company founders with innovative ideas, and high-level government guys, like the powers that be at NASA HQ."

Helen nodded and pressed further. "So what you and Tess are saying is, unless we get close to success with good ideas, we're left alone. But if it looks like we're going to get something important done, we get zapped somehow? Is that right?"

"Yep. Looks that way," said Stonger, finishing the last drop of his coffee.

"Wow."

"Exactly."

"Not that I buy it, but it explains a lot, doesn't it?"

"Yep."

Sighing, Helen gazed at the broken tarmac outside the building's dirty window. "So what now?" she asked of nobody in particular. "What are we supposed to do about all this?"

"I'm glad you asked." Stonger replied. "Because it brings me to the Club."

7

The Awakened

As the Time of Examinations progressed, it became clear that an increasing number of Keepers who underwent a probe by X emerged with reduced rank in Tandoran society—not because they had been discovered as the Questioner, but because they were judged, either by X or their colleagues, to be less dedicated to the Plan than they should have been or less able to contribute to the joined mind of the mentally-merged Community than previously thought.

As a result, most never returned to their family pods, not wanting to bring disgrace on their lifemates. Separated from all they had known and all they had been in previous cycles, they soon came to be known as the Drifters, pod-less adult Tandorans who wandered from task-center to task-center offering their labor to pods that needed temporary help, then moving on.

Although the growth of this new class of Tandorans was distressing to many in their rigidly hierarchal society, some secretly wondered what it might be like to Drift, free from their preprogrammed pod lives and able to choose each day's tasks for themselves. Of course, no Tandoran actually expressed this thought aloud where they would be subject to their pod's censure, but the thought still remained.

Sern, already feeling alone and separated from Tandoran society by its internal questioning, became increasingly curious about the life of the Drifters and hungry for the possibility that they might be able to offer new insights into its emerging fears about the Plan.

Then, early one cycle, Sern announced to its podmates that it was going to take a supply of hajra to the Drifter encampment that was forming near their home in the hope of harvest work becoming available.

"Why encourage those lowlifes?" asked Delft. "They should be ashamed to even approach high-status communities such as ours."

"Quite right," Mernd agreed, always in tune with the pronouncements of its agemate.

"But are they hungry?" Lelt asked, concerned about the welfare of any fellow Tandoran, regardless of status.

"Do you think they're dangerous?" asked Pert, who sought safety at all times.

"Of course they're dangerous," declared Delft. "Any Tandoran rejected by X who drifts pod-less is apt to do anything!"

"Even so," Sern declared. "They are still our fellow beings and deserve enough hajra to survive. We have enough to share after the last batch task, so I will take some to them in case they are in want."

"That's good of you, Sern," encouraged Lelt. "No one should be in want on Tandor."

"What about us?" demanded Delft. "What if we need that extra hajra for our own use?"

"Then I would hope our fellow Tandorans would share with us

just as I intend to share with the Drifters," Sern responded as it turned away from its podmates, gathered several containers of hajra, and began its journey to the Drifter encampment.

~

Having lived most of its existence within the confines of its family pod, Sern had never encountered anything like the gathering at the encampment. Adult Tandorans aimlessly wandering from sleep pad to sleep pad or crouching on the bare ground that surrounded Sern's village. Without podmates, individuals lived up to their title as a Drifter by remaining aloof from one another and society as a whole.

As Sern approached the ad hoc community, several older Drifters barked at him from a distance.

"What do you want from us?" yelled one particularly stooped Drifter. "We have nothing to take or give. Go away!"

The elder Tandoran reminded Sern of Delft, so it ignored the order to depart, as it would have ignored Delft during one of its many tirades, and continued its approach.

"Have we injured you in some way?" called a younger, smaller Drifter hiding behind one of the angry elders. "Have you come to hurt us, like the Examiner?"

"I have not," Sern reassured the small one whose body posture mimicked Lelt when it was frightened. "I have come to offer you hajra, if you need it."

"Why?" the Angry Drifter shouted. "We have not labored for your pod. Why would you give us hajra?"

"Because you may be in want," answered Sern, as calmly as it could. "And, as the ancient texts tell us, no Tandoran should ever be in want if others have plenty."

"What ancient texts? I never heard of texts being part of the

Plan," challenged another Angry one.

"The texts were written before the Plan came into being," Sern said. "Do you not remember your early learnings?"

"All we remember is the injustice done to us by the Examiner after we gave good service to the Plan. All we know now is labor, and misery, and loss," said yet another Angry Drifter. "Look at that one, by the rock," it continued, pointing to a shivering form sitting on the ground. "After its Examination, it couldn't even remember its designation. It just sits and quakes and mumbles apologies. And it wasn't even the Questioner—just a Keeper whose mind was damaged by X. And it's not the only one! We feed it and bring it along with us, but it cannot work and will soon be gone."

"Nevertheless," Sern insisted. "I bring hajra because my pod has plenty and you have want, and it is my duty to do so, according to the texts."

As Sern circulated slowly among the throng, offering small portions of hajra to any who appeared to be in want, it noticed that several Drifters who stood apart, but did not yell or quake or run, were following it carefully from a measured distance—not approaching, but also not fleeing. When it had distributed all that it had brought, Sern spoke directly to one of the following Drifters.

"What is it you seek, citizen? How can I be of service to you?"

After a long interval, the follower responded.

"It is not the old texts that brought you here. It is something else, something deeply hidden, is it not? What is your designation?"

"I am known as Sern."

The ensuing pause was so long that Sern thought it might be the end of the interaction. Finally, the Drifter replied.

"You are a Keeper, are you not?"

When Sern bowed its acknowledgment, the Drifter continued.

"Why do you seek us, the rejected of our class? What do you

fear? That your superiors will ask you to do us further harm or that you will one day be forced to join us—or worse?"

Now it was Sern's turn to pause.

"I seek to understand what you came to know about the Plan from your experience with the Examiner."

"Why? If you are a Keeper, you must already believe the Plan is perfect and that adherence to it is the duty of all Tandorans," said the questioner, parroting the catechism spoken by all Tandorans when they entered the ranks of the Keepers.

"Yes, that is what we are taught. But of late, I have been plagued by thoughts I cannot escape—thoughts that you and your fellow Drifters might help me to understand," admitted Sern who was suddenly terrified that it had exposed more than it intended to some possibly dangerous individuals.

"Come with us," beckoned the Drifter as it turned away from the encampment and led a small party of its fellows out into the wasteland between pod communities.

After what seemed like a very long journey, the leader slowed and turned to face Sern who was then surrounded by the others who had flowed along with them.

"Now tell us about these thoughts," the leader demanded. "No one can hear us out here, not even X."

Sern inhaled the cold, dry air, gathered its form as tightly as it could, and plunged ahead, relieved to finally share the mental demons that plagued it more every cycle. "I sometimes wonder if the Plan might not be perfect for all life-forms. I wonder if it might only be good for Tandorans. Then I wonder how it came to be that every citizen became compelled to echo the pronouncements of the Plan in such unity," Sern admitted, looking down at the bare, cracked soil in shame.

"And where do such wonderings lead you?" pressed the lead

Drifter.

Sern hesitated, searching the visage of each Drifter pressing against its form. Deciding it had come too far to retreat, it revealed its guilty secret to the group.

"To think that X may not be the Supreme Tandoran Being, but that it might be a monstrous evil leading our people—and all peoples—to ultimate destruction."

The group forming the tight circle around Sern then initiated a local mind merge, inviting Sern to enter. When it complied, one thought hung in the air.

"We have a Keeper who has awakened without being Examined. There may be hope, after all."

8

The Clubhouse

The machine shop behind the rusted remains of the Giant Planet Test Facility at NASA Ames hadn't been used since the Galileo mission to Jupiter in 1995. Like many other promising avenues of exploration, NASA had given up on sending probes to the gas giants because, according to the politicians in charge of the Agency's budget, "the scientific data gathered by these probes had no practical purpose on Earth." So the hundreds of millions of tax dollars spent to build the test facilities and hire the experts needed to make spacecraft that could withstand journeys to high-gravity environments was allowed to fall into the fiscal hole of "sunk costs," which would later be used to show how money spent on the space program was, essentially, wasted.

So when Richard Stonger submitted a handwritten request to Max Greeber in Facilities to use the old shop as a social club, offering to evict the rats, putty up the cracks, sweep it out and paint the inside, Max saw it as a win-win-win for all concerned. With one less crumbling structure to oversee, he could use more of his dwindling personnel resources to respond to the daily infrastructure emergencies that plagued the underfunded Center.

"Great," Max responded in a handwritten note of his own which he left in Stonger's mail slot. Everyone knew Stonger was unreliable when it came to phone messages and email. "Just don't ask for any help or materials from me, and I'll leave you to it."

Stonger couldn't have been more pleased. "Leaving him to it" was exactly what he wanted.

But when he and Tess braced their shoulders against the unlocked door of the old shop and pushed with all their strength, nothing budged.

"Something's blocking the entrance," the old scientist said, puffing from the exertion. "Something heavy."

"Stop, Richard," Tess pleaded. "I don't want you having a heart attack before we even get in!"

"Fat chance! Let's peek in that high window and see what's in the way."

As directed, Tess climbed up onto a rickety table left outside the shop and peered through the dusty glass to see several large filing cabinets stationed across the inside entrance. How, she wondered, had someone done that and still managed to exit the building?

"It's an old trick we used to use when we didn't want the NASA auditors stripping all our machine tools from shops that got closed after missions were completed, or more often, abandoned," explained Stonger. "If they needed heavy equipment to open a door to an abandoned building, they usually left it and went on to an easier carcass to pick."

Moving around to the back of the structure, Stonger poked and pulled at a few side panels until two jiggled loose.

"Aha!" he crowed. "Good old Murphy! He was in charge of this place until they shut it down along with the Giant Planet program. He's gone now, retired I think, but he knew every square inch of this shop and could make anything you could think up with the tools inside—as long as it was made out of metal."

The two explorers pried the loose panels apart far enough to squeeze through the gap and enter the musty cavern that once held a vibrant workforce of scientists, mechanics, and engineers.

"Geez, Richard," Tess exclaimed, waving aside the dust and cobwebs floating in the newly disturbed air. "Look at all this equipment! There must be two hundred thousand dollars worth of machine tools in this place!"

Sweeping her flashlight beam around the shop and into the darkened corners, she found bins of metal fabrication supplies, specialized hand tools, and some custom-made parts that had obviously been crafted right there under the now-sagging roof.

"See? I told you this would be a bonanza if we could get access to it and keep it under wraps at the same time! There isn't anything that couldn't be made here with the right people working on it!"

"Under wraps? How are we going to keep the brass thinking this is just a social club once we start making things? The power use alone, not to mention the noise, will give us away in a heartbeat!"

Stonger chuckled.

"Not to worry, my girl. I've got it all figured out. We use solar panels and battery backup systems for power and build an insulation envelope around the big machines that will hide and muffle their operation, like a false front in the Old West. And we keep elevator music playing in the background twenty-four-seven blaring out the most annoying seventies and eighties pieces you can find to cover activity inside."

Ignoring Tess's skeptical stare, Stonger started ticking off requirements for the project on his fingers.

"First, we need a crew, members of the Club, so to speak. If this were the old days, I'd pull together a team with a project scientist—which could be me, if I last that long—a chief engineer to honcho all the how-tos, a mission design engineer to figure out the exo-atmospheric trajectories we'll need to tackle, a systems engineer to make sure everyone works and plays well together, mechanical design engineers—notice I said 'engineers' as this might mean structural guys, material guys, aerospace guys, and such—a propulsion expert to make sure we can deliver enough juice to get where we want to go, a GNC guy with a really good handle on communication systems, and of course, a test engineer or two.

So let's see, that means our Club needs about ten more people, besides you and me. Then, of course, there's the hardware, but we can figure that out as we go."

Tess stared at her friend for a moment, wondering how to bring him back to reality without robbing him of the enthusiasm this fantasy plan had sparked in his previously gloomy demeanor.

"Richard, let's talk about this and take things one at a time."

"Okay. Talk."

"We agree, for now, that someone or something is messing with the genes of certain people on Earth to keep them from helping us evolve in a positive way. Right?"

"Right."

"But we don't know for sure how it's being done yet. Right?" Tess asked.

"Your friend Eric thinks it's some kind of force coming from off-planet."

Tess sighed. "Yes, he does, but the only way to test that theory is to detect that force either as it's being introduced into our biosphere or as it's being applied to someone's DNA."

"Exactly! And since nobody we know has the means or power or position to monitor the world of genetic manipulation, we've got to use the means, power, and position we do have to detect that force as it comes to us from somewhere in space."

"What means?" Tess asked, her voice rising in the frustration she felt trying to explain a simple concept to someone who wasn't listening. "What position? What power? We are one elderly, discredited physicist—sorry, Richard, but you know it's true—one failed female entrepreneur who has been consistently ignored by everyone in the venture capital community, and one runaway biotechnologist with a set of pirated data and an outlandish theory about how the world works based on one data set. How, exactly, do we use those resources to detect an invading force from outer space?"

Stonger took a step toward Tess, placed two wrinkled hands on her hunched shoulders, and answered her complaint in a voice that Tess had never heard him use before—a strong, confident voice from a man who needed to be heard. "By enlisting the talent, vision, drive, and genius of people that NASA has discarded or pushed aside over the years to join a team—a club, if you will—and pursue an underground mission. Together, we'll design, build, and launch a small spacecraft into high Earth orbit that will look for any unexplained forces entering our biosphere. And if we're successful, and Eric is right, that discovery should be enough for the governments of the world, not just the US, to help us figure out a way to stop it. That's how."

In the space left between the two friends and the thoughts lingering in the musty air of the abandoned machine shop, Tess began to visualize what might be possible in this most unlikely of environments if "the club" ever became a reality.

Several weeks later, in less time than Tess had imagined, they were holding their first meeting in Tess's studio apartment.

9

The Hilbert Spacers

Tess hadn't believed six adults could fit into the small living area in her studio apartment, let alone a dozen, but somehow everyone found a space to stand in or a surface to sit on.

Richard Stonger, standing in the kitchen alcove with Tess and Eric on either side, addressed the gathering.

"Thank you all for coming. I know I wasn't very clear on what this meeting was all about when I called you. I told you it would be worth your while to listen to what we've got to say, but I didn't tell you why. Before we go any further, you should all know that what you hear tonight and what we're proposing to do about it is not without risk, either to you personally or to your careers. So I want you to ask yourselves if you're comfortable with pushing some boundaries—some of them possibly legal. If you're not, then please help yourself to some coffee and cookies and leave without any knowledge of what we may be undertaking. Take a minute or two to think about it. No hard feelings, honest. I'll tell you right now, it's going to be a rough ride; exciting as hell, but sort of like one of those early Moon launches when the astronauts didn't have parachutes or escape vehicles."

The old scientist paused for a few minutes to search the faces of each person in the room. To his satisfaction, nobody looked uncertain or made any moves toward the door. But given their personal histories, it was not surprising that they were all-in, even at this first step.

"Okay. With no apparent objections or defections, I'll get right to the point. I've asked you all here to be part of a clandestine team that will design, build, launch, and operate a small spacecraft, a CubeSat actually, that is utterly unsanctioned by any government or organization on the planet. We'll do it in secret by using what you all have in buckets—brains, talent, experience, and a can-do attitude."

A cough came from the audience, followed by a hand in the air.

"Yes, Mike?" Stonger acknowledged a gray-haired man sitting on the arm of Tess's sofa bed. "Ladies and gentlemen, if you don't already know, this is the legendary Michael Murphy, former guru of all things mechanical at NASA Ames."

"Thanks for the props, Richard," said Murphy. "But what we don't have in buckets, to do this thing you're talking about, is money. Unless I haven't heard about someone in here winning the lottery, where, exactly, is the funding going to come from to do something like this?"

"Ah," Stonger replied. "Now I want to introduce you to your hostess, Tess Bailey, whom many of you already know if you've ever published anything in your field. Tess, you want to answer Mike's question?"

Tess stepped forward to stand by Stonger, looking around the room as curiosity grew on the gathered faces. "Hi, there. Welcome to my little home. Some of you I know, and I look forward to meeting the rest of you."

As her heart pounded in her ears, Tess felt like she was inhabiting someone else's body. All her life she'd prided herself on dealing in and carefully explaining real, hard science. She'd come to NASA Ames with solid academic credentials in mathematics, chemistry, biology, and business, eager to put her skills to use to help the people she considered to be the smartest on Earth reveal the wonders of their discoveries to the rest of the world. Yet here she was, about to ask these very people to take a leap of faith with her into the unscientific realm of conspiracy theories. It was almost surreal.

"You may or may not know that I've been pitching your ideas to local venture capitalists for a few years now, ideas which they have universally declined to fund. This worried me because they were great ideas, full of promise for improving things like energy use, building materials, and airline fuels. Things we all agree humanity needs. Then about six months ago, my friend here, Dr. Eric Chow, stumbled onto what might be an explanation for it all. Eric is a geneticist—a biotechnologist, if you will. I know that's a subject area foreign to most of you, but it's at the heart of why we're going to try to send up a skunk-works satellite. Eric found—and I'll explain how later if you're interested—that some of the higher-ups around here may have had their DNA altered when they came into positions of power. We think this was done to influence their decisions about which technologies to foster and which to suppress. And yes, he does have anecdotal and mathematical proof of his theory. What he doesn't have is experimental proof. That's what this project is all about. Getting the hard data to prove whether this is happening so we can bring it to the attention of the world."

When she saw keen interest replace skeptical curiosity in her audience, Tess motioned to the nervous researcher standing on the other side of Stonger to come forward and face the group. "Eric, you're on."

Before speaking, Eric held each gaze in the room for a heartbeat or two. As was his habit, he got right to the point. "I'm Eric Chow, and as Tess said, I work with genes—specifically human genes. It's well known, at least among geneticists, that there's a section in our DNA that tells our nervous systems, our brains, to be open to new ideas or to run away from them and hunker down in our caves. Humans who tolerate new ideas and high-risk situations have a slightly different genetic structure—I call it the IV region for innovative vision—than the majority of the population, which instinctively perceives anything new as dangerous and avoids it. These IV folks are the ones we usually call innovators until recently, when many, if not most, of them turned away from truly innovative leaps in favor of safer, older ways of thinking and acting. My data show that they made this turn when scans of their genomes showed their original IV regions had been altered to look more like the general population. In effect, they'd been blunted."

A hand shot up from one of the younger members of the group. "Hi. Ben Fischer, here. NASA Ames, Electronics and Communications—at least when we had something electronic to communicate with other than the ISS and the Mars rovers. Eric, is it?"

Chow nodded.

"Eric, how did this happen to these people? What caused this 'blunting' in your opinion?"

Eric looked down and then back up. "I don't know for sure. But in my experience in the genetics labs at UCSF, the only force we know of that can accomplish such a modification is radiation of some kind. Unfortunately, all the frequencies we use in medicine have such a broad spectrum—they're used to kill cancer cells, you know—that I don't know which portion of the spectrum modifies genetic structures. And nobody is looking at that yet because there's no money in it."

"Well what about that gene-editing thing that's getting so much press these days? Couldn't these guys have been CRISPR-ed by a competitor or something?" Fischer asked.

Eric shot Tess a look that said, *See? I told you so!*

"In theory, yes. But it would take the full knowledge and cooperation of the person whose DNA is being edited, which is why clinical trials in humans are only happening with people trying to get rid of a genetic disease. Also, the process is painful and time-consuming. So what we have here is genetic alteration without consent, let alone knowledge," replied Chow, plowing on. "Now you might ask why Tess and I and Dr. Stonger, and probably all of you, haven't been edited too. We think it's because none of us are visible to the general public or keep positions of power, meaning we're not gatekeepers. So whoever or whatever is doing this feels no need to attack people at our level."

Tess stepped forward, putting a hand on Eric's shoulder to take the floor again.

"But there's one more thing you need to know. This whole thing came about because Eric discovered that my own IV region is structurally unique, making me immune to this type of genetic editing. From that data point, Eric has identified several other individuals here in the Valley who get medical services from UCSF and have a similar genetic anomaly. As you might expect, they are known as lone wolves, outliers in the start-up culture. But because they haven't been blunted, they've been able to push forward one or two truly progressive ideas that allowed them to achieve some wealth before their boards of directors or our government managed to push them out. So to answer your question, Mike, this is where our money is going to come from. I've already pitched the plan to these people, and they are on board for whatever it takes, as long as they remain anonymous and we stay completely underground and off the radar."

The silence that had descended on the assembly was suddenly broken by a chorus of exclamations: "Wow!" "Really?" "Good God!"

When the cacophony finally settled down, a young, attractive Asian woman sitting on the sofa bed next to Murphy spoke up.

"This is a lot to take in all at once. Before I hear any more, I'd like to know who my fellow conspirators are. How about we go around the room and introduce ourselves? As for me, I'm Anna Tran, materials scientist by title, but generally ignored lab rat to my male colleagues."

"I know how that feels," agreed the middle-aged woman standing near the door. "Helen Miranski, soon-to-be-retired-against-my-will project manager and systems engineer for most of the missions flown at NASA over the past twenty years. Apparently they don't like my age, gender, or outspoken nature anymore. Makes the brass at my company, ARM, uncomfortable."

An older man sitting on the other side of Anna Tran cleared his throat and spoke next.

"I'm Dick Rauch. Sort of like Mike over there, I was a chief engineer at Ames for a few decades until someone in HQ decided I'd outlived my usefulness and was 'defunded' into an early retirement. Since then, I've been contracting with coastal cities to help them figure out how to build defenses against the rising sea levels we're seeing everywhere. But it's shoveling sand against the tide, and I'm getting tired of being on the losing end of things. As an engineer, though, I'd want to know what this CubeSat was supposed to accomplish before signing up to make one. What's it supposed to do, exactly?"

Stonger stepped forward to answer Rauch's question.

"Dick, it's going scan for, detect, and communicate the existence of the unknown radiation beam or beams we think have been messing with our best and brightest, that's what."

"Hmm," Rauch replied. "Let me think about that for a while."

Turning to face the tall, graying, dark-skinned man standing behind the sofa bed, Rauch asked, "What's your take, Prasad?"

"Being asked for my opinion is indeed refreshing. Thank you, Dick. I am Prasad Shandra, Aerospace Engineer. At least I try to be. Since this appears to be a group of current or soon-to-be outsiders in the Ames community, I'll share my background with you to show how I qualify for that distinction. Although I came to this country to work for NASA twenty-eight years ago, I finally decided to become a US citizen last year, whereupon my family in India demanded that I return home to work for the Indian Space Agency. And in truth, India is making more progress in space science these days than the US has, but I refused to return and told them that America is now my home. Since then, they have basically disowned me. On top of that, the growing distrust of all brown people in this country has made me somewhat of a target at NASA—not overt, but pernicious. So in a sense, I am a rocket scientist without a country, looking for a way to ply my trade with people I respect. What do I think, Dick? I think anything is possible with the right combination of people, resources, and passion. And yes, depending upon the skill of those here, I think we may be able to construct and launch this detection device you want. But it still remains to be seen."

Another white-haired Caucasian man shifted on his chair to address the group in a low-pitched voice.

"Greg Banyon. They used to call me a mission design engineer, doing guidance, navigation, and control. Of course, that was back when we *had* missions to design, guide, navigate, and control. Now I'm mostly an on-call math geek, I guess, because I can still whisper to the supercomputers, but my bosses have made it clear I'm mostly extra baggage and that I should be looking for some other way to make a living. But what I love, what I've always loved, is figuring out trajectories for spacecraft flying outside our atmosphere—trajectories that I can guarantee will get the ships where we want them to go.

I just can't imagine finding something else to do that I'd even want to try. So if you're planning to fly anything up there, count me in."

"That's great, Greg, but first we've got to design and build that puppy," boomed a robust middle-aged man who looked more like a weight lifter than a scientist or engineer. "I'm Chuck Maddock. You've told us what you want this little spacecraft to do, so I can tell you how to build it. Back in the day, we used to call that structural engineering when NASA still paid for people to engineer structures. Like Dick and Mike, I was put out to pasture when they started doing more tearing down than building up around here. I still build stuff, office towers and the like, but that stuff usually stays put. The real fun is building something that can fly, hold up under launch and re-entry pressures, and survive in space for however long it's needed. If that's what you're proposing we take on here, for whatever reason, even if it's on our own, deal me in. As far as I'm concerned, it's high time we got back to the work we started out to do!"

Stonger waited for a few beats, then walked up to the only person in the room who hadn't spoken yet.

"Well, Ernie? What about you?"

Ernie Scott, a smallish bearded man in his late fifties, remained quiet until others in the room began to shift their weight and shuffle. Finally, he responded to the question Stonger left hanging in the air.

"I have a wife and two kids in college. Even if my working life isn't as fulfilling as it used to be, I don't know that what you're proposing is worth risking their futures for. You all know that at least one out of three missions fail at some stage or other, even *with* the backing of NASA management. So far, I haven't heard anything about anyone being able to implement the functional test protocols that every mission we've ever undertaken has needed to have a good chance of success. Remember LCROSS? If it hadn't been for my mission management and test algorithms, that satellite never would have made it to the moon, let alone created the impact we needed to find water in the lunar dust."

The group grunted their acknowledgment of the inherent risks in working on any aerospace project.

"So if it does fail, what then?" Scott said. "We're all fired? Disgraced? Broke? Or maybe even jailed? I don't know, Richard, it just sounds awfully thin to me."

Stonger took a chair opposite Scott and spoke to him one-on-one, with everyone else in the room hanging on the exchange. "That's exactly why we need you, Ernie. You're the best damn test engineer NASA ever saw, when you had something to test. You've found flaws that nobody else even thought to look for and gave mission teams time to fix them. We all know that the last Mars Rover would never have made a successful descent without your input three days before it was launched. We need you to do the same thing for us. Bring your special way of seeing things to the party so we have a chance to be successful. That's all most of us in aerospace want and have ever wanted—a chance to succeed."

"But if we take that chance and still fail? What happens then?" repeated the reluctant engineer. "I'm not hearing a good enough answer."

Tess stepped up. She knew everyone else was secretly pondering the question Scott had raised. "Then mankind, your wife and children included, will continue to go down somebody else's idea of our evolutionary path instead of having the chance to create our own destiny. Yes, it's a long shot. But you, like everyone else in this room, have seen and lived through the seemingly incomprehensible wrong turns humanity is making more and more of these days. At some level, we all feel the wrongness and fear of where these turns are taking us. This mission, our mission, is about trying to figure out how and why it's happening, and then maybe we'll have a chance to get back on track. Everyone in this room has been invited for the same reason. Without your special capabilities, it can't be done. But if we all sign up to give it our best, we may, at least, have a chance."

Taking the handoff from Tess to make a final pitch, Stonger concluded his appeal.

"Look, Ernie. There are no sure things in this life, but your special skill is to test the hell out of every step in this process."

Scott looked around the room at the people he'd worked with throughout his professional life and who had trusted him to be their backup throughout theirs. Finally, he drilled Stonger and Tess with a straightforward gaze.

"Okay, I'm in. But understand, I get to pull the plug on this thing if and when I see holes that can only be filled by wishful thinking and alien conspiracy theories."

"Done," replied Stonger with obvious relief. "Done."

After a collective sigh throughout the room, Helen Miranski spoke up.

"Okay, Richard, you've got your team. Now where, physically, will we be doing all this, and just as importantly, what will we call ourselves? You know every mission team needs a great name for the history books!"

"We'll be headquartered in the old boarded-up machine shop behind what used to be the Giant Planet Test Facility before they tore it down for scrap metal. Tess and I have already checked it out, and as Mike can tell you, he managed to discourage the scavenger corps from appropriating the machine tools in there."

Murphy nodded with authority.

"Nobody strips my workshops but me, even when I'm not there anymore!"

Then Tess took the floor once again.

"I think I have the perfect name both for the mission and our cover story of being a social club for bridge players. We'll use the name that was given to a lounge in one of the Ames Reentry Branch buildings. They called it the Hilbert Space as a nod to their math geeks. So we'll call our club the Hilbert Spacers, and our mission will be known as 'Small Slam'!"

***

When everyone finally left, Eric offered to stay behind to help Tess clean up the apartment.

"Thanks, Eric, but I'm just going pile everything in the sink tonight. It's getting late, and I'm really beat," she said through a yawn.

"Um, actually, I wanted to talk to you about something else," Eric said. "I didn't want to mention it until I knew for sure this was really going to happen. But now that it looks like you have an actual team pulled together, I need to tell you that UCSF officially cut me loose this week."

When Tess looked up from the sink to stare at him, Eric went on quickly.

"I guess Puccinelli finally convinced the administration it wasn't worth the trouble to keep me around, even in the labs. So as of this Friday, I've got no visible means of support and may not be able to stick around."

"Whoa! Wait a minute! You're telling me this now? When Richard and I just put our reputations on the line to back your theory? What the hell, Eric?"

"Yeah, I know, Tess. Bad timing all around."

"You think?"

"There *is* a way to keep it going, though, if you'll agree to it."

"And what is that?"

"Look. I'm not totally destitute. I've got a few dollars in the bank and can probably get a part-time lab tech job nearby to cover food and gas, but without the job at UCSF, I can't pay Bay Area rents anymore. So how about letting me bunk here with you? That way, I can be closer to the action and on-call for Small Slam, if I'm needed."

Leaning on the sink, Tess sighed and shook her head.

"In case you haven't noticed, Eric, there's only one bed in this place, and I have no intentions of sharing it with you or anyone else. So forget it. Not gonna happen."

"No one else? Really?"

"Look. I've known for a very long time that I'm never going to be anybody's idea of a prom queen. I'm smart, I say what I mean, and I have a really low bullshit tolerance, which automatically makes me a threat to most men and a lot of women. And I'm sick a lot, always have been. I decided some time back that being on my own was probably best for everyone. It's just who I am, and more importantly, who I'm not."

"What do you mean? Who you're not?"

"I'm not that female you see rising to the top of anything because she slept her way there. If I ever get anywhere in this life, it'll be because I earned it with what I've got from the neck up, not the waist down!"

After a moment, Eric blew out the breath he'd been holding and chuckled.

"Well, Tess, you've got no worries in that department with me. Truth is, I'm not all that interested in women. Men, either, for that matter."

"Seriously?"

"Scout's honor, even though I've never been a scout," he said, grinning. "In case you haven't noticed yet, the only thing I really care about is science and getting to the heart of things. Relationships just get in the way. So how about it? Can I stay? I won't be a bother, honest!"

“Oh, please! You’ve been nothing but a bother since I met you. But you’re right. If we’re going to go forward with this project, you’ll have to be around to keep us moving in the right direction. Fine. You can stay. But you’ll bunk on the floor in a sleeping bag, or the deal is off. And if you snore, you’ll sleep in the bathtub!”

10

Examination

It was almost a relief when the summons for Examination finally arrived at Sern's pod. So many cycles had passed since the interrogations had started that Sern began to feel it was slowly being run to ground as more and more Keepers either passed or failed the ordeal and joined the growing number of Drifters.

As expected, Delft received the dreaded summons with a mixture of alarm and triumph, alarm at its pod being the focus of any of X's thoughts and triumph at the possibility of being correct about its predictions that Sern would someday bring ruin and disgrace to the family.

"Sern is to appear for Examination at X's Domain before the next cycle begins," announced Delft with its customary ominous overtones.

Groans emerged from everyone, including Sern. It was one thing to be relieved of the stress of waiting, but quite another to be facing the trial itself.

"Oh, Sern," wailed Lelt. "What will become of you if X is displeased? How will you survive?"

"For that matter," howled Pert, "how will our pod survive?"

"Do not be concerned," Sern assured them. "I am confident that X will find me acceptable."

"And what do you base this confidence on?" demanded Delft. "Older, more experienced Keepers than you have gone before X and have been found wanting. What makes you believe you will come out whole when many before you have been broken? You, one of the youngest of all Keepers! You, who questions the authority of your own pod elders!"

Backing up its lifemate, Mernd expressed the thought that had plagued the entire pod for some time, though it had been left unspoken.

"Perhaps, if X finds you unacceptable to remain within the Keeper Community, you will return to your original station within this pod and take up the duties for which you were designed—to humbly serve and provide for the needs of this family. What you were meant to do, Sern. Serve and provide, not question."

"When have I ever failed to serve and provide for the needs of this family? Have we not all enjoyed increased status and larger portions of the haj harvest since I was accepted into the Keepers?" asked Sern, bristling at the combined attack of its elders.

"But you still oppose and question elders to whom you should offer total obedience," answered Delft. "It is that opposition in your nature that makes you a danger to this family, and perhaps, even to the Plan. But X will know of your defective nature soon enough. And when it does, know this: you will not be allowed to further disgrace this family by reentering the pod, at any level."

"So to you, it's pass the Examination or die. Is that right, Delft?"

asked Sern quietly.

"No!" cried Lelt. "It didn't mean that. Did you, Delft?"

"You are correct, Sern. Take the knowledge with you into X's Domain that your acceptance in this pod depends on the outcome of its Examination. And I will hear no more about the matter from you or anyone else until the results are known," Delft declared, moving away from its assembled podmates to the sounds of distress being broadcast in its wake.

~

Holding station by the entrance to X's Domain, the senior Keeper, Grendi, gestured to Sern as it approached, halting its progress.

"Your designation, Keeper," demanded the elder guard.

"Sern, from Jailar Pod."

"You are prompt," the guard acknowledged after referring to the list of Keepers summoned to appear before the end of the cycle. "Eager to be in the presence of X, are you?"

Ignoring the implied disrespect in the guard's tone, Sern simply bowed.

"Follow me," barked the elder. "And don't lag. X has others to examine before the end of this session."

Immediately upon entering the lofted chamber that held the personage of the most powerful being on the planet, Sern felt a sense of heaviness in the air, pushing it to breathe faster than normal, which in turn, began to make it a bit dizzy.

Be calm, Sern cautioned itself. *You've been warned of this.*

Perched on an elevated platform at the end of the hall stood a Tandoran unlike any Sern had ever seen. Older, with more layers than seemed possible for one body to uphold in any form, this being occupied the entire stage, edge to edge. As the young Keeper made its way toward to platform, it heard a booming voice within its mind.

"COME CLOSER!"

Upon reaching the edge of the platform, Sern halted its progress and remained looking down before the object of its terror.

"OPEN YOUR MIND TO ME. NOW!" X commanded.

Sern felt blown backward by the force of the mentality thrown against it, but so far, the force remained outside its inner thoughts, scouring only those surface images Sern had placed so carefully for X to detect.

"OPEN, I SAY, OR I WILL END YOUR ABILITY TO THINK AT ALL!"

With practiced reluctance, Sern opened one small section of its mind at a time to the invasion of X's powerful presence, each section revealing a deeper and deeper reverence for the Plan, for X's leadership, and for Sern's role in assisting the Keeper Community to adjust the evolutionary trajectories of non-Tandoran species.

But X was looking for more than loyalty and reverence. It was looking for passions that could drive the young Tandoran, passions that X might appropriate to use and enjoy for itself.

Soon the mental invasion broadened into Sern's emotional psyche, a place it had not thought to protect. There X found roiling anger held under tight control, anger that could kill if ever released. Anger at what, though, was unclear.

Interesting, thought X. *This young Keeper could be an effective weapon if that rage was properly directed. It seems to worship me and the Plan, but it is too dangerous a being to leave out in the population.*

"STAY, SERN," X commanded unexpectedly. "GRENDI, TAKE UP YOUR STATION. EXAMINATIONS ARE FINISHED FOR THIS CYCLE."

"But, Master," the old guard protested, "many more await your inspection."

"PUT THEM INTO THE NEXT CYCLE AND SEND THEM AWAY. NOW!"

After all the waiting and worrying and preparing and withstanding, Sern felt so drained it might have collapsed had X not flowed from its platform to hover over the young Tandoran.

"YOU ARE YOUNG AND STRONG AND APPARENTLY LOYAL. YOU WILL SERVE HERE IN MY DOMAIN, IN MY BODYWATCH."

With this pronouncement, Sern did collapse, but only after the immense persona of X had left the hall. When it returned to consciousness, Grendi was instructing several lower-level members of the Domain to take Sern to its new quarters, allow it to feed, and make it ready to serve their master. Exactly how Sern was to do that was not yet clear.

~

Delft was not pleased. It had looked forward to Sern being pushed down into its rightful place at the lowest level of Tandoran society. Instead, notice had come that Sern was to be promoted to serve the great X personally, living in its Domain. Of course, such an honor brought great respect and even higher status to Delft's pod for having brought forth such a worthy Keeper at such a young age. But Delft hungered for vindication in the eyes of its podmates, vindication of its distrust of Sern and its constant denigration of Sern's abilities.

It was just too bitter to take in, and not at all fair.

~

In the Drifter encampments scattered across the Tandoran plains, a thin tendril of hope made its way from outcast to outcast as one of their own crossed the threshold into the halls of power.

11

Slamming

When Max Greeber finally put in an appearance at Stonger's club, officially designated the Hilbert Space in the facilities inventory, he could hardly believe the transformation that had taken place in the few months since Stonger had submitted his request to use the ramshackle old building for social gatherings.

Although the outside still looked like a candidate for demolition with its rusting metal panels and faded stencils announcing a once-useful purpose as a machine shop, there was now a new, hand-painted sign over the freely swinging entrance doors that said:

HOME OF THE HILBERT SPACERS.
COME IN AND PLAY WITH US!

Inside, Greeber saw that the members of Stonger's club had come through, not only with the cosmetic improvements the old physicist had promised, but with some very sharp structural upgrades as well.

Interior walls, once covered with dust and cobwebs, were now lined with a new-looking pocked beige quilting material that gave the inside space a cozy feeling while deadening any sound that might emanate from activities inside—not that the NASA retirees playing cards at the tables scattered throughout the room would be having any wild, noisy parties. But still, Max was pleased that the elevator music coming from speakers in the corners of the room could not be heard from the outside.

And then there was the space itself. It looked like the group had decided to concentrate their refurbishing efforts on the front part of the building, walling off the back area where old, rusting machine tools would have been stored. The new wall was obviously a prefab from the local home improvement store, but solidly installed and lined with the same, sound-deadening material that enhanced the other interior walls. No door or other entrance could be detected through the new wall to the back area, so Greeber decided not to worry about that part of the building.

New appliances like a mini refrigerator, microwave oven, and small portable heaters and air conditioners completed the picture of a comfortable clubhouse that could adequately serve the needs of one or two dozen members in winter or summer.

"You've done a great job here, Richard," Greeber announced loudly to be heard over the music. "Everything looks solid and tidy—a good use of unused resources. What about the roof? Any problems there I should know about?"

Stonger stepped to Greeber's side and gazed up at the underside of the metallic roof panes.

"Nope. It's solid as the day it was built, Max. No leaks, no erosion, and most important, no asbestos to worry about! We're fine!" the scientist declared, obviously pleased with his accomplishment.

"How about power, Richard? You know we're under tight usage constraints right now. Every time the arc jet fires up, we practically need a pardon from Congress."

"No worries, Max. I've donated some solar panels and a small backup battery from my home system if the little we use for lights and the fridge gets to be a problem. All permitted, consumer stuff. And after all, didn't we help those solar guys invent that technology back in the eighties before we gave away the patents? I know I was in on that project."

"Sorry, Richard. That was before my time. Just make sure that battery is well insulated, and you know you need to notify me if you ever turn it on."

"Right you are, Max. You'll be the first call I make. Promise," said Stonger, blinking innocently. "Say, would you like to join us for a few rubbers of bridge? The guys are getting pretty good now, but we always welcome newcomers!"

Greeber held up both hands, backing away. "No thanks, Richard. Unlike you guys, I've still got a schedule to work," he said, pointedly glancing toward a table occupied by four white-haired men dealing cards. "And besides, poker's more my game. Texas hold 'em? When you start playing those kind of games, let me know. In the meantime, thanks for keeping me in the loop and doing it all yourself. I appreciate it and won't be bothering you again until the facilities audit next year."

With that, the harried buildings manager exited the club, climbed into his officially labeled NASA electric cart, and headed back toward the "real" Ames facilities he was tasked with maintaining.

As Stonger watched the cart recede across the overgrown field between their building and the rest of NASA Ames, he pressed a small button next to the newly oiled door hinges. Abruptly, the music stopped, the card players gathered up their decks, and the new wall rose into the vaulted space under the metallic roof to reveal a back room lined with whiteboards and populated by polished, functioning machine tools, the latest computer hardware, an array of modeling equipment, and workbenches at which the Hilbert Spacers resumed their suspended labors.

"No, no, no!" barked the young Fischer, standing toe-to-toe with the towering structural engineer who stood over him. "Look, Chuck. I know you want to stay in your comfort zone and build the kind of satellite you used to put up there in the good old days, but this job requires as much stealth as it does capability, and your 'super cube' just won't cut it!"

"And why not?" challenged Maddock. "What's wrong with my super cube?"

"For one, it's only a single point in space trying to scan a three-hundred-and-sixty-degree range. Super or not, there will always be blind spots in its pickup, no matter how fancy the trajectory is. Second, it's too 'super!' It would stand out against all the other sats up there and be just as easy to detect as a flying toaster! We're supposed to be doing this thing under cover, remember? And third, getting your sat up as a secondary payload would require too many cooks in the kitchen—clandestine cooks at that. It makes me nervous just thinking about how many people we'd have to bring into our little gang to get it up there under the radar."

As Maddock's face began to take on color, he bellowed, "Well, Wonder Boy, what's your grand plan, then, if us old gummers just don't get it?"

Hearing the rising volume in the discussion Maddock and Fischer were having, Helen Miranski rose from behind her computer and walked over to the whiteboard where the two scientists were arguing.

"What's up, fellas?" she asked calmly. "Not having fun today?"

Helen had a way of disarming the most difficult prima donnas on project teams, but these two were examples of polar opposites in every way—oil and water, high and low, quick and slow, young and not-so-young. Somehow they needed to find enough common ground to work together. Keeping them on track was her job, so she got to it.

"Look. You're both right, and you're both wrong," she said, taking the combatants by surprise. "Mostly, you're both wrong."

"How so?" asked Maddock, not used to being overruled by a woman and definitely not used to ever being told he was wrong.

"Chuck, you're right when you say this thing we're building has to do something no sat has done before—detect, verify, and transmit data for a radiation wavelength we don't even know how to see yet. So yes, it has to be 'super.' Ben, you're right when you say it can't be one point in space, it can't be easily detectable, and it can't be complicated to get up there because it has to be nearly invisible to the powers that be."

"Fine," said Ben, a bit smugly. "So we're both right. How are we both wrong?"

Helen noticed with satisfaction that Ben was now saying "we" instead of his usual "I." It was a start.

"You're both wrong because you're thinking too small. You're concentrating on just one or two elements of the problem. Let's look at the bigger picture."

As she spoke, other members of the team gravitated to the whiteboard where Helen started to draw a series of large concentric circles, one within another.

"Here's Earth." She pointed to the center circle with her colored marker. "Here's the region of space that could be generating the wavelength or wavelengths we're hunting for." She pointed to the largest, outermost circle. "And here are the various known, well-used, and occupied geosynchronous orbits of satellites already up there." Then she tapped the progressively smaller set of circles surrounding the Earth. "So here's the problem: we need data from everywhere. What can we build that will get us that data and still be 'off the radar,' so to speak?"

From the back of the room, Prasad Shandra spoke up with authority.

"A network. We don't just need a satellite, we need a satellite network with interlocking, overlapping scan programs that can cover the entire region of space surrounding Earth. Greg, could you calculate the number of sats it would take to do this along with the range, trajectory, and attitude each would need?"

Banyon looked around from the drawing he was making on a whiteboard at the other side of the room.

"Sure, I could. Just give me a day or two to set up the parameters for a simulation, and I'll tickle my supercomputers with the problem. But I can tell you right now that we'd need at least a dozen sats to do the job. Maybe two dozen."

"Great, guys. A network," Fischer said with skepticism. "Exactly how does turning one super sat into dozens make it less visible or easier to deploy?"

Tess approached the group from her place at a workbench where she'd been examining a model of a standard CubeSat.

"By hiding it in plain sight. We pitch it as a University Research project looking for something so boring that even the academic committee sanctioning the work won't think to check on our progress till we've got the network in place and humming," she said, thinking out loud as she walked toward Helen's drawing. "Only we don't tell them we're looking into space. We say we're looking for something on Earth, like sludge deposit migrations from chemical plants or minute temperature changes around oceanic algae forests. And if you brilliant engineers can figure out a way make each sat in our network small enough, we can pack them all together in a secondary payload on some milk run launch like the supply ships going to the ISS every month and deploy on the way up at whatever point Greg says we need to place it."

With everyone in the room now listening closely, Tess began to see the pieces of the plan swirl into a vision of what could be—an innovative vision.

"Ben, can you program a CubeSat to reorient post-deployment? To basically point up instead of down?" she asked the now-thoughtful scientist, who began nodding slowly.

"Chuck, can you build a CubeSat with the ability to fly itself to a designated point in space when given the proper command?" The scowling engineer began rubbing his stubbled chin and scribbling notes on yellow pad.

"Anna, can you come up with a kind of lightweight stealth material that would make our sats invisible to the normal imaging radar used to track objects in orbit?" she asked the quiet young woman standing by the workbench.

"You bet I can," Tran replied. "Is that all you need from me?"

"No," said Tess. "We're still counting on you to help us figure out how to see the radiation wavelengths we're interested in, but we'll tackle that after we see if these fine gentlemen can hold up their end of the stick. How about it, guys? Ready to do some heavy lifting?"

"You mean launching?" said Dick Rauch. "I take it that part's in my court?"

"You read my mind," said Tess. "See what you can find out about deployment and attachment busses being used these days for secondary payloads and who's using them. Thanks, Dick. In the meantime, I'll start writing a grant proposal that will get some University science department the NSF funds and blessings we need to get out there under the NASA and DoD radar."

Turning to face Stonger, who was standing in the doorway between the false front of the Hilbert Space and the workshop in the back, Tess asked, "Well, Richard, what do you think? Are we on the right track?"

"Only time and Ernie Scott will tell." He replied with a smile. "But either way, it's going to be one hell of a ride!"

12

The Winnowing

Never, in its short life, had Sern imagined the existence that was enjoyed by those in X's Domain.

The hajra that comprised the primary diet of all Tandorans in various proportions was served only as an accompaniment to the daily exotic fare usually reserved for the most solemn occasions by the rest of the population. *Trenk*, the intoxicating beverage brewed by solitary Tandorans living in the high country, was available to anyone at any time. Pots of *lemsha*, rendered from the flesh of creatures kept for sacrificial rites, dotted the common tables to enrich the hajra. Prized spices of many forms abounded in various containers. But most amazing of all were the daily allotments of *denski*, an indulgence Sern had only heard about when Delft recounted ritual feasts it had attended before X's Plan had taken over Tandoran society. According to Delft, X had declared consumption of the delectable substance to be a decadence that righteous Tandorans must forego to be truly in harmony with its Plan. And yet, here, in its own Domain, *denski* was freely available to all, with X being the primary consumer of the banned delight.

And then there were the spaces reserved for inhabitants of the Domain. Of course, none came close to the size and palatial elegance of the areas X inhabited, but each member of the Domain was given its own comfortable niche, unlike the communal living arrangements typical for Tandorans living in family pods. No sharing of sleep spaces according to age and status was required, although some chose to seek out the company of one or more like-minded Domain members for sleep and other enjoyments.

Never having had space to itself before, Sern was at first alarmed by the silence in its niche. Over time, however, it came to treasure the mental calm available in solitude, retreating to its niche whenever X released it from its Bodywatcher duties.

But while the accommodations and sustenance were beyond any luxury Sern had ever known, the duties of Bodywatcher were more loathsome than any hardship Sern had ever endured.

Bodywatchers, it seemed, must bear witness to each and every mental assault X perpetrated on members of the Keeper Community, then they must assist elders like Grendi in gathering up the broken remains of the Examined to be escorted out or simply disposed of if the subject had not survived. Over the several cycles of its service, Sern calculated that it had seen dozens of Keepers perish under X's mental assault.

Of those who survived and found to be 'acceptable,' most needed to return to their pods for prolonged periods of recuperation. Any who were pronounced to be 'wanting' by X were told to leave the Keeper Community and Tandoran society in general.

As Drifters, Sern found these former Keepers could be seen as falling into four groups: the Angry, who felt unfairly removed from their peers and their power; the Damaged, who had resisted X's probe to emerge with severely wounded minds; the Anxious, who feared everyone and everything in their new, unstructured lives; and the Awakened, who saw in X's Plan what Sern had long feared to be true and had decided to be no part of it.

Whenever Sern assisted the elder Keepers in ejecting a Drifter-to-be from X's Domain, it embedded a connection into the minds of those it felt to be a member of the last group, the Awakened. Although still unsure how to proceed, Sern hoped these connections could be called upon sometime, if and when it conceived of a way to interrupt the cruel winnowing taking place in its new home, a winnowing it was forced to enable in order to survive.

~

Xfrenda was becoming bored.

As it worked its way down the ranks of Keepers, it found less and less resistance to its lascivious probes, uncovering fewer and fewer guilty passions to exploit. While many of the older, more intelligent Keepers had been an interesting challenge to grapple with and ultimately break, the prospect of examining the younger, less skillful Keepers that remained in the pool held fewer excitements for X than when the winnowing began. Although the original Questioner had not yet been found, X had long since allowed for the possibility that the guilty party may have abandoned the Community to avoid detection. Nevertheless, X had pressed on with the Examinations to ensure that all unfit Keepers would be discovered and eliminated, one way or another.

And so it went, cycle after cycle, until most Tandorans forgot the original reason for the Examinations, only knowing that many of the

Examined now wandered with the growing population Drifters. As the Examinations became more and more routine, X decided it needed a new way to demonstrate its ongoing power to Tandoran society. To do this, it needed to identify a new enemy, someone or something it could hold up as a threat to the population while making a grand show of destroying that threat.

"SUMMON SERN," X bellowed. "I HAVE A TASK FOR IT TO PERFORM."

Bowed and cringing, Sern approached the immense platform that now sagged under X's growing bulk. "How may I serve you, Master?" asked Sern, unsure of what had caused X to call for its presence when Examinations were not in progress.

"OF ALL MY BODYWATCHERS, YOU HAVE SHOWN ME TO BE THE MOST HARDENED. IS IT THE ANGER I FOUND THAT FEEDS THIS IN YOU?"

"The only quality I know of is my desire to serve the Plan, the Community of Keepers and yourself," Sern replied with a great show of submission. *It's seen my anger and did not detect the source,* Sern thought. *Curious. And hopeful!*

"THEN SERVE ME BY GOING OUT AMONG THE UNFIT TO SEE WHAT PLOTS MAY HAVE ARISEN TO ENDANGER THE PLAN. GO OUT AS ONE OF THEM, THEN RETURN TO MY DOMAIN SO I MAY IDENTIFY AND PURGE ANY WHO WOULD RISE AGAINST THE PLAN AND ITS KEEPERS."

"But Master, I am known as your Bodywatcher, a position of high status among our people. Surely the Unfit would not accept me among them."

"WHEN I OFFICIALLY DECLARE YOU TO BE 'WANTING' AND STRIP YOU OF YOUR POSITION, ALL WILL BELIEVE YOU TO BE OUTCAST, EVEN YOUR OWN POD."

Especially my own pod. Sern imagined how pleased its disgrace would make Delft. "But how will I rejoin the Community of Keepers, Master? How will I identify the resistors to you if I am disgraced and outcast?"

"WHEN THE EXAMINATIONS ARE COMPLETED AND THE NEXT CONCLAVE IS ANNOUNCED, OFFER YOUR KNOWLEDGE TO THE REMAINING COMMUNITY SO THAT WE MAY ACT UPON IT AND SWEEP AWAY ALL WHO WOULD STAND AGAINST THE PLAN. DO THIS IN SERVICE TO ME AND YOU SHALL REPLACE GRENDI IN OVERSIGHT OF MY DOMAIN."

Infused with wonder at the possibilities this turn of events opened before it, Sern bowed as low as it could while backing away from X's presence. As it flowed back to its niche, alarms sounded throughout the Domain announcing the detection of a traitor and calling inhabitants to witness its expulsion, or worse. All at once, the burden of a preordained destiny fell away from Sern's consciousness—a burden it had not known it was carrying. Both the excitement and terror of an unknown future opened before it as it envisioned a life on Tandor utterly unlike any it or any of its fellow Tandorans had ever known, a life where each individual might decide what lay ahead for itself, its pod, and its planet.

~

I am coming, Sern broadcast to its network of connections within the Drifter Community. *Prepare!*

The contrast between the luxuries of X's Domain and the stark conditions in the Drifter encampment was all the more evident to Sern as it approached the gathering of ragged, gaunt Tandorans. Having been the recipient of the excesses and pampering enjoyed by Domain inhabitants for so long, Sern had forgotten how cold, hungry, and desperate life among the Drifters was—a life it had only sampled when connecting to the Awakened, a life it must now endure if anything was to come of its exile.

"So they found you out, did they?" growled a hunched, Angry Drifter, defending its place by the hajra pot. "Why come here? You'll only bring more misery to us the way you did as X's Bodywatcher! Keep on going! We don't want you here, and we don't need another failed Keeper to feed!"

Sern searched the gathered, looking for individuals who might have heard its summons. Here and there it detected a knowing nod, an accepting gesture.

"I seek those who would form a new pod with me," Sern announced. "A pod whose members have no predestined roles but share a common purpose."

"And what purpose would that be, Bodywatcher?" sneered another Angry One. "To further degrade and humiliate any who do not join you? What more could you take from us, other than our very existences?"

"The members of my pod would seek a new kind of existence," Sern replied. "An existence not based on the Plan, but on our own ways of thinking and being and serving."

When the mumbling and shuffling in the crowd died down, one of the Drifters who had nodded its understanding when Sern first arrived came forward.

"How do we know that this is not a trap? Perhaps it is an elaborate scheme of X to finish us off. How can we know you are no longer a Bodywatcher in mind and spirit? Just because you reached out to some of us when we were ejected from the Domain, and then were ejected yourself, why should we offer you our trust?"

Sern met the challenge by approaching the Drifter to make direct physical contact. "Examine me yourself," said Sern, opening its whole mind and psyche. "See who and what I am, then decide."

A gasp came forth from the questioner as Sern exposed layer after layer of its thoughts and experiences, until finally, the two exhausted beings separated.

"It was *you!*" breathed the challenger with a mixture of awe and anger. "*You* questioned the merged minds in the Conclave. *You* started X on its path of torture and revenge!"

"Yes," Sern sighed. "But the question I asked was not meant to harm anyone. I simply wanted to understand why things I felt might be wrong could not be explained or even mentioned. I did not know then, could not have known, that my small, quiet question would have been seen as such a threat to those who rule our lives. Had I known, it is likely I would not have had the courage to ask the question. But I did ask it. I asked 'why,' and we are all here now because I did."

"My designation is Butlr," said the challenger. "You may not have known that your question was a forbidden act, but I did, which is why I never came forth within the Community with the same question. I silently cheered when you did, and my silent support is why I was found to be unfit for the Community of Keepers. X saw it during my Examination. Does it know you are the Questioner? Is that why you were ejected from the Domain?"

"No. I was able to conceal my true self beneath the raging anger X found during my Examination. It revels in the strong feelings of others. It feeds on them. It wants to use my rage as a weapon against those who would question the Plan. It believes I am its hardened Agent and has sent me here to seek out and identify any who oppose it. Strange, isn't it? That X would send a hidden enemy to find an imagined one?"

"We knew you were a spy!" shouted the Angry One. "We knew it! Let us destroy this creature now, before it can report back to X!"

As the crowd began to close in around Sern, Butlr came between the mob and its target. "Enough, all of you! If Sern is a spy, it works for us, not for X. I have seen into this one's being as well as its mind. Put down your fear and your hatred long enough to use what is left of your minds to hear its thoughts. I, for one, think I could join such a pod as the one Sern wants to form. Perhaps you will too," Butlr declared.

Slowly, cautiously, former Keepers who had not engaged in a mental merge since the last conclave extended tendrils of thought toward Sern and each other. After many tries and many failures, old familiar skills began to emerge as the Community of failed Keepers explored each other's minds, seeking the harmony that such merges once offered. At long last, the dissonant images from angry, wounded, fearful minds were subsumed beneath the common bond of being Tandoran, a bond that had once defined what was essential to their species, a bond that was being renewed, one member of society at a time, as each finally Awakened to the truth of their world.

13

Wavelengths

Richard Stonger hadn't felt so good in more years than he cared to remember. After inhabiting the persona of a passed-over pariah, a relic of a bygone era, the elder physicist was once again seen by colleagues as a key contributor to a project in which they were all heavily invested. The aches, pains, and other artifacts of an aging body were temporarily forgotten as each new day brought the prospect of discovery and achievement, not to mention getting to know some new friends to add to the dwindling number of those who still remained. And it was the respect of those new friends for his still-acute knowledge of advanced physics that touched Stonger most deeply. Seeing admiration in the eyes of younger scientists was worth any price, any risk of failure or detection. With the advent of Tess's project, Dr. Richard Stonger had found a new reason to get up in the morning and face the challenges of the life he had chosen—a life of scientific exploration and wonder.

Stonger's newfound enthusiasm, however, was not rubbing off on Eric Chow, who keenly felt the rising pressure from Tess's team to identify the type of radiation they were supposed to detect—radiation that could theoretically accomplish the genetic manipulations Eric had discovered in the highest echelons of Silicon Valley society.

"So what's the holdup?" asked Stonger one afternoon as the rest of the team worked on trajectories, communications protocols, and grant proposals. "We know that electromagnetic waves, what you call radiation, vary in frequency and length. The shorter the frequency of the wave heights, the longer the wavelengths, right?"

Eric nodded, but he was distracted. He wasn't enthusiastic about getting a physics lecture when he was trying to concentrate on genomic science.

"So which wavelengths are known to mess up DNA when you treat cancer?" Stonger pressed. "Are they long or short? In other words, how much energy do they contain?"

This was an area Eric could address, having worked for so long at the UCSF. "Cancer is treated by what we call 'ionizing' radiation, typically beams or waves, I guess, that have enough energy to knock electrons out of their atomic orbits or molecules out of their compound bonds. When exposed to this kind of radiation, cells usually die. We hope that pointing the beams as precisely as possible at cancer cells will kill more cancer cells than healthy cells. But there's always collateral damage because these beams can only be aimed in the general region of a tumor and can't be stopped once they hit the body. So you get burns and tissue death and a whole bunch of injuries that stay with you even if the cancer is knocked out."

"Sort of like living on a battlefield after the fighting is over?"

"Exactly. Now from what I can tell, electromagnetic waves that produce ionizing radiation go from frequencies of around 430 terahertz for the kind of ultraviolet radiation that can fry your skin and give you melanoma all the way up to billions and billions of hertz for the gamma rays used in cancer-treating radiation beams."

"Thank you, Eric. I'll remember to stay out of the sun and as far away from clinical linear accelerators as possible," Stonger commented wryly. "So if I'm understanding you correctly, and I usually do, ionizing, high frequency radiation in the EM spectrum is something we would notice if it were being pointed it at us. So how about the nonionizing type? What happens when those beams are pointed at us?"

"It varies," Eric admitted. "At the high end of the nonionizing spectrum, relatively low-frequency ultraviolet, visible, and infrared light can excite electrons to cause photochemical effects in plant and animal life, nothing really harmful but definitely detectable. In the middle of the spectrum, radio waves and microwaves are thought to mess with our bodies, but it hasn't been proven yet. And at the low end, things get fuzzy."

"What do you mean, fuzzy? Fuzzy how?"

"From what I've been reading—and remember that particle and quantum physics are not my fields—NASA has defined radiation with frequencies of zero to three hundred hertz as ELF, which apparently stands for Extremely Low Frequency radiation."

"Great," Stonger quipped. "One more NASA three-letter acronym. Someday I'm going to put out a dictionary with all of them. But go on. What does ELF radiation do? With that low a frequency, the wavelengths must be pretty long."

"You got that right. They figure about six thousand kilometers between wave peaks, which puts it out of the detection range of nearly all of the Earth-based antennae. And no, we have no idea what it does because it's so hard to detect with current equipment."

"Hmm… Now I'm intrigued," mused Stonger.

"But tell me, Richard," Eric asked with a growing level of frustration. "You're a NASA guy. How do we even know it's there if we haven't been able to detect it?"

"Mathematically, of course. Just like we know there may be a fourth dimension or even alternate timelines using relativistic and quantum calculations to detect them."

"That's what I was afraid of," Eric sighed. "Every time I get near physics, someone launches into the theoretical mathematics that drove me into biology in the first place! Look, Richard, if we're going to build a device that can detect something, I need to know what it's looking for, not what to calculate. Hasn't anyone ever 'seen' ELF wavelengths on any of the instruments you guys are always inventing?"

Stonger rose from his chair to pace the area of the workshop he and Eric were occupying. "Now that you mention it, I think I remember a researcher here at Ames having some success imaging what you are calling ELF waves in the shock tube they used to use to simulate the effects of atmospheric reentry by spacecraft. Let me get into it, and I'll get back to you. But I think we may be on to something here. If it's an area neither physics nor biology has explored, we might have found a clue to what's been happening to us, and more importantly, how it's being done."

"I hope so," Eric replied, "because time's running out. If we don't zero in on what we're looking for soon, Small Slam is going slam the door on all of us!"

***

Three days later, Richard Stonger and Eric Chow literally danced into the Hilbert Space, arm in arm. Doing a jig in a small circle, the two unlikely colleagues announced to all those assembled the reason for their euphoria.

"Hallelujah, Spacers!" they cried as the team gathered around. "We found it! We know what we're going to look for up there!"

"Well, don't keep us in suspense," called Helen Miranski from across the room.

Stonger looked at Eric, who looked back at Stonger. Both were grinning. "You tell them," they said simultaneously, falling into each other's arms with high-pitched laughter.

"Knock it off, fellas," growled Chuck Maddock. "Get to the point so we can all get back to work."

"Right," said Eric, sobering. "We're looking for an extremely low frequency electromagnetic wave, an ELF to put it in NASA terms, that has an exact frequency of 7.8 hertz. Right, Richard?"

"Precisely," Stonger replied through a wide smile. "With the unintended help of some shock tube researchers and a bit of quantum mechanical calculation—yes, Greg, we gave one of your friends in the quantum computer lab a hypothetical problem to grind on—Eric and I believe the ELF wave we're trying to find has been slipping into our ionosphere undetected until now because its wavelength is approximately equal to that of the Earth's circumference, so it's been thought to be a natural phenomenon."

"Hold on," said Prasad Shandra, who had been listening intently to what his two giddy teammates had been saying. "I know something about the ELF frequency of 7.8 hertz. It's called the Schumann resonance. Everyone in aeroscience knows that the wave peaks in this EM range are the source of, and sometimes the result of, lightning. Tesla figured it out a century ago but was ahead of his time. Schumann proved it again in the 1950s. It's just the natural occurrence of the electrical tension that happens in the cavity between the undersurface of the ionosphere and the surface of the Earth. It's physics, not physiology!"

"Yes, it *is* physiology," Eric shot back, "and physics, too. Koenig proved that Schumann resonance frequencies were an exact match to those seen in alpha waves in the mammalian brain. Since then, we found that blocking exposure to those naturally occurring ELF waves disrupts the immune system. Like when those volunteers were shielded from EM waves in a cave in the UK some years back, they all developed the autoimmune problems usually seen in old age. And when they were restored to the natural environment, their health was restored as well. Now I know this information has triggered a lot of hype in the alternative medicine world about the healing power of crystal frequency energies, and I'm not saying anything about that. What I am saying is, this particular frequency, or resonance, has been proven to get into the human brain. So why couldn't it be used to get into the human genome as well?"

As the Spacers contemplated what had just been explained to them, smiles began to form on a several faces.

"Yes," said Tess. "It makes sense. Especially the part about the immune system. If my IV gene protects me from this resonance, it could also be the cause of some of my autoimmune problems."

"You got those problems, Tess?" asked Dick Rauch. "I do, too, but it didn't start for me till I was past sixty. You're too young for that."

"It's a small price to pay, Dick, if it shields me from the tinkering going on around here." Turning to face the team, Tess settled the matter. "Okay. We've got our target. We look for ELF waves with a 7.8 Hz frequency coming from outside our atmosphere. Now, how are we going to detect them without Earth-based tools or antennae?"

When none of the senior team members stepped forward with any ideas, Anna Tran raised her hand shyly.

"Yes, Anna," Tess acknowledged. "What have you got?"

"How about using diatoms?" she asked.

"You lost me," said Rauch, who was used to knowing nearly everything about any mission he directed. "What's a diatom?"

"It's a type of microscopic sea creature with an incredibly complex shell pattern," Anna answered, sure that everyone on the team was familiar with her area of expertise given their reputations as leaders in their fields.

"Great. A tiny shrimp," Rauch said, eyes rolling. "Come on, Anna, how do we tell a little critter like that to go looking for an ELF wave?"

Anna paused, surprised the renowned Mission Director didn't already know the answer. "By selecting the diatom with a shell pattern that disrupts that exact radiation frequency, of course! Didn't you read the paper from our Materials Branch on the potential use of diatom shell patterns to protect astronauts from ionizing radiation in space? I thought everyone had read that!"

"Must have missed it," said Rauch, somewhat chastened. "Did the theory pan out?"

"It should have," said Anna, "but the project was defunded before further research could be conducted. Then it was abandoned when NASA stopped sending people into space. I always thought it was going to be a truly enabling technology, but someone else in NASA HQ obviously didn't, or it wouldn't have been cancelled."

"Not necessarily," Tess surmised. "Maybe that someone in HQ had their DNA 'altered' to make sure we wouldn't follow that path. I think it's those kind of alterations that may be keeping us from getting on with the progress in space we started to achieve in the last century. Has anyone besides Richard and I noticed how that effort has been progressively stalled by 'the powers that be' whenever we get close to making headway on something?"

Heads nodded all around the room.

"Well, we've got the funding now," Helen volunteered, "and with Anna's help, the brains to develop the technology, so let's see if it works."

"Yes," said Anna, feeling more confident about her role in this exciting effort. "Let's just see!"

14

Launch

No one ever asked why cars could be seen parked around an old machine shop on the back of the Ames campus at all hours of the day and night. If they had, someone might have noticed the ebb and flow of activity taking place there every day over the months since the Hilbert Space card club had opened.

Daily deliveries from Spacers came in the form of materials brought from overstock in NASA laboratories, machine tools that had been sitting in storage waiting to be scrapped, precision instruments intended for use in assembling nanomachines if and when authorization to proceed with such projects ever came through from HQ, specialized metallic components tucked under a tattered canvas cover in the back of Mike Murphy's old pickup truck, plus a dizzying array of the latest electronic gadgets acquired through internet purchases and brought to the club in takeout boxes for pizza and Chinese food.

To the casual eye, the Hilbert Space was just a popular place for retirees to play games and eat fast food—lots and lots and lots of fast food. In reality, it became a cutting-edge manufacturing facility—inventing, developing, and assembling technologies never before seen, let alone used—in the US Space Program.

Most nights, Ernie Scott dropped by after his regular work hours to test the revolutionary satellite system being developed, identifying false starts and suggesting alternate approaches to particularly tricky problems. And no matter the enthusiasiasm of any Spacer about a particularly promising idea, all agreed that Scott had the final say about whether time and resources would be put into pursuing it. He acknowledged that his role as final arbiter of every go/no-go decision often meant he would be the recipient of frustrated grumbles from team members, but he was no less exacting in his standards of excellence in spite of the people who occasionally wanted him to examine an alternative.

So when Ernie gave a short nod and two thumbs up to the launch package the Spacers finally completed, cheers could be heard spilling from the shop, momentarily drowning out the nonstop elevator music that had masked the sounds of metallic grinding needed for the construction of one of the most sophisticated monitoring and communications devices ever made.

"Okay, Tess," said Scott. "You've got your satellite package. Now it's up to you and your team to get it up there and deployed. I'm assuming you've arranged to hitch a ride as a secondary payload on a regularly scheduled launch?"

"Absolutely, Ernie. It's all set. We've only been waiting for your say-so," Tess replied, satisfied that the months of planning and focused labor were finally going to get the chance to pay off.

Turning to her chief engineer, Tess asked, "Dick, is your friend at Kennedy ready to attach our payload?"

"He's just waiting for the final payment from your grant funder before locking it into place beneath the commercial communications satellite that's bankrolling the main launch. Will the university folks be able to wire him the money by tomorrow?"

"Yep," said Tess with a smirk. "The Earth Science Department at the University of Montana can't wait to get an exclusive data feed from a dedicated satellite on algae temperatures in the South Pacific. Especially since their department received that large donation from an anonymous benefactor who told them to study it. Greg, how long will it take for the launch vehicle to deploy our package after it reaches orbit for the primary payload?"

"About three hours, if all goes well, and if Ben can tell the package to let go of the docking collar when the clamps are removed," Banyon said.

"Don't you worry about my communication protocols," the young tech whiz replied defensively. "Let's just hope our package does its job without raising any alarms from eyes in the sky or on the ground."

"Look," said Helen, attempting to take the edge off both the excitement and the worry. "We all know it's been done before, so we know the basic concept is sound. A mothership in a CubeSat grouping sending out a dozen little cubes to do stuff and check back in was shown to work long ago. It just hasn't been done with the number of CubeSats or on the scan coverage scale that we're attempting. So for now, everyone take a breath. Chuck, can your transport guys get this thing to Florida in time for Dick's friend to get it loaded?"

"Better than that," answered the big engineer, with a grin. "Dick and I are taking it ourselves. He's got a friend with a private plane who wants to do some marlin fishing off the Keys, so we're going along for the ride, with a stopover at Kennedy."

Nodding, Tess turned to address the group at large. "For the next few days, then, it's out of our hands. We've all done our jobs, which, in my opinion, has been some of the best work I have ever seen in satellite design, GNC programming, instrumentation, and materials development. You should all be proud. Honestly!"

When the back-slapping and high-fiving subsided, a tired voice could be heard coming from the far corner of the shop where Eric Chow had set up his workstation. "Guys, remind me again how this single package of CubeSats is going to become an entire, Earth-circling network of satellites?"

Over the past few months, Eric had struggled to keep up with the aeroscience part of the project and wanted to be sure he understood what everyone else was cheering about.

Prasad Shandra sighed conspicuously, accepting the fact he'd have to explain it to the geneticist one more time. "Okay, you understand that we get it up there and kick it out into space while it still looks like a single object, right?"

"Right," Eric replied, not minding Shandra's patronizing tone as long as he was willing to revisit the topic.

"Then Ben sends a signal to the package that tells all twenty-two CubeSats inside of it to move away from each other into a three-hundred-and sixty-degree circular space. Once separated from their original configuration, each CubeSat gets an instruction to proceed to its assigned, preprogrammed network node site. With me so far?"

"That much I've got. It's the next part that rattles my brain a bit."

"The part about telling each CubeSat to orient its scanning instruments away from Earth or the part about the network disappearing from Earth-based monitors?"

"Both."

"It's a simple matter of communication protocols," said Fischer.

"And stealth technology," added Tran.

"Indulge me," said Eric. "What may be simple to you still takes me a while to figure out."

"I'll take it from here, guys," said Tess, recognizing the need to bring her special 'geek translation skills' to the conversation.

"You know that we've given each little cube its own solar-powered, micropropulsion system that takes orders from the tiny communication chip we embedded inside it."

When Eric nodded, she continued.

"So in a sense, each cube is smart enough to do what it's told to do. Remember the Winter Olympics in South Korea back in 2018? When all those drones came swarming in to dance with each other in the closing ceremonies?"

Eric nodded silently.

"Well, our CubeSats are just like those little drones—only smarter. Ben sends them a special signal on a communication frequency not currently used by any other satellite system that we know about. With that signal, he tells them where to put themselves on the network grid Greg developed. When each little guy is in position, Ben sends them all a command to turn themselves so that the surfaces that Anna has coated with stealth material are facing down toward us on Earth and the surfaces carrying the diatom-based monitors are facing outward toward the rest of space. When that happens, normal, Earth-based monitors won't be able to see them because the stealth materials will absorb light instead of reflect it. So as far as the University of Montana will know, some kind of technical glitch will be blamed for losing contact with the satellites, and everyone will go back to their drawing boards to figure out what went wrong. In the meantime, we will have the only eyes and ears that can get information to and from our 'invisible' network. Does that make more sense to you now?"

"Yeah, thanks. I'm sorry to be the short straw in the brains department, but this flying around space stuff is just not what I ever learned about," Eric confessed.

"Well your genetic modification stuff is just as Greek to us," Shandra admitted. "But I am confident that if and when our little diatoms tell us we're being approached from outside our planet by someone else's Schumann waves, you will be as patient with us when you explain how those waves are turning smart, reasonable people into the mind-blind toads we're up against."

"You can count on it," Eric replied. He felt buoyed by the assurance that his area of expertise was valued as much as the rocket jockeys and space science guys who had been taking point on the project until now.

"Okay, everyone," said Helen, closing out the discussion. "The next step is launch. All we can do until it's up there and deployed is watch and hope, so let's all take a break and try to enjoy the ride!"

***

The twin aromas of hot pizza and spicy chicken wings filled the air at the sports bar where the Spacers gathered to celebrate the successful conclusion of the first phase of their clandestine project. As pitchers of cold beer were brought to the table, the normally reserved group of scientists, engineers, and researchers mixed freely with other bar patrons as well as each other. When glasses had all been refilled several times and chicken bones formed piles on the empty pizza pans, Chuck Maddock rose from his place at the head of the table to address everyone with slightly slurred speech.

"Guys, I gotta admit. I had m' doubts going into this thing. What're the odds a bunch 'a science stiffs like us could pull off somthin' even NASA couldn't do—or wouldn't do? Not good, I tell ya. Odds were not good! But here we are tonight with our li'l package signed, sealed, and almost delivered. Good on ya! All o' ya!"

To a chorus of "Here, Here!" and "Whoo hoo!" Maddock raised his glass to his colleagues at the table, downed the last of his beer, and went on, reluctant to give up the floor.

"Now, why don't you young folks go out for a change and have some real fun? Get drunk! Maybe make a few babies! You don' wanna spend all your time with old farts like me 'n' Dick 'n' Richard there. Or ol' Murphy, for that matter."

In the embarrassed silence that followed Maddock's exhortation, Ben Fischer unsteadily rose to his feet.

"Chuck, I'm all for the getting drunk part. Working on that right now, as a matter of fact. But I don't know about the making babies part. Could get complicated."

Then someone at the table called out "Don't worry Ben, we'll show you how!" and a chorus of raucous laughter erupted.

"Okay, fine. So how about it, ladies?" Ben asked gesturing toward Anna and Tess. "Anyone up for some proactive procreation?"

As the laughter subsided, Anna Tran shook her head slightly, held up her hands, and murmured, "Sorry, Ben. I'll pass."

At that, Maddock picked up the ball and threw it toward Tess.

"How about you, Bailey? You and Eric thinking about making any little Chows any time soon?"

When Eric stopped smiling and put his glass back down on the table, Dick Rauch took charge.

"Chuck, you're out of line, here. Will somebody take his glass? He's had too much to drink tonight. Sorry, Tess, Eric. Just ignore him."

As Tess considered the possibility that everyone knowing she and Eric roomed together might become an issue for the team, she decided to deal with it head-on, like she had done with everything else in her life. "That's okay, Dick. Eric, I'll take this one, if it's okay with you."

When he nodded, still without smiling, Tess addressed the group in the matter-of-fact way she used to bring them all to attention. "It's true Eric and I share an apartment. But we're friends, like you and Dick, not lovers. As for making babies, I have no intention of passing on my DNA until we get a much better handle on what each and every one of my genes does and doesn't do, which is kind of what this whole thing has been about, hasn't it? Getting a handle on how DNA is being used to mess things up for people."

The sober nods and grunts of agreement that followed her speech said Tess had made her point, but that point had broken the upbeat mood in the room. So she picked up her glass, and smiling at those assembled, made one last point. "So here's to the mystery we're chasing and the very special people chasing it! To the Spacers!"

This time, the toast was joined by all present in a thoughtful and heartfelt way.

Mike Murphy, feeling his own drink, then lumbered up to a standing position at the opposite end of the table from Maddock to add with a twinkle and a slight Irish brogue, "And to Tess's DNA. May she pass it on in good health!"

15

Conclave

When the remaining Keepers finally received the call to assemble for Conclave, so many cycles had passed since the last gathering that many were unsure of what to expect. Of course they came, hopeful that X had finally put things right among the members of the Community, but at once terrified that some new reason for more Examinations might be found.

One by one, the Keepers assembled in the large outdoor expanse that had been set aside for such events, noticing that there were far fewer in attendance than the last time they were called together. After a seemingly endless period of nervous waiting, X entered the space, supported by its troop of Bodywatchers.

When all present had quieted and X was certain it had their full attention, it spoke. "OUR COMMUNITY IS SMALLER THAN IT ONCE WAS, BUT IT IS ALSO STRONGER. THROUGH OUR EFFORTS, ALL

WHO REMAIN IN THE COMMUNITY HAVE BEEN TESTED AND FOUND TO BE AT ONE WITH THE PLAN."

Sighs of relief echoed through the throng as it became clear no further testing would take place that day.

"LET US ONCE AGAIN JOIN MINDS TO SING IN HARMONY AND SPREAD THE WISDOM OF TANDOR AMONG THOSE WHO DO NOT YET SHARE OUR VISION OF THE UNIVERSAL ORDER TO WHICH ALL SPECIES SHOULD ASPIRE."

Slowly, softly, the assembled Keepers began to commune with each other. As each mind joined the merge, the pitch of mental music rose until a harmonic chord was achieved that resonated throughout the Conclave. When X finally added its mental might to the symphony, an entirely new level of brilliance and energy arose from the joined minds of the Community. Relaxing into its role as leader of the merge, X began to send out the focused, resonant wavelengths that could penetrate the barriers between quantum universes.

At first, the Keepers simply observed the civilizations previously being guided by the Plan, noting how they were progressing along their predetermined paths and where adjustments would need to be made. Because many cycles had passed in their own timeline between the last observations and the present ones, X anticipated that some major adjustment might be needed to bring things back into order, but it had not foreseen the possibility that the Community's efforts might be detected or even blocked!

Of course, this could only have happened in the humonid universe, that reality where the naturally occurring mental chaos had to be continually adjusted to keep the dominant sentient species on an evolutionary track determined by X to be one that would prevent them from becoming a threat to Tandor. Somehow, the humonids had placed a barrier between their planet and the Tandoran wavefronts. Although X and its supporting Keepers could have easily overwhelmed the new obstacle, the very fact of its existence demanded that X reevaluate its strategy for dealing with this most troublesome species. With the dissonance that resulted from disruption of their mental approach, tentative though it was, the Conclave once again fell out of harmony.

"ENOUGH! IT IS CLEAR THAT HUMANS ARE OPPOSING THE PLAN."

As gasps of horror rippled throughout the Community, an elder Keeper voiced the thought being involuntarily shared with its fellows.

"If they can oppose the Plan, have we lost control of their timeline? Will the humans now evolve into the marauding species we fear?"

Recognizing that its abrupt withdrawal from the Conclave at the first sign of human opposition may have instilled more uncertainty among the Keepers than the disruption of their wavefront warranted, X moved quickly to reassure its followers.

"NO SPECIES CAN STAND AGAINST OUR JOINED EFFORT TO BRING TANDORAN ORDER TO ALL THINGS. THIS FEEBLE ATTEMPT TO SHIELD THEMSELVES FROM US IS EASILY OVERCOME NOW THAT WE KNOW OF ITS EXISTENCE. RETURN TO YOUR PODS. REFRESH YOURSELVES AND PREPARE FOR OUR NEXT CONCLAVE, TO BEGIN IN THREE CYCLES. AT THAT TIME, I WILL LEAD US TO VICTORY OVER THESE PITIFUL CREATURES AND INSTILL THE TANDORAN PLAN FOR ORDER IN ALL THINGS INTO THEIR VERY BEINGS!"

With such an all-out assurance from the strongest mind on the planet that there was nothing to fear from the humans, the Conclave disbanded to recover their mental center, confident in the knowledge that X would triumph, as it had ever since the Plan had begun thousands of cycles ago.

X, however, was not so sure. When its Bodywatchers brought it back to its Domain, X turned to address its loyal troop of supporters. "I NEED TO KNOW EXACTLY HOW MANY AND HOW STRONG MY COMMUNITY OF KEEPERS ARE. GO OUT AMONG THE POPULATION TO SEEK OUT ANY WHO DID NOT HEED THE CALL TO CONCLAVE TODAY, ESPECIALLY SERN, AND BRING THEM TO ME."

"But, Lord," protested Kerlbt, one of the most senior of the Bodywatchers. "Sern and the other Keepers who did not come were judged to be unfit and are likely to be moving among the Drifters now."

"SO MOVE AMONG THE DRIFTERS YOURSELVES. FIND SERN. IF IT RETURNS TO ME WITH THE INFORMATION I SENT IT OUT TO FIND, IT MAY REJOIN OUR COMMUNITY WITH HONOR. IF IT DOES NOT, ITS EXISTENCE WILL BE TERMINATED."

Puzzled, but obedient, the Bodywatchers set out in all directions from X's Domain to find Drifter encampments that could be harboring the missing Keepers X was seeking.

~

Never had Xfrenda been opposed so directly. Never had it encountered such a pushback by any species it had sought to control. For the first time in its long existence, X felt the presence of an actual threat—a threat to itself and to the Plan. Nothing like it had ever occurred in its or any other Tandoran's memory, and X was at a loss for how to proceed.

Even though it had made a great show of the need to ferret out opposition within the Community of Keepers as the existence of the original Questioner had suggested, X had not really feared that these flawed individuals could actually pose a threat to its position of authority. However, when it encountered opposition from a species using technological progress to thwart implementation of the Plan, that was another matter entirely. Failure to implement the Plan

while leading the merged Conclave could imperil the long-held belief among the population of Tandor that only X had the ability to continue leading the Community and thus continue enjoying its lifestyle of unparalleled luxury.

For the first time in its multimillennial existence, X knew fear. But unlike the guilty enjoyment it felt while indulging in the fear of others, its own fear rose up before it like a black wall that it could not see beyond, bringing a sense of vulnerability it had only experienced when causing it in others during their Examinations.

As its unbidden waves of panic slowly subsided, X began to regain control of its formidable mental powers and decided on a course of action. First, it must determine exactly how the human pushback was accomplished. Then, it must assemble the mental weaponry that would be needed to overcome this upstart species' opposition. When sufficient forces were gathered, X would lead an invasion so overwhelming in its ferocity and effectiveness that no species in the humonid universe would consider repeating their criminal act of defiance, now or in their shared futures.

~

When X's call for Conclave first went out among the Community of Keepers, Sern and its Drifter podmates were engaged in a Conclave of their own. More intimate, more personal, and thus more wholehearted in submersion of the individual into the merged mind, Sern's Conclave noted and dismissed the order from X to assemble on the plain outside its Domain, considering it to be an external annoyance.

After the refreshment of mutual connection and support, Sern's new podmates assembled quietly in their hastily built shelter at the base of the Tandoran high country to reflect on what they had earned and what was to come.

Butlr, who had become Sern's lieutenant despite its advanced age, began the exchange with the mantra that had come to define their new pod. "As we grow in spirit, so do we grow in strength. As we value each other's view of the world, so do we grow in our own value," Butlr intoned.

Sern then came forward to address its pod.

"How do you feel we should respond to the call by X for Conclave?" Sern asked.

"We should reject it, of course," answered Tebla, newly admitted Drifter who was trying to become Awakened instead of Angry. "It is either a false call to further imperil our existence or a call for us to reengage with the Plan, which we no longer support!"

General murmurs of agreement floated about the shelter.

After a time, Sern pushed its podmates to think more deeply about their situation. "If Tebla is correct, and X is hunting us for its own reasons, how long do you think we can remain apart from the rest of Tandor? How long will it be before the Bodywatchers discover us and our purpose?" Sern asked.

"Long enough to gather more members and fight off the Bodywatchers!" declared Tebla. "Long enough to make a plan to protect ourselves and our new way of being!"

Butlr moved to Tebla's side to engage its podmate directly. "Make a plan, perhaps. But bring that plan to fruition? Most likely not. Sern is wise in raising the question of time. It is the one resource we need and may not have in great quantity if we are to bring about the changes to our world we all seek. It might be satisfying to fight the forces of X before we are ready, but it would not be successful. Too few Tandorans have ever questioned the Plan to feel any connection with those of us who do. Somehow, we must hide from the scrutiny of the Community long enough to grow into a force of our own, one that has a chance of succeeding. Our plan must give us time to oper

the minds of those who have always done what they were told in the belief that no other way of life could exist. The question now is, how do we continue to hide while being hunted and not fuel the fire that hunts us?"

"By hiding in plain sight," Sern responded sadly. "It is the most difficult and painful course to take, but it is the only one that will deflect the power that X controls away from our movement long enough for us to gather the strength we need to survive."

From the puzzled looks it received from its new podmates, Sern decided to explain further. "X believes I am here among you as its Agent seeking out those who would oppose the Plan. It sent me here to identify its enemies and bring them back for further 'adjustment.' If I return with a few failed Keepers and declare that they are the only enemies that remain, X will turn its attention back to implementing the Plan."

"Adjustment," cried Pelt, a newly Awakened Keeper. "You mean another Examination and perhaps extermination! Who among us would willingly return to undergo such torture? And if any revealed our movement during its next Examination, would not X become aware of what we are doing? It makes no sense!"

"It is a risk," Sern admitted. "But you forget that I underwent Examination and was able to shield my mind from X beneath a level of anger it could not penetrate. If we have a cycle or two before the Bodywatchers come, I believe I could build such shields within the minds of any who volunteer to return with me."

"Are you certain that these shields would protect us?" asked Butlr. "Are we not risking everything on the hope that X will be unable to see into the minds of those who return?"

"Yes, we are," Sern answered. "But I am also certain that if we do not try, X and its Bodywatchers will ultimately sweep us from the world, and the time we do have will have no import for our people or our planet. For me, risking failure is far better than having no chance of success."

Many more such discussions took place in Sern's pod before all podmates were convinced that Sern's plan was the only hope they had to continue their efforts to liberate their world from the Tandoran Plan for Order in All Things.

By the time the Bodywatchers appeared in the high country, Sern and its small group of volunteers were prepared for capture and return to X's Domain.

In its absence, Sern appointed Butlr to lead the Awakened pod with orders to implement their plan of recruitment among the Drifters and eventually extend it into normal Tandoran society to seek out any who may never have expressed dissatisfaction with the unyielding order of their lives, but who may be open to considering another way to exist.

16

Alarm Bells

When Ben Fischer programmed his smartphone to play the theme from *Star Wars* if the diatoms in the Spacer's network of CubeSats ever started sending back signals that Schumann resonance waves were hitting them from outside Earth's atmosphere, he didn't really believe he'd ever get that call. It had been seven months since the excitement had worn off from the successful launch and deployment of their satellite network, long enough for most Spacers to drift back into their former lives, although they did check in with Ben from time to time to verify that the communication protocol he'd set up on an obscure X-band frequency was still working.

Tess went back to polishing the scientific papers scheduled to be presented at an upcoming space weather conference at NASA Goddard.

Stonger spent most of his time in his portable building on the Ames back lot learning everything he could about genetic engineering from Eric Chow.

Helen Miranski finally accepted the fact that ARM was going to cut her loose at the end of the fiscal year and began cleaning out her office.

Mike Murphy decided he would take his newly acknowledged status as "someone who could fix anything" on the road and hired out to oversee maintenance of some 3D printing shops in the area and show customers how to make tools that actually worked.

Anna Tran returned to her small cubicle in the Ames materials lab, unable to share the incredible breakthroughs she had achieved in stealth and radiation detection materials, but more secure in her own capabilities knowing she had the respect of her fellow Spacers.

In the continued absence of any new spacecraft missions being planned or funded by Congress, Prasad Shandra focused on his day job of predicting asteroid and comet strikes on the Earth to give the newly established Planetary Protector Division enough time to figure out how to avoid disasters.

NASA Management moved Greg Banyon into quantum computing, an area of research that very few people understood or believed had any chance of success. Although he knew he was being set up to fail, Greg decided to hang on as long as NASA allowed him to draw a paycheck.

Dick Rauch found that his trip to Florida to hand off their CubeSat package to his friend at Kennedy Space Center and go fishing off the Keys was such fun, he decided to invite Chuck Maddock to come back there with him to spend some time exploring the area in a two-man sailing ketch.

And then it happened. With the unmistakable notes of the Star Wars theme music ringing loudly on Ben Fischer's phone at 4 a.m PST, the world changed forever, for everyone.

***

"Are you sure?" Tess demanded when she came barreling into Ben's office at six that morning. "Could it have been a battery failure or somebody just calling you on a strange ring tone?"

"No, no, Tess. I checked it out, honest. The X band on the CubeSat downloaded a boatload of data onto my station in the Hilbert Space. In fact, it's still coming in. I've never seen a dataset like that before, and I don't think anyone else has, either. It's almost like a storm!"

"Call everyone back in," Tess ordered. "We've got to get a handle on this fast, while the signals are still new."

"Way ahead of you. I sent out an all-call right after I called you. It's going to take Dick and Chuck a day or two to get here, but we can conference them in on their satellite phones. Wow! Until this morning, I've got to admit I didn't think it was real! I mean, I understood it could be, but let's face it. It sounded more like a sci-fi plot than an actual project, didn't it? But it's real, Tess, it's really real!"

"Calm down, Ben. We're still under cover, remember? Nobody can know about this yet. Not until we've figured out what we've got and what we're going to do with it. Take a breath. Then take another for me. I'm headed over to the Hilbert."

With that, Tess disappeared into the early morning mist rising above the quiet airfield.

***

By noon, all the Spacers were gathered in the card room, asking what had happened to prompt Ben Fischer to sound the "come–a–running" alarm.

"Okay, people," said Stonger in a firm tone to the group. "Settle down. Let's go over it, slowly. Ben, what precisely do we have, and what exactly does it mean?"

"Right," said Fischer, who'd had a few hours to come to grips with the situation. "Here's the story. Schumann resonances are supposed to come from the space between Earth and the ionosphere, generated by the electrical imbalances that result in lightning, right?"

Fischer saw nods all around.

"So in theory, our diatom monitors in the CubeSats that are keyed to recognizing and disrupting only Schumann radiation frequencies should never actually encounter any because they are all pointed away from Earth. Also right?"

Again, nods.

"But very early this morning, too early in fact, I got an alert on my cell that our diatoms were all going nuts, all at the same time! When I rushed over here to check my download station, I found terabytes of data streaming in—data that only stopped just now. There's so much, I haven't even begun to do a complete analysis. Greg, I'm going to need your help with that, by the way, but what I can tell you is that it looks like wavefront after wavefront tried to enter our atmosphere at the exact resonance we predicted!"

"What was the point of origin?" asked Shandra, obviously skeptical of the young scientist's claims.

"That's what I need everyone's help with," Ben admitted. "From what I can tell, the wavefronts came from all over, from everywhere, but they were all pointed toward Earth!"

"Good God," whispered Helen who was still in the dusty jeans and work shirt she'd worn to pack up her office that morning.

"Indeed," replied Stonger, softly.

"Wait a minute," said Eric Chow, who had arrived with Stonger

"Are you saying that the someone or something we think ha been messing with our DNA is from outside our solar system?"

As the Spacers looked to each other for confirmation of thi

unimaginable possibility, Shandra offered an even more frightening thought. "Or perhaps from outside our universe," he offered.

"What do you mean, Prasad?" asked Ernie Scott. "There is nothing outside our universe, at least nothing that we can interact with." He paused, sure of himself, but only at first. "*Is* there?"

Shandra turned to Greg Banyon, who had been unusually quiet during the entire exchange. "Tell them, Greg. Explain quantum realities, if you can."

Banyon looked around the room at his colleagues, trying to collect the thoughts that had been racing around in his head. After all, quantum theory was just that—a theory, something for mathematicians and physicists to kick around. Could this really be experimental proof of a theory that even his supercomputers were having trouble tackling? With all eyes turned toward him, Banyon offered an explanation of events that even he had difficulty grasping.

"Quantum theory allows for the possibility of many realities to exist at the same time, sort of like parallel universes, with each reality having its own timeline and following its own physical laws. You've got to be able to wrap your head around the concept of infinity to get a sense of how vast and complex this theory can be. But for now, let's just say that if the point of origin of these wavefronts is three-hundred-and-sixty degrees around Earth, they may be coming from a quantum reality that is either very close to our own or inhabiting the same relative space we do. Either way, it's the only thing I can think of that might explain these results."

"If that's the case," said Dick Rauch over his satellite phone hookup, "do you think it might be an accident? Could we be getting radiation backwash from something going on in some other universe?"

"No," Eric declared. "Whatever else they might be, these wavefronts are no accident. The genetic effects are too specific and the outcomes of exposure too predictable for it to be a random act of space weather!"

"I agree with Eric," said Tess, stepping forward. "This seems like more than just another space-based occurrence we can't explain yet. And if it is something more, something intentional meant to change how things play out here in our little universe, then we aren't just gathering experimental data on a physics phenomenon, we're looking at proof of an actual invasion."

"Whoa! Hold on there, folks," hollered Chuck over the long-distance hookup. "You're saying we're being invaded by aliens to change the way we think about things? To change the way we do things?"

"Yes, Chuck," said Tess. "That's exactly what I'm saying."

"Well that's just plain crazy," said Maddock. "Why would anyone do that? It doesn't make sense!"

"To make us say 'yes' to some things and 'no' to others," said Tess. "Look, quantum mechanics, X bands and wavelengths aside, we're all agreed that too many of the people in power these days—whether it's in this country or some other country—are saying 'no' to ideas for innovative technologies that could solve a lot of our problems and help us get out there among the stars, while saying 'yes' to things that distract and divide us."

"Such as?" challenged Ernie.

"Such as Richard's last pitch to the Sand Hill venture capitalists for an energy-generating system based on chemical phase change that would be inexpensive, nonpolluting, and triple the conversion rates of solar or wind power," said Tess. "And that's just the latest one. Over the past ten years, I've brought half a dozen great ideas for technologies that could really make a difference to the powers that be at NASA and in the business world. But for some reason, they're more interested in making addicting toys than tackling real world needs."

"Maybe they're just more interested in making a quick buck,"

Maddock suggested over the static of his conference feed. "Not everyone is out to save the planet, Tess. Me included. Hell, I only signed on to this party because we were building something that could fly, and the concepts were cool, and I had nothing to lose but my time. But I didn't sign on to become the next nutcase spouting UFO and alien invasion theories!"

"Nutcase?" yelled Eric. "How do you explain these data then, Chuck? It's clear the wavefronts are coming from outside of our world. Doesn't that mean there is an extraterrestrial link somewhere?"

"Clear to whom?" pressed Ernie Scott, quietly. "I have to agree with Chuck on this. It's been satisfying to get back into the business of launching spacecraft just to see if we could still do it. But I cannot be a party to taking this thing any further, data or no data."

"What are you afraid of, Ernie?" asked Stonger. "What's really bothering you here?"

Turning to Stonger, Scott replied. "I'm afraid that my position at NASA will be compromised if these results are ever published or leak out with my name attached to them. Like I told you all in the beginning, I have a family and an uncertain financial future to consider. At my age, this will likely be the last job I'll ever have, so I need to hold onto it."

With that, Ernie Scott turned to address the group at large. "As of right now, please remove all references to me or my contribution to this project from any written or digital record you have. For my part, I give you all my personal pledge that I will never reveal the details of how we put Small Slam up in space or why we put it there. I'm sorry, guys. I just can't be part of this anymore."

In the space of time that followed Ernie's departure from the club, the remaining Spacers began to think, perhaps for the first time, about what it all might mean to each of them going forward.

"I take it Ernie left?" asked Maddock through the static.

"Yes, he did," Stonger replied. "And now might be a good time to decide if anyone else wants out, because from here on out, it's going to get bumpy."

"Bumpy how?" asked Anna Tran. "What do you mean?"

Stonger looked to Tess for confirmation of what he was about to say. From the look in her eyes and the set of her chin, that's exactly what he received.

"We can't just sit on this information and pretend it didn't happen. Period." Stonger began. "We have to get the word out, somehow, about what we are being exposed to, and what we think the effects of that exposure might be. It's our duty as scientists, and more than that, as members of the species being attacked."

Now it was Dick Rauch's turn to enter the conference call.

"Get the word out how, Richard?" asked Rauch. "Publish a paper that nobody will believe or give credit to? Notify the media that we've detected aliens from another dimension trying to break into our brains? I have no doubt the *National Enquirer* will pay well for the story, but it would have to be enough to support all of us for the rest of our working lives because after it goes to press, none of us will be employable in science or technology ever again!"

"Let's back up for a minute, guys," said Helen, trying to calm the situation before anyone else walked out. "Ben, Greg, how long will it take you to run a full analysis on the diatom data you've downloaded? More than that, what will that analysis show us?"

Ben dropped the shoulders he was unaware he'd been hunching as the discussion returned to a subject area he could manage—data analysis. "If we work at night, Greg, when computer core usage is low, could we get it done in a week or so?" Ben asked.

"Maybe faster," said Greg. "It depends on the character of the information, how much there is, and how you want it broken out."

As Tess would likely be the person tapped to make sense of it all to the outside world, she gave Greg her requirements. “First, find out what the exact frequency of the incoming wavefronts were as closely as possible. That way, we can tie the phenomena to Schumann resonances, or not. Next, try to determine the strength of the encounter so we can say how much energy it would take, in our terms, to generate the contact. And finally, and probably most important, verify Ben’s claim about point or points of origin relative to timing of the event. With that data, I can put together a presentation that should hold up long enough to get the information into the hands of someone who can appreciate its significance and do something about it.”

“I’m still stuck on the bumpy part,” Anna pressed. “What’s going to happen when you present what we found to the world? Won’t we all be hosed for doing it underground? Maybe even jailed for misappropriation of government property? We agreed going in to keep this thing secret, and so far it’s worked because nobody seemed to care about what we were doing out here. Don’t you think that will change when we make it known we’re seeing aliens?”

“Don’t worry, Anna,” said Tess. “We’re not going to tell the whole world, at least not yet. We’re only going to tell people we don’t think have been ‘adjusted,’ people still in positions of influence who might want to join the cause.”

“And who might that be, Tess?” asked Helen. “Do you have someone in mind?”

“As a matter of fact, I do. She works at Goddard and is expecting me to present a paper there at the Space Weather conference in a few weeks. She’s wicked smart, and I think she could be trustworthy, but I’ll have to feel her out first before opening the door on what we’ve got, once we know for sure what that is.”

“In the meantime,” said Stonger, “if anyone else feels they need to bail, please speak up. Otherwise, let’s all get back to work!”

When no other dissenting voices were heard except for the inarticulate grumblings of Chuck Maddock over the conference line, the Spacers did just that.

17

Defense

Zachary Rojas was unlike any scientist Tess Bailey had ever met. In spite of a laundry list of academic awards for breakthroughs in protein and genetic engineering, Rojas was generally considered to be an outsider in the scientific community. Billing himself as a CRISPR expert, Rojas had been a frequent guest on popular radio and TV talk shows to promote the rapidly evolving field of genetic editing and how it could one day cure everything from cancer to the common cold.

Tess was not surprised that Eric Chow knew Rojas personally. The two men were both prone to coloring outside the lines when it came to biotechnology and genetics. What did surprise Tess was how compelling and charismatic Rojas was when she and Eric met with him two days after Ben Fischer's alarm bell had rung.

Clocktower Coffee in Mountain View was a well-known hangout for NASA Ames workers who needed a caffeine fix. Strong lattes and a barista staff that anticipated the drink preferences of regular customers kept counter personnel busy in the late afternoon when Eric and Tess walked in to find Rojas camped with his laptop at a small table in the corner. As they pulled up chairs to join him, Rojas glanced up from his screen to acknowledge their entry into his mental space, then went back to his keyboard.

"Hey, Zach," Eric began. "What's happening?"

Without looking up again, Rojas responded. "You tell me. It's your meeting."

"Zach, this is Tess Bailey," said Eric, waiting for Rojas to greet his friend. When that didn't happen, he pressed on. "The one I told you about? The one who's interested in your tabletop CRISPR work?"

When Rojas still didn't respond, Tess took over.

"Look, Mr. Rojas. I get it that you don't think much of most establishment types—types like me who work at NASA. I saw your YouTube video slamming us for being the robotic henchmen of brain-dead leaders. And quite frankly, I think you're right."

With that, Rojas lifted his gaze to look straight at Tess. "So?" he countered. "You get it. What of it? What do you want from me? A quick fix for having the wrong color eyes?"

Perhaps it was his forelock of dyed purple hair or his easily understandable articles on both mainstream and social media that so put off would-be colleagues. Whatever it was, Tess knew she had encountered someone who would not be intimidated by out-of-this-world theories or the social risks they carried. In fact, from what she had read about his well-publicized battles with the scientific establishment, Rojas would probably embrace such risks for the excitement they promised and the publicity they could generate.

"What makes you think I want something from you?" asked Tess. "Maybe I'm just here for the espresso and hoping to get a selfie with a famous scientific rebel!"

"Yeah, right." Rojas laughed. "You could've photoshopped one of those without getting in my face."

Rojas sat back in his chair and turned to face Eric, dropping the rebel-without-a-cause attitude. "Seriously. What do you want, Eric? I've got two articles to finish for my blog before COB, and I'm already running behind. What's up?"

"Okay, Zach, here's the deal. First, you've got to swear on your nose rings that we won't see anything about what we're about to tell you on the internet, or anywhere else for that matter, until we agree to go public, which may or may not ever happen."

"Fine," said Rojas, waiting for the next shoe to drop.

"Second," Eric continued, "you need to know that there may be some risk if you decide to come on board with what we're doing."

"What kind of risk?"

"It could be a physical risk. We just don't know yet, but it will definitely be a professional one. If you join us and this thing blows up, it's likely nobody will take you seriously for a very long time, assuming we have a long time!"

"Now I'm interested," said Rojas. "Being called 'crazy' and shut out of the conference circuit is what I'm used to. It's being ignored that actually makes me crazy, so I can deal with a bit of risk. Not a problem. Now get to the point, Chow. What's going on?"

"Actually," Tess interrupted. "We need to know what's going on with you before we go any further. You claimed on TV that you've invented a way to put CRISPR into the hands of kitchen table tinkerers. Is that right? Can you splice and dice genetic code in your garage?"

Rojas smiled. "Technically, it's called biohacking. And yes, I can. In fact, there's a small community of biotech hackers working with my processes to see if we can make stuff like yeast that eats hydrocarbon pollutants or bacteria that could live on Pluto. In fact, I've got an online start-up selling supply kits to these guys. Want to invest? The VCs don't seem to be interested in my little enterprise, but it could really change the world if I get it going."

"Yeah, I know about blind spots in the VC world," said Tess. "But if what we're working on pans out, we may be able to open their eyes a bit."

"Last time I'm going to ask you folks," said Rojas. "What's going on and how do I fit in?"

Over the next two hours, Tess and Eric explained the Small Slam project to an increasingly enthusiastic Zachary Rojas. When they'd finished, Rojas drained the last of his espresso and leaned across the table to address them both. "Man! I know where Eric's coming from. He's tired of the big guys telling him he has no business thinking and discovering the things that could really matter. So am I. But you, Bailey, you just might be the key to why it's all happening in the first place. What I still don't get, though, is *why you need me*," said Rojas, with special emphasis on the last phrase.

"Actually," said Eric flatly, "we're hoping you can come up with a genetic fix to help us play defense against whoever or whatever is messing with human DNA. If I give you a template for Tess's IV gene, the one that shields her from alteration, can you replicate it and get it into someone who doesn't have it?"

Zach sat back to consider the question carefully.

"It's possible. Not sure of the delivery method for a multicelled organism yet. So far, I've just been biohacking single-celled stuff like bacteria or yeast. But just because I haven't done it yet doesn't mean I can't figure out a way. What kind of time are we looking at before I have to give you an answer?"

"I'm going to meet with a friend at NASA Goddard to see if she can corroborate our diatom findings," said Tess. "If she can and she agrees to put the stamp of approval on them, the next step will be to bundle the whole thing together to present to NASA HQ. But there's no point in telling them the sky is falling unless we can offer some kind of shelter from the storm. You, Zach, will have to provide that shelter, if you can, in the form of a genetic defense. At the outside, I'd say we have six months before we'll have to go public."

"Then I'd better get to it," said Rojas, standing up and stretching. "Eric, show me this template for the Tess Bailey supergene. Where are you staying these days? I'll follow you home."

With some evident embarrassment, Eric admitted he'd been camping out at Tess's apartment. "It was the only place that was safe to continue my research. And with no visible means of support other than part-time lab tech work, it's the only way I can keep from becoming homeless."

"Don't apologize, man," said Rojas. "Some of my best friends have been couch surfing for years, what with the cost of housing these days. Okay, folks, take me to your data!"

***

On the third day after Ben's alarm system went off, Anna Tran decided to walk the back lot at Ames to clear her head. She had listened to the data analysis as Ben and Greg were compiling it; had sympathized with Ernie as he fled from possible exposure of his involvement in their enterprise; had wondered what the fallout would be when Dick and Chuck returned from their sailing trip to face the Spacers in person; and had sat in silent horror when Eric and Tess revealed their plan to recruit a gene-editing rogue to work on a way to immunize them all from the next wavefront attack.

It wasn't that Anna didn't understand the concept of gene editing; she just didn't want anyone messing with her or her family's DNA. Not good guys, not bad guys, not aliens, not anyone. That kind of defense didn't feel like any defense at all as far as she was concerned.

As she walked out among the weeds and broken pavement near the fence separating Moffett Field from San Francisco Bay, Anna's mind turned to what she knew best for a way to protect herself and those she loved. She thought about materials. After all, it was her development of the filtering process for diatomaceous earths that had allowed the Spacers to isolate marine fossils with the exact shell pattern that could disrupt Schumann resonances. True, it had taken the better part of three months to gather enough of the little critters to supply their warning systems in the CubeSats, but somewhere deep down, Tran felt those diatoms might hold the key to another way to defend people against the invading wavefronts.

But how?

Small quantities like the ones used in the CubeSats would never do the job. And besides, they probably didn't have the time to search for, mine, and filter the naturally occurring fossils. If only they could spit them out on a massive scale somehow, like the little plastic toys being given away in fast-food diners for children. Or…

Tran stopped, suddenly thinking faster than she was walking. Hadn't she read somewhere that Tech Shops were opening all over the valley where regular people could manufacture just about anything on 3D printers as long as they had a good CAD pattern file? Hadn't Mike Murphy been telling them about a consultant job he'd just finished making sure those printers were working reliably? Why couldn't they print diatoms with the right shell pattern from the plastic substrate that was used in those children's toys? She certainly had the pattern specs! All she'd have to do is get Prasad to feed them into an engineering program, AutoCAD or Pro-E maybe, to make a file that 3D printers could use!

That's it, she thought. *That's how we're going to get enough diatoms to make materials that might be able to shield us*.

No, she didn't have a plan for using such materials yet, but the first step was to fabricate them. Then she'd have something to bring to the other Spacers who might not want their genes tinkered with but who still wanted protection.

Tran made the run back to her materials lab in record time.

18

Reconnaissance

"HAVE YOU IDENTIFIED THE REMAINING OPPOSERS AS I ORDERED, SERN?" X demanded.

"I have, Lord. Your Bodywatchers and I have delivered them to your Domain. They are few in number but retain much of the mental strength they had as Keepers. If their minds can be repaired, I believe they may still be of service to the Plan," Sern responded, keeping its eyes trained on the floor while in the presence of the overbearing leader.

"REPAIRED HOW?" asked X, suddenly interested in the prospect of adding some mental muscle to the force it was building before the next Conclave began.

"With my meager skills, I was able to see into their minds deeply enough to detect a longing for independent thought and action. With your superior abilities, Lord, I believe you could replace these misguided desires with feelings of loyalty to the rightness of the Plan and to yourself as our undisputed leader in all things."

"OF COURSE I COULD DO THIS IF SUCH WERE MY DESIRE. BUT THEIR TIME AMONG THE OUTCASTS MAY HAVE SO POLLUTED THEM TO MAKE IT UNWORTHY OF MY EFFORTS. ELIMINATION FROM EXISTENCE WOULD BE THE MORE PRUDENT COURSE."

"True," Sern replied, taking the utmost care to keep its body posture and mental tone as neutral as possible. "But consider the extra power they could bring to the next Conclave if they could be salvaged. It is my understanding that several were highly placed in the Community before becoming infected with these radical attitudes. Surely you could determine if they could be saved through a casual Examination. Those found to be beyond your healing could be eliminated easily enough. But any who could be made whole again by your reprogramming would surely become even stronger allies in the next merge."

Reprogramming, X thought. Yes, it might be worth the time and effort if I need to call upon more minds to move against the humans.

"VERY WELL. HAVE THE OPPOSERS BROUGHT BEFORE ME THAT I MAY DETERMINE THEIR WORTHINESS TO BE SAVED AND RETURNED TO OUR COMMUNITY."

~

To Sern's profound sorrow, not all of its new podmates were "saved." Of the dozen who had volunteered to be returned, three were found to be unworthy of continued existence when X succeeded in penetrating the mental shields they had built to withstand another Examination. But the nine who survived, along with Sern, were welcomed back into the Community of Keepers and given exalted status among the growing number of Bodywatchers that X was recruiting to prepare for the upcoming merge.

While all this was taking place, another group of Tandorans was adding to its numbers as well. Disguised to look like every other ragged outcast, members of Sern's Awakened pod brought their message of hope for a new way to live to the Drifter encampments scattered across the planet.

Slowly, the ranks of the Awakened grew until many, if not most, Drifters no longer thought of themselves as outcasts, but as Awakened Tandorans. By the time X called for the next Conclave of Keepers, Butlr was ready to call for a Conclave of the Awakened, formed utterly apart from the forces of X, but able to offer its merged resources to podmates inside the Community.

~

Once again gathered on the outdoor expanse near X's Domain, the assembled Keepers joined minds with a newly determined X. Once again, the mental music arising from the throng pulsed with the energy of resonant harmonies that echoed throughout the population of the planet. Through these echoes, all Tandorans knew when Conclaves were happening, although direct participation was traditionally limited to members of the Community. This particular Conclave, however, was to be anything but traditional, if Sern and its Awakened allies had anything to do with it.

Focused on its need to discover how members of the humonid universe had detected and turned back the wavefronts sent by the previous Conclave, X pushed the merged probe into the quantum space occupied by humans. There, instead of the great barrier it had feared, X perceived only a fragile network of devices armed with miniscule creatures encircling the planet where the human civilization had taken root. Reassured that this pitiful attempt by humans to defend themselves could be easily overcome, X summoned the power of its merge to push beyond their insignificant barrier to dive deeply into the minds of humans already identified as being both powerful within their society and susceptible to alteration.

Once again, X had to pause as it encountered what appeared to be a general weakening of the determination of its targets to turn away from new ideas that could help their species reach out into space. Research had already begun in areas of science X believed should be forbidden to humans as it might allow them to discover truths governing life in all realities—truths reserved, in X's view, for Tandorans to use in maintaining control of all sentient life.

Hardening its resolve to bring this troublesome species back under control, X instructed the merge to blanket these known individuals with more powerful resonant frequencies than had ever been used when altering molecular structures in genetic code. Fear of change, of losing control, fear of each other, and fear of the future must emerge as the dominant drivers in the minds of these humans.

As Sern watched the Conclave push its way into the minds of the highest placed humans, it summoned its own forces through the network of the Awakened to quietly pull against the onslaught so that X's merge found it increasingly difficult to continue their attack as time went on.

When X saw that the merge was near exhaustion and about to collapse, it broke off the invasion and retreated back to the plains of Tandor, furious that it had been unable to reestablish complete control in the humonid universe.

"WEAKLINGS!" it bellowed with such force that all Tandorans cringed before its echoing anger. "WHAT HAS BECOME OF THE COMMUNITY OF KEEPERS IF A SIMPLE ADJUSTMENT OF THE HUMAN CIVILIZATION IS TOO DIFFICULT FOR YOU? WILL YOU

SHRINK FROM IMPLEMENTING OUR SACRED PLAN IN THE FACE OF THIS INSIGNIFICANT CHALLENGE? WHERE IS YOUR PASSION? WHERE IS YOUR STRENGTH? AM I NOW THE ONLY TANDORAN WILLING TO POUR ITSELF INTO THE HOLY PURSUIT OF ENSURING THE PLAN BECOMES UNIVERSAL LAW?"

But the Keepers who broke apart from the Conclave were not listening to their leader at that moment. More than spent, they were wounded. Some lay prostrate, in solid form, on the gathering grounds, staring silently into the air. Some flowed about the area, keening their mental pain. Some huddled together to provide comfort to their brethren, hoping that X would allow them to rest now that they had given their all in its service.

Sern and the rest of the Bodywatchers remained near X's pulsating, bloated form, ready to help if its bulk required support. For some reason, this group did not appear to be as tired or damaged as the other Keepers, something X noted with both satisfaction and suspicion.

"RETURN ME TO MY DOMAIN," X commanded when its rage began to cool. "WE MUST PLAN OUR NEXT CAMPAIGN NOW THAT WE KNOW WHAT WILL BE NEEDED TO OVERWHELM THE HUMANS. THE TIME FOR RECONNAISSANCE IS PAST. THE TIME FOR WAR HAS ARRIVED."

As the troop of Bodywatchers retreated with their leader back into its halls of power, Sern silently hoped it could buy its podmates enough time to mount a campaign of their own, one that might open a second front on Tandor itself.

19

Real Time

As Tess assembled her speaking notes on the podium at NASA Goddard's largest auditorium, she noticed that although the gallery was nearly empty, the main floor was almost full. When the title of her presentation, "DETECTION OF SCHUMANN WAVE STORMS IN 360-DEGREE GEOSYNCHRONOUS ORBITS," appeared on the large screen behind her, courtesy of a technician giving her a thumbs-up in the AV booth at the back of the hall, the lights dimmed and the ambient noise subsided.

"Good afternoon," Tess began. "I'd like to thank the conference organizers for allowing this last-minute addition to the program. Due to the lateness of the entry, we were unable to provide the usual content summary and source documentation in your conference materials, but my colleague, Dr. Richard Stonger, will pass these out to anyone who raises their hand during the presentation.

"So let's begin. How many of you know what Schumann resonances are?"

When a scattering of hands shot up, Tess nodded to Stonger to give the hand-raisers a copy of the presentation documents.

"Not most, I see. So for those who did not raise their hands, let me explain."

As Tess began narrating her carefully crafted slide show, flashing pictures of lightning, satellite networks, and the electromagnetic spectrum on the screen, she noticed a dozen men wearing black suits and dark glasses entering the hall from side doors. As they moved down the outer aisles, she could see some speaking into their wrists while others pressed their fingers against listening devices embedded in their ears.

Tightening her belly to control her rising fear at seeing what she assumed to be "government agents" coming toward her, Tess looked out over the audience to see that heads were turning in the direction of the intruders who, by then, had encircled the audience.

Determined not to be intimidated, Tess lifted her chin and began to tell the audience about the diatomaceous radiation detectors she and her colleagues had developed, when the screen behind her suddenly went blank.

"Hello?" Tess called to the AV booth in the back of the darkened auditorium. "I'm not sure what the trouble is, but can someone hit the lights so I can continue?"

When the ambient lights in the hall came back on, Tess saw that the person formerly running the AV booth was gone, replaced by one of the black-suited men.

Speaking into the microphone on the podium, Tess found that it, too, had been cut off. It was then she saw the black suits moving among the audience members, gathering up the documents Richard had distributed.

When the sound came back on with a piercing whine, a harsh male voice made an announcement to the crowd that was protesting the surrender of materials. "Please proceed to the exit at the back of auditorium. Quickly and quietly, please. Leave your materials and any notes you may have taken with the gentlemen passing among you. Lack of cooperation will result in your being taken into custody," boomed the speaker.

"Wait a minute!" Tess shouted as loudly as she could over the shuffling of people heading for the exit. "What's going on here? What are you doing? Who are you?"

Just then, a black suit crept up behind Tess where she was still standing behind the podium.

"Please come with us, Ms. Bailey," he ordered in a tone that ordered compliance. "It's for your own protection."

"Protection from what?" she demanded.

With that, the man applied a paralyzing grip to Tess's elbow and dragged her with him to the side door of the auditorium where she saw that Richard was receiving the same attention from other black suits.

"Let me go, goddam it!" yelled her friend as he was unceremoniously ushered out of the building and shoved toward a waiting black SUV.

Seeing that her protests were not likely to stop what was happening, Tess jerked her arm away from her abductor and climbed into the back seat of the vehicle to sit beside Richard, who was still complaining loudly.

"Tess, we're being kidnapped!" yelled the old scientist over the roar of the car engine being revved as a black suit took the front seat.

"Seat belts, please," the driver said calmly to his two passengers.

"Fuck your seatbelts. We want out of this car right now!" yelled Stonger.

"Buckle your belt, Dr. Stonger. You, too, Ms. Bailey, or I will buckle it for you," threatened a second black suit riding shotgun.

"Do as he says, Richard," said Tess, trying to calm her friend. "I don't think we have much choice in the matter right now."

"Very wise, Ms. Bailey. As a matter of fact, you don't."

As their SUV and several chase cars turned onto the highway, Tess shook her head at Stonger to prevent any further outbursts, wondering where they were being taken, and hoping beyond hope that it wasn't to some undisclosed location.

***

The conference room in the bowels of CIA Headquarters in Langley, Virginia looked like every other government conference room Tess had seen. It contained the standard-issue oval table made of polished oak and surrounded by twelve black plastic, ergonomic rolling chairs. But this windowless room felt different. Maybe it was the blank expressions on the faces of the officials sitting around the table or the fact that she was the only woman inside or outside the room, as far as she could tell. Whatever the reason, Tess was getting the distinct impression she and Richard were in a situation you might see in the middle of a spy thriller movie and that the conference room was a set up for the big plot reveal, where the hero and heroine are told either that they've been chosen to go on some dangerous mission or that their lives were about to come to an end.

If she hadn't been so nervous, Tess might have chuckled when the occupants of the rolling desk chairs all stood in unison to acknowledge the entrance of a young man obviously in charge, someone neither Tess or Richard had ever seen before. Although he seemed too young to be in charge of such a serious group, he carried the unmistakable air of authority in his manner and body language. This was someone who was used to being obeyed.

"Good afternoon," said the newcomer, walking around to occupy the space at the head of the table. "Please, everyone, take a seat."

When the shuffling died down, he looked directly at Richard and Tess and began.

"As some of you already know, my name is Taylor Ormage. I'm special advisor to the president of the United States. As such, I head the National Nuclear Safety Agency, the NNSA, and am tasked with ensuring interagency collaboration in matters of Homeland Security. Which is why you, Ms. Bailey, and you, Dr. Stonger, have been asked to join me at this meeting today."

"'Asked' is not exactly how I'd put it," Richard growled. "More like hijacked."

"Perhaps that's how it felt, Dr. Stonger, but let me assure you, that was not my intention," said Ormage with practiced ease. "You must admit, however, that the information you were presenting to the conference at Goddard was somewhat alarming. Naturally, my people responded as they would to any revelation of a potential threat to the security of our nation."

"Wait a minute, son," said Stonger, challenging the explanation for their high-handed treatment. "First of all, we were presenting a paper at a NASA conference, which, in case you don't know, is a place where scientists, not government cops, get together to figure stuff out, something we were just starting to do when your bully boys busted in and broke up the party. What gives you the right to interfere with a NASA conference, anyway? NASA's a civilian organization, not an arm of the military or the Department of Energy, which I assume runs your NNSA. We don't deal in weapons, nuclear or otherwise. We deal in science, pure and simple, and sometimes discoveries that can end up helping people. We don't threaten them, whether they live in this or any other nation!"

Tess reached over to put a calming hand on Stonger's arm.

Unlike Richard, she wasn't about to challenge these people until she knew the extent of their interest in and power over their discovery.

Ormage let the ensuing silence hover over the table before responding to the scientist's statement.

"Actually, Dr. Stonger, the president of the United States gives me the right. And I have to disagree with you that science presents no threat to our security. I'm sure you remember that it was our best scientists who discovered nuclear energy in the last century and developed the weapons to use it—weapons that still present the greatest threat to global survival to this day. So perhaps you can understand how someone like myself and the gentlemen in this room, might take more than a passing interest in what scientists are discovering these days. But let me assure you once again, this meeting is just our way of trying to determine the possible implications of your discovery in this dangerous world we live in."

Pressing down on Richard's arm to restrain him from responding, Tess finally spoke.

"Who exactly are the other gentlemen in this room, Mr. Ormage? Are we speaking to the military or the civilian branch of government here?"

"Both, Ms. Bailey. And if you are really as smart as my staff tells me you are, you already know that there's no real dividing line between the two. When Congress slashed the NASA budget in the 1970s and '80s, your bosses had to look elsewhere for the dollars to keep your science projects going. What was the phrase used by John Glenn back in the day? *No bucks, no Buck Rogers!* Where do you think they found those dollars, Ms. Bailey? The American people didn't want to pay more taxes to keep you in the business of stargazing. They were, and still are, more concerned with safety than science. So the money went to the military. Fortunately for NASA, our military had some scientists of its own working for DARPA."

At Tess's puzzled expression, Ormage elaborated.

"The Defense Advanced Research Projects Agency, tasked with developing emerging technologies. Surely you've heard of them. Dr. Bennett, on your left is one of their chief scientists, I believe in your field, Dr. Stonger. He heads up their physics research programs."

Stonger stared at the sallow-faced man sitting on the other side of Tess.

"Yes, I know Dr. Bennett," said Stonger dismissively. "We booted him out of NASA twenty years ago for sloppy science and questionable motives. I see he's found a home that suits his talents. Who else is in this rogue's gallery?"

Ignoring the insult from Stonger, Bennett introduced several of his colleagues in the room as top minds in the fields of chemistry, biology, communications, computer science, and propulsion, all the specialties needed to develop advanced weapons systems.

"Okay, Mr. Ormage," said Tess. "It's your meeting. What do you want from us?"

"Please repeat to these gentlemen the discovery you and Dr. Stonger were presenting at the conference. I'm sure you will find them most attentive."

After exchanging confused and dubious looks, Tess and Richard recounted the series of events leading up their appearance at the conference, taking care to omit any specifics about how their data were developed or who, beside themselves, were involved in the project. While they were speaking, Tess took note of the facial expressions of the scientists in the room. To her amazement, they actually appeared to be not only interested, but enthusiastic about what they were hearing. Although the still-anonymous power brokers scattered around the table continued to be guarded in posture and language, Tess felt their audience might actually be open to accepting the extraordinary possibilities associated with their discovery of extraterrestrial ELF waves bombarding the planet.

Then, just as Richard began fielding questions from the scientists in the room, Tess glanced at her smartphone to see it flashing a silent alarm signaling detection of another wavefront bombardment from their CubeSat network.

Her heart pounded as her brain swirled with questions about how this latest invasion might be affecting people. When she looked up from her phone, Tess was horrified to see that the wavestorm was having an impact right in front of her eyes, in real time. Body language and attitudes in the higher ranked scientists began to change. From one moment to the next, she saw faces go from open and questioning to closed and shut off. It was like watching a slow-motion ballet where the dancers suddenly shifted from fluid movements to stiff march steps.

More ominous was the change she saw in Ormage. At first guarded but interested, he now declared himself to be an outright adversary. Sucking the oxygen out of the room, he stood, interrupting Richard's answer to a question about the connection between ELF frequencies and alpha waves in the human brain, to signal the end of the meeting. "Gentlemen, thank you for your time, but I think we can all see that these wild speculations about space wave invasions are simply that, wild speculations."

As the others filed out in lockstep into the underground corridor, he turned to Tess and Richard with a deadly serious expression on his face. "Dr. Stonger, Ms. Bailey, I warn you to stop these attempts to go public with your supposed discovery. What you are stating as fact is not only implausible, but patently impossible. And I'm telling you, I intend to report your unauthorized use of government resources to NASA HQ, which I am confident will be contacting you for restitution. Before that happens, though, it would be wise to stop whatever it is you are doing right here and now."

"And what if we don't?" shot Stonger, pushing back against

Ormage's naked threat.

"Then you will be putting not only yourselves, but whoever you're working with at risk, personally and professionally, and let me assure you, we'll find out who they are," Ormage warned.

"We understand," said Tess, cutting off another challenge by her enraged friend. Somehow she had to get Richard alone long enough to tell him what had happened in the room.

"Will your driver take us back to Goddard so we can make arrangements to return home?" she asked as meekly as possible.

"Fine," said Ormage. "But remember what I said. This ends now!"

***

"What the hell were you thinking, Tess?" demanded Richard after the black SUV disgorged them in front of the Goddard entry gate and peeled off. "Why did you let that bastard push us around?"

"Quiet, Richard," said Tess, looking around nervously. "I'll fill you in when we're on the plane home. Till then, you'll just have to keep your head down and trust that I'm trying to get us to safety in one piece!"

"Safety? You don't think that little pipsqueak would actually harm us, do you?" Richard asked, lowering his voice a bit.

"I know he would, Richard," Tess replied under her breath. "And I think I finally know why. But I also know our only chance to get out of this alive is to look like frightened, whipped puppies to whatever surveillance assets are trained on us right now so that Ormage and the rest of his crew think they've scared us off. Seriously, Richard, try to look old and defeated. I'll take care of looking scared, which is exactly what I am and what you should be too!"

***

Instead of meeting at her apartment, which Tess now assumed was compromised, the Spacers gathered at the Baylands Open Space where she and Eric first spoke almost two years ago of the incredible discovery that had brought them all to this moment in time.

It was not a happy reunion.

Standing around the same rotting picnic table while the late autumn sun sank behind the coastal hills, the group waited for Tess to fill them in.

"You're not going to believe what I'm about to tell you," she said. "Seriously, I'm having a hard time believing it myself, and I was there to see it. You all got the alarm yesterday signaling the second wavefront storm, right?"

Seeing nods all around, she went on.

"Well, my alarm went off while Richard and I were explaining our findings to some NNSA honcho at the CIA Headquarters in Langley."

"Langley?" said Ben Fischer, clearly upset with Tess's revelation. "You told us you were headed to Goddard to feel out your friend about the situation before going public with the data. What made you think you could take it to the CIA without even checking with us?"

"Geez, Tess," said Mike Murphy, agreeing with Ben about the wisdom of revealing themselves to the higher-ups. "Don't you know those guys are dangerous? Don't you know you could have been 'disappeared' if they'd wanted you to? That we all could be? My god!"

"I know, I know," said Tess, looking at Stonger for support in defending their actions. "But we didn't exactly have a choice in the matter after they crashed the conference and forcibly escorted us into their lair."

"It's true, folks," said Richard, confirming Tess's assertion that they'd been strong-armed. "The only thing they didn't do was blindfold us during the ride from Goddard and Langley."

When the growing agitation everyone felt began to plateau,

Helen Miranski stepped forward to speak for the Spacers. "Keep talking, Richard. What happened next?"

"Well, when they got us into their underground bunker or conference room or whatever, the head guy, a young man named Orange or something, actually treated us with some respect at first. He introduced us to some science types from DARPA and a few brass hats from the DOE, who mostly wanted to know what we'd begun to tell people at the space weather conference. After we filled them in, they asked some good questions, bounced a few ideas around, and even offered thoughts about what the whole thing might mean."

"Wow," Murphy muttered. "I figured they'd hook you up to electrodes or something to get what they wanted."

"Yeah," said Tess, "so did I. But just as Richard and the DARPA guys were swapping ideas and everything looked like it might work out, the wheels came off the wagon."

"What do you mean?" Helen asked, huddling inside her heavy jacket as dusk faded and stars came out. "What happened?"

"I saw, first hand, what those wavefronts can do, Helen. During the twenty minutes the alarm was signaling, I watched people in that room who had given every indication they were intrigued by our findings turn first into skeptics and then into outright enemies. Ormage—that was his name, Richard—went from curious to threatening. He warned us that there could be grave consequences if we pursued this in any way or spoke to anyone else about it. And there's no doubt in my mind that he not only meant every word he said, but that he had the power to make good on his threat."

"So what are you saying?" Helen pressed. "You think the wavefronts turn good guys into dangerous jerks? Don't you think it's more likely they got that way naturally rather than being brainwashed by ELF waves? I've known a lot of jerks in my time around here, and to account for what made them all that way, we'd have to prove they've been bathed in these waves twenty-four-seven for a couple of years!"

Feeling the cold herself, Tess sat down on the table's ragged bench, blowing on her hands and rubbing them together. "I don't know how it works, Helen, but I know what I saw. Richard saw it too. During the last wave storm, these people in obvious positions of power closed their minds to anything that might be new and reverted to a threat-response behavior. And now that they've identified Richard and me—and probably all of you—as that imagined threat, we're going to have to decide how to defend ourselves against their response."

"Defend ourselves," said Prasad who had been listening stoically to the disturbing news that they all might be targeted by the very country he'd so recently pledged to serve, "against the power of the United States Government? How would we ever be able to do that? It's over, fellows. We're dead, professionally, and maybe for real. Personally, I would tell them anything to avoid having their electrodes inserted into my anatomy. That was standard practice in the world I left behind, and I can tell you, it was very effective."

"Don't panic, Prasad," said Anna, who had also been silent during the discussion. "Before Tess and Richard went to Goddard, Mike and I were working on something that might offer us some protection."

"From the government or the wavefronts?" asked Ben, clearly frightened by Prasad's vivid imagery of what could be in store for them all.

"From both," said Tran, with a level of confidence she hadn't previously shown to her fellow Spacers. "Although Eric's friend Zach has said he might be able to biohack our DNA to immunize us from the ELF waves, I wasn't really comfortable with that option, so Mike and I decided to get serious about manufacturing building materials stuffed with enough diatoms to deflect the Schumann resonances. Mike, why don't you tell them where it's being installed while we're out here freezing our brains off."

Murphy grinned at Anna, happy to be able offer solutions instead of problems.

"You know the Mothership being remodeled in Cupertino?" asked Murphy, referring to the iconic circular structure that was home to the world's largest computer company. "Well, I happen to be the uncle of the guy in charge of resurfacing the underground research labs. Turns out he was coming in late and over budget for the job, so I offered him enough free 'mud' to finish off the entire enclosure on time with money to spare. In return, he has authorized unrestricted access to the labs for those of us who want it, for as long as we want it. And no, the company won't disclose our identities to the government because he's linked them to the encryption files the Supreme Court finally said they could keep secret."

"Good lord, Mike," said Tess, grinning from ear to ear. "We might just have to make you and Anna leaders of this group if you keep coming up with goal-line saves like that!"

"But what about our work?" asked Greg Banyon. "Surely we'll all be fired when this Ormage person puts a bug in NASA's ear. And we can forget returning to the Hilbert Space. That's going to be the first place they look for us."

"Way ahead of you," said Dick Rauch, who'd been waiting to join the conversation and share what he and Maddock had been doing since their return from Florida. "Chuck and I have been removing the tech stuff we had in there, little by little, and stashing it in a private storage facility in town under a false name. If anybody goes into the Hilbert now, all they'll find is card tables, chairs, stale food, and a lot of empty work benches along the walls."

"How did you know to do that?" asked Stonger, astonished that the group was still working together even when they had been physically apart.

"Let's just say we had a feeling it might come to this when the first wave alarm went off and you said you had to tell someone about it," said Maddock, obviously pleased with himself. "Dick and I have been around the block enough times to know that it's always better to hope for the best and plan for the worst."

"That's all fine and dandy," said Banyon, "but how can we keep going without using the NASA supercomputers? When they kick me out of there, I won't be able to do the kind of data analysis that got us this information in the first place, or pay my mortgage, or feed my family or, well, you get the picture."

"Weren't you listening, Greg?" asked Murphy. "We'll be hanging out in the basement of the largest, most sophisticated computer company on the planet. And you know how you'll be able to keep working and feed your family at the same time? Just tell their corporate branch you've got an idea on how to build and operate the first practical quantum computer, and you'll not only have a job, but I'll bet they'll authorize you to hire a team to help you get it done. A team, get it? Us. All of us. We're going to be your team!"

Stunned by the pace of rapidly unfolding events, the Spacers looked to each other for reassurance. Finally, Richard Stonger stepped up to speak for them all.

"It's settled, then," he decided. "First thing tomorrow, Greg and Prasad will give their bosses notice that they are taking that early retirement offer NASA HQ has been trying to shove down our throats since they cancelled the Shuttle program. After a few weeks, due to 'medical problems,' I'll follow. We do it quietly, no testimonials, no retirement parties. In fact, it might be best if we just send our managers an email. Though I must admit, my boss might throw a party when I tell him I'm finally on my way to Sun City."

"No problem," said Helen, shaking her head. "After all my years of working for my corporate masters in the service of NASA, my notice of 'get-thee-hence' came just that way—in an email."

"Fine," said Stonger. "Those no longer actively employed here, like Chuck and Dick and Mike, will just let their visitor badges expire—no fuss, no muss. As for Tess, Ben, and Anna, you three are too young to retire and too visible to disappear. But like Greg, it's not unreasonable to believe you could be hired away into the private sector now that space travel is becoming a product to be sold on the open market. The only question is, how do we make that happen in the minds of those watching us, without making it happen for real?"

"I got this," said Tess, with a coalescing vision of how this next phase in the life Hilbert Spacers was going to unfold. "Remember those anonymous benefactors who've been bankrolling us? They're all entrepreneurs who got rich starting companies nobody ever heard of till they were worth enough money for somebody else to buy. I think they're going to come together to start a new space ventures company that will need a start-up team made up by the three of us. Then, not too long after we get hired, the CEO will have to replace us with other 'more experienced' marketers and financial types, so we can fade into the background like the rest of you while living on our generous severance packages."

"What about Eric and his friend, Zach?" asked Anna. "How do we protect them?"

"For now," Tess answered," they're off everyone's radar. None of the information we disclosed at the conference included the work they've been doing. You all know Eric's been crashing at my place, but I think he and Zach will have to move in together at another location to keep that work going while staying out of the line of fire. I'll take care of it."

Dick and Chuck both started nodding as they considered the practicality of the plan.

"That might work," agreed the two NASA veterans. "But we can't ever go back to the Hilbert Space. And we can't communicate or contact each other in any way that can be detected by government spooks. Seriously. From right now, we're out of each other's digital family. No social media exchanges, no old-fashioned telephone calls, no snail mail, no carrier pigeons, no nothing till we all get clear."

"But how do we stay in touch to know what's going on?" asked Anna.

Tess turned to Greg Banyon, who had been fantasizing about what life might be like with all the resources he needed to do the kind of cutting-edge computer research he'd always envisioned.

"Would you be able to develop some kind of superencryption to build a Spacers-only code that can run on a smartphone and install it remotely?"

"Sure, if you give me all your device IDs. But it could take a month or two after I get clear, and my new employer gives me access to their family secrets, so to speak."

Tess nodded. "Fine. While that's happening, we all pursue our own escape plans, totally apart from each other," she said. "When Greg is established at his new job and gets a secure SpacerNet code up and running, he'll send us a text—something like those phony warnings you always see on the internet like 'Scientists find broccoli causes irreversible brain damage! Click on this link to purchase the antidote!'" That link will be our notice to download the entry credentials Mike's nephew has agreed to prepare along with a date, Mothership room number, and time the Spacers will reconvene to figure out our next move!"

And with that, they slowly dispersed to begin their individual disappearances into the background of Silicon Valley life.

20

Infiltration

After the violent collapse of the last conclave, Sern realized it may not have much time to act before X unleashed its full remaining power against the humonid universe. And although the number of Awakened Tandorans was growing, the group was not yet sufficient in size or strength to offer any real resistance to a united Community of Keepers intent on implementing the Plan across the known quantum universes.

Somehow, Sern must keep X's focus on its campaign against the humans long enough for the Awakened to establish a foothold in Tandoran Society. At the same time, however, it must find a way to protect what was left of the human population's natural capacity for innovation and species growth from the next onslaught of X's genetic tampering.

To that end, Sern had a plan.

At the conclusion of the last Conclave when the merge was violently reinforcing the adjustments already made in identified humans, Sern noted that one individual in one of the species' power centers appeared to be completely unaffected by exposure to Tandoran quantum energies. Looking more closely into this human's genomic structure, Sern had found an uncommon molecular arrangement that made the type of adjustment being performed on others of its species to be quite impossible. There was simply no place in this individual's genome for the tampering that instilled fear at all levels of sentience.

Also, to Sern's knowledge, this particular human had never been identified as a target for manipulation, despite close proximity to others who occupied high stations in human society. Could this genetic anomaly make this human invisible to X? If others in positions of power who were not yet adjusted could gain access to this molecular arrangement, wouldn't the influence of Tandoran adjustments be diminished?

Sern decided to conduct its own research into that theory, quietly, privately, from a place on the planet where neither X nor its troop of Bodywatchers would want to go.

At the next gathering for daily consumption, Sern rose to address X, who boomed, "WHAT IS IT?"

"Lord, sufficient quantities of trenk no longer seem to be available in the Domain," Sern announced with feigned agitation. "Shipments from the high country have slowed while the need among the Community has risen, especially after the last merge."

When gasps and rumbles from the assembled Bodywatchers reinforced Sern's agitation, X, who had been indulging in larger-than-usual quantities of the intoxicating beverage, silenced the gathering with an unwelcome question. "WHO WILL GO TO THE HIGH COUNTRY TO CORRECT THIS STATE OF AFFAIRS?"

As expected, no Bodywatcher volunteered to give up its comfortable existence in the Domain to venture into the lands of those who preferred to live apart from the rest of Tandoran society and who were rumored to be fierce in the protection of their isolation.

"I will go, Lord," Sern announced finally, making a great show of resignation. "As the youngest of your Bodywatchers, your comfort and health must be my main concern."

"ONCE AGAIN, YOU PROVE YOUR WORTH, SERN. LET THOSE HERMITS KNOW THAT IF MORE SHIPMENTS OF TRENK ARE NOT DELIVERED TO MY DOMAIN WITHIN THIS VERY CYCLE, THEY WILL BE BROUGHT BEFORE ME TO ANSWER FOR THEIR INDOLENCE. "

"As you command, Lord," said Sern, ducking its head and turning toward the exit of the great structure that housed those in power on Tandor.

~

The swift journey Sern made to the high country easily yielded increased shipments of trenk for delivery to the Domain as the Tandorans that made it were natural allies of the Awakened and any others who opposed control over their life choices.

With its task accomplished, Sern sent a light call to several of its podmates working in the area to initiate a private merge to observe human society.

Upon entering the humonid universe, Sern could easily see the waves of anger, aggression, and outright violence being perpetrated against humans by those of their species who'd had their genomic adjustments reinforced during X's latest attack. As identified leaders and individuals of power, the behavior of these beings were seen as examples for other humans to emulate—behavior that would ensure the Tandoran Plan for Order in All Things would become the norm and prevent humans from engaging peacefully with each other to further the progress of their kind.

And yet, the waves of dissonance and hardening of control were not universally effective. Many humans in lesser positions within their society appeared to resist the efforts of adjusted ones to enlist them in acts of violence and hatred against each other. Some of these humans also appeared to be developing the seeds of advanced technologies that could overcome some of the challenges facing them in their universe. Still others seemed to offer public protests to the power structures that were unknowingly implementing X's Plan. So there was hope, yet, that humans could be rescued and allowed to return to their natural evolutionary path. But that hope would be short-lived if those standing against the power of adjusted ones were not assisted in some way.

Scanning for the genetic anomaly that made that one human immune to the destructive quantum energies sent by X, Sern located several dozen individuals within the larger population, but very few in positions of power. Perhaps, if these individuals could be seen as worthy of advancement within human society, they could offer an alternative example of behavior for the population to emulate.

Unlike the citizens of Tandor, Sern observed that the sentient beings of Earth did not often honor those of their species who attained the wisdom of advanced age. Possibly this was due to the prevalence of a mental defect that appeared to develop in older humans, but it was a defect that Sern saw could be cured or even prevented with a simple genetic fix.

Genetic fix! That was it!

It was genetic manipulation that had enabled X to interfere with the evolution of humans. Perhaps humans could use genetic manipulation to increase the numbers of immune individuals to rescue their species from X's control!

But humans had not yet advanced their knowledge of the science of life to a point where it could be used for their benefit. As with many other promising areas of technological advancement, humans seemed to fear the progress genetic engineering offered their kind—a fear, no doubt, encouraged by adjusted humans or those who saw some advantage to keeping fellow humans with damaged genomes from becoming whole again. Either way, humans in positions of power were preventing others from using their species' natural curiosity and talent for invention to gain the technology that could be used to blunt the forces X had sent against them.

Sern decided it needed to consult with its podmates to find a way to help the still-curious, non-adjusted humans see that engineering their own genome was the best way to regain control of their universe.

As it disengaged from its private merge, Sern put out the call to all its new podmates throughout the planet to gather at the base of the high country, where the majority of the Awakened were housed to determine their path forward.

~

"Are you saying that the sentient beings in the humonid universe have no knowledge of how life is constructed?" asked an incredulous Tebla, still fighting against its tendency toward Anger to embody the calm certainty of an Awakened Tandoran. "Without this understanding, how can you call this species sentient?"

"Sentience is not defined by knowledge, Tebla," responded Butlr on Sern's behalf. "It is defined by wisdom gained from knowledge. The rak from which lemsha is made knows it needs to eat and drink to remain alive, but it continues to be unwise about how those needs lead it into rendering pots near the Domain."

"It is our Tandoran wisdom," Sern continued," that has allowed us to use our knowledge of genomic science to develop the mental capabilities we use to connect with each other so that we may share our life experiences and become even more knowledgeable."

"If that is so, where was that wisdom when we allowed X's Plan to predetermine Tandoran lifepaths?" challenged Tebla. "Did we lose our own sentience when we gave up the ability to choose for ourselves?"

Clearly, the newly Awakened Tandoran was still harboring much of its Anger.

"That ability remains, Tebla," answered Sern patiently. "If it did not, we would not now be joined in our understanding of the great struggle it will take to regain the right for each being to choose its own fate. But having the right to choose does not always mean the choices made will be wise ones. When unwise choices are made, it requires wisdom to recognize them as missteps and summon the courage to correct them."

"So how do you propose to give humans the wisdom they need to make good choices when engineering their own genome?" asked Pelt, still the youngest of the assembled podmates and somewhat in awe of their acknowledged leader.

"I don't," said Sern. "I propose to offer them some of the knowledge they need to understand how the molecular structure of their genome affects the quality of their lives and hope that this knowledge develops into the wisdom to use the information for the protection and advancement of their species."

"Knowledge? Hope?" asked Butlr. "Is that enough to ensure their defense against the power of X and its cohorts?"

"Knowledge and hope are as much as one sentient species should offer another," Sern answered with newly found conviction. "To do more would be to assume the role of X in manipulating the progress of a species toward a fate of our choosing, not theirs."

"But what if the humans make bad choices with this knowledge?" Pelt pressed. "Could they engineer their genome to a point where they become the threat to their own and other universes the Plan warns us about?"

"Yes," acknowledged Sern. "Allowing sentient lifeforms to find their own evolutionary paths accepts the risk that those paths may be dangerous ones. But without risk of bad choices, there can be no possibility of good ones, as frightening as that may be. Look at us. Tandorans have made some very bad choices in the past. But they were our choices to make. And now, because we still have that ability for choice, we have the opportunity to make better ones, guided by the knowledge of our past mistakes—knowledge we would not have gained had we not had the choices to make in the first place."

As this concept permeated the minds of the gathered, a newly evangelized member of the Tandoran Awakened asked the question that hovered in the air.

"Noble Sern, if X and the Keepers have already made the alterations to humans that prevent them from making their own free choices, how can we few give humans genomic knowledge without altering them again, something you are forbidding us to do?"

"X has not altered all members of the human species, only those identified as having a predisposition to fearing change and placed in positions of sufficient power to ensure that other, non-altered humans react with the same fear. But I have seen that many humans still resist the efforts of the altered ones, much as we resist the efforts of the Community of Keepers. It is to these humans that we will offer the knowledge they could use to defend themselves against X's attacks, not through alteration, but through direct communication."

"Communicate how?" asked Tebla. "Do humans form merges that we could join to impart this knowledge?"

"As strange as it may seem to we who can see into each other's minds, humans can only connect with each other through a system of visual symbols they call *writing* and sonic waves they call *speech*," said Sern to the obvious dismay of its audience. "And unfortunately, the wavelengths that carry their *speech* are too short to cross the quantum barrier, but I believe their visual symbols can be recreated with the longer wavefronts we use to enter their space if we use the devices in orbit around their planet they developed to detect our presence. The *writing* message we create would have to be very short, as humans only have limited technology, and it must be a message that can be recognized as different from X's assault and purposefully sent to inform them."

Butlr then came forward to extend its mental reach to include all those gathered and any Awakened located in different parts of the planet.

"Let us commune, then, to determine what this message shall be," it decreed with the steady authority the Awakened had come to respect.

Over the course of the next quarter cycle, the merged Awakened worked together to develop both the best message and the best way to deliver it into the humonid universe. All that was left, then, was to make it happen, and return to their lives to hope the message got through.

21

Warning!

Greg Banyon had not been this happy in his working life since before NASA had announced it no longer had the money to pursue a manned space program. Set up in what his new employer called "the tombs," he had access to all the hardware and software he needed to construct his very own, high-efficiency, quantum-based computer system, along with a research budget that would make his colleagues at Ames resent the hell out of him!

For several months after being hired by the computer giant, Banyon had labored quietly in his basement laboratory, content in the knowledge that neither wave storms nor storm troopers could get to him. Then last week, he'd completed the encrypted SpacerNet code that would allow him to call in his own troops to see where they were heading next.

After sending the Spacers the fake phishing link they'd talked about at the Baylands last autumn and noting that they'd all downloaded the code that contained the date, time, room number, and entry credentials Mike's nephew had secured for them, Greg looked forward to rejoining his friends in what had become the most exciting adventure he'd ever had, one that even rivaled the exploratory work NASA had once been engaged in.

When the appointed day and time came, Greg watched for the light on the inside door of his lab to tell him that his friends had arrived.

He didn't have long to wait.

There on the monitor, smiling and waving up at the security cameras were Tess Bailey, Richard Stonger, Prasad Shandra, Anna Tran, Helen Miranski, and Ben Fischer. As Greg buzzed them in, Dick Rauch, Chuck Maddock, and Mike Murphy emerged from the elevator and joined the group entering Banyon's lab.

"Where's Eric?" Greg asked. "Do you think he got the message?"

"He's working with his biohacker friend nailing down the molecular codes in those mysteriously altered genes he found," said Tess, obviously annoyed that the person who'd started this whole thing had decided to skip the meeting. "They get together in that tiny genetics lab I rented for them and don't come out for days. Sometimes I think they're having an affair!"

Ben Fischer smiled. "Come on, Tess," he remarked. "You should be used to us serious geeks by now! When we get the chance to work on something that really grabs us, nothing else matters until our bodies or our funds give out!"

"Then I guess I'll have to cut off his pizza supply and cancel his credit card to get his attention," said Tess. "What do you think, Helen?"

"Don't worry," said Helen. "We'll get the bio boys up to speed as soon we figure out our next move. Agreed?"

Voices in the room rose in agreement.

"So, Greg," Helen continued. "What's the story with the CubeSat network? Are we still hooked up way down here?"

Banyon's grin said more than any technical recap could convey, but he answered anyway. "Sure are. In fact, it's better here than it ever could have been in the Hilbert. Ben, I'm bouncing your X-band off two private communications satellites the company uses to keep their cloud services running and routing it right down into this little beauty here."

Banyon walked over to a mysterious looking, black metallic cube about the size of a small van. "You wouldn't know to look at it, but this baby has more computing power and is connected to more global databases than any machine I've ever worked with or even heard about. Instead of having to run weeklong analyses of input data from the CubeSats to find out what's happening, I can get a nearly instantaneous report right here telling me what's being detected, how strong it is, and with any luck, a more accurate point of origin than we had before, assuming of course that we ever get any more alarms. I'm telling you guys, this little machine the closest thing to HAL I've ever seen!" Greg said, referring to the mythical AI computer from an old science fiction movie. "So close, in fact, that I'm calling it Halley!"

"It looks like you're all set up here," said Stonger. "So where do we Spacers fit in?"

Helen and Tess smiled at each other when Stonger included himself as part of the working group. His self-identification as a Spacer had a rejuvenating effect on the old scientist. No longer bent and grouchy, Richard Stonger spoke and moved with the energy he'd been famous for earlier in his life, and it was good to see.

"We keep the whole thing going on the ground and in space until we do get another alarm," said Helen with the authority of a seasoned manager. "After all, we got it up and running on a shoestring and a prayer. We should be able to maintain it with robust resources like these at our disposal."

"And I firmly believe another alarm will be coming," Tess stated flatly.

"Aren't you the gloomy one, though?" said Murphy. "Why do you think it will ever happen again, let alone in our lifetimes?"

"Just look at what's happening in the world today, Mike," Tess replied. "Every time people seem to be figuring out it's better to come together than to fight each other, something or someone shuts it all down. It's like at NASA when someone comes up with something that might solve a global problem, someone in Legal finds a way to bury it so that it never sees the light of day. Or when some university puts money into aerospace or biotech studies, somehow, the money always dries up just as the researchers are starting to make real progress. You can't tell me it's a random phenomenon or that humans are just built that way, built to self-destruct. If we were, we'd have done it before this. I think we're being pushed in that direction somehow by those wavefronts. The problem is, we don't have the hard data to go public with proof. But if we ever do, I think we should push back with all the brains and muscle we can muster. How about you guys? What do you think?"

"Pushing back has always been my specialty," said Maddock with a cocky grin.

"Mine, too," Murphy agreed. "If I know who or what I'm pushing against. Correct me if I'm wrong, guys, but we really don't know that yet, do we?"

"No," said Dick Rauch. "We don't know who or what is sending the waves, but we do know who's being affected by them. It's the same people that got the Hilbert bulldozed about a month after we all left."

"Demoed? Really?" Stonger exclaimed. "It's gone?"

"Scraped the site clean as far as I could tell. I only got back on base once before my pass ran out. When I saw what Facilities was up to, I hightailed it out of there before I ran into anyone who knew me. At least I hope I did."

When Tess shook her head, Rauch went on.

"Listen. Until we know for sure what's happening, until we have the proof we need to tell the world what's going on, I think we should lie low. What is it you computer guys say? Go dark?"

"I suppose you're right," said Banyon. "It would be foolish to give the enemy a target until we're ready for the fight, which we are not right now."

"Fight? What fight?" asked Anna, not sure she wanted to fight with anyone or anything.

Tess turned to the young woman. "Anna, your diatomaceous drywall is keeping us safe down here for the moment, but what about everyone else? We can't build a suit of armor around the world to shield it from the wave storms. Right now, the best we can do is warn people of the danger, then join with whoever wants to fight this thing. People need to be out there exploring new worlds, not cringing inside bunkers, afraid of each other. Back in the day, NASA was created to help us get out there among the stars, not to be the obstacle to space flight that it's become."

"But Tess," Tran whined, "Right now we don't have anything to warn them about, just paranoid theories that even I wouldn't take seriously before I met you all."

"This is true," said Prasad. "But if we do get the proof—proof that cannot be disputed by any rational person—then we must also be ready with a battle plan to offer those who do want to fight."

Facing his colleagues, Shandra spoke decisively.

"I propose that this is what we should undertake while we are maintaining the CubeSat network and helping Greg build his quantum computer. If we begin by assuming the proof will someday exist, we need to work out what should be done when it does. Who do we tell? How do we get the information to them without running up against the Ormages of the world? What do we ask of those who want to join us? Who will be in charge? Will we be pushing back only on the wave storms or on the people who have been influenced by them? And if it's both, which I believe it will be, how do we manage a two-front war?"

As the Spacers considered the questions Shandra posed, it became clear to them that they were part of something that could consume whatever remained of their working lives. It was a sobering thought, especially for the younger members of the group.

"But what if no more alarms come?" Tran asked, hoping that she and her fellow Spacers were all in the midst of a wild fantasy and that, when it ended, she could have her normal life back again.

"Then we'll have spent some time brainstorming with each other to plan for a war that doesn't happen," Tess answered, trying to calm Anna's fears and lighten the rapidly darkening mood in the room. "At the very least, we'll have great scenarios to sell to video game makers when we walk away from it all, not to mention the money we'll have banked from our angel investors and being part of Greg's team down here."

"Really, Anna," said Banyon, "I would never have made the move to the private sector if all this hadn't happened. And I wouldn't have met and gotten to know all of you. Personally, I hope we don't get any more alarms and that this has all been just a one-off, a scientific curiosity. But hoping won't make it so. Like Dick and Chuck told us, hope for the best, but plan like hell for the worst. If those CubeSat alarms do go off again, I want to be as prepared as we can be for whatever comes next."

Seeing that her fears were only in her mind, Anna straightened her back and answered her friends. "You're right, Greg. Being prepared doesn't mean it's going to happen. It just means that if it does, we'll be ready for it," she said. "So let's get ready."

***

When Greg lit up the SpacerNet that following August to alert the team about new impacts on the CubeSat network, it took everyone by surprise.

After months of maintaining the satellite code, punctuated by occasional detours into the rarified fields of quantum mathematics and game theory, the Spacers had settled into a comfortable routine. They were enjoying coming to work each day in the tombs to spend time with respected colleagues who had become real friends.

Now, suddenly, the reassuring rhythm of their new lives was shattered by the alarm they had anticipated and planned for, but hoped would never come, at least not so soon.

It was late at night by the time everyone made their way into the lab. Security guards at the company gate took no notice of the fact that so many employees were showing up at that hour as IT workers often came in whenever inspiration struck them, no matter the time.

Due to the urgency of the call, every Spacer was present, even Eric Chow who was still spending most of his time with Zach Rojas working on the genetic research he needed to verify his original findings.

"Please tell us it's all a big mistake, a software glitch or a Comsat collision!" pleaded Anna. "I'm throwing a big birthday party for my mother tomorrow. The whole family is coming, even an uncle from Hong Kong!"

"I don't think Greg would have activated the alarm signal in the middle of the night unless he had something real to tell us, Anna," Tess replied. "At least I hope he wouldn't."

"It's no glitch, and the system seems to be working fine," said Banyon, sporting several days of beard stubble and looking like he'd been sleeping in his clothes for a while. "In fact, I didn't even call you when the first signals came through yesterday so Halley could chew on them and spit out an analysis before you came."

"So did she?" asked Fischer.

"Yes, but I don't understand what she's telling me, and its driving me nuts!" Banyon admitted.

"Show us what you're getting!" demanded Prasad, losing his typically calm demeanor.

Banyon hit the refresh key as the group gathered around Halley's large I/O monitor where a seemingly endless column of digits streamed by. After several minutes, the digital display stopped, but before anyone could comment, the entire data set reappeared and began streaming again.

"Geez," said Murphy. "I'm no IT guy, so you all need to tell me what we're seeing."

"Well I *am* an IT guy," said Greg, "and like I said, I don't understand it either. It's in a format I don't recognize, but more than that, I think it's a pattern because it repeats like this, time delayed by thirty seconds, then by forty seconds, then by thirty seconds, over and over again."

"Wait a minute," Tess interrupted. "When you say pattern, do you mean a code? Like a coded message?"

Banyon turned from the monitor to present a worried but excited face to the colleagues who had become his closest friends. "I'm afraid so," he conceded. "But it's not like the signals we intercepted before. Yeah, it's using the same kind of wavelengths, but before, the CubeSats detected a constant, unrelenting set of impacts, like a storm passing. This time, the impacts occur over a repeating set of time delays. What's more, the amplitudes of the ELF frequencies change in a very specific pattern, also repeated with each data set."

"What do you mean, amplitude?" asked Murphy.

"Amplitude is like a wave height," said Stonger. "If the waves we're detecting still come in very low frequencies, like Greg says, they can vary somewhat in how big they are. And if that variation is repeated in a way that seems like a pattern, it's probably not a natural phenomenon, which could mean there's a message of some kind hidden in the wave impacts."

"Holy Mother of God!" said Murphy, blowing out his breath. "Are you saying we've got an ET that wants to phone home?"

"Or rather, phone us at home," Banyon answered. "But yeah, Mike. Looks that way."

The room exploded with exclamations, then Helen's voice rose over the general chorus. "Ben, what do you make of it?" she asked, trying to get the team back on track.

"I don't know," Ben said. "There's something familiar about the data format. Let me watch it for a few cycles."

"Here you go," said Greg, hitting the key that would initiate a replay of the display. "Please tell me you've seen this before somewhere."

Several minutes went by as the Spacers waited for their IT experts to shed some light on the situation. Finally, Ben slapped his forehead and let out a yelp.

"Of course! What an idiot I am! It's hex code! You remember, Greg, we had to study hexadecimal code when we first learned to program as an historical reference, like COBOL or Basic. You didn't recognize it because nobody's used it for years."

"Damn it. You're right!" Greg answered with a self-deprecating snort. "I should have seen that yesterday! Now that we know the base code, we can tell Halley to translate it into something we can read. Hold on. Here we go!"

Everyone gathered around the display again, waiting with bated breath for Halley to tell them what the message was. Unfortunately, when the answer appeared on the screen, they were just as much in the dark as before.

"It's just a random series of letters," said Greg, frustrated by the continuing mystery. "It's not even English, or at least it's not a language that Halley or I recognize! Crap!"

"It *is* a language," said Eric Chow, stepping forward. "It's my language. It's the language of genetics. You're looking at the description of a gene."

"What do you mean, Eric?" Greg challenged. "Genetics isn't a language."

"Actually, it is," said Chow, finally on solid ground with his fellow scientists. "The language of DNA is digital, just like any other computer language, but it's not binary. Instead of the two positions we're used to in binary codes—you know, zeros and ones—DNA code has four positions that correspond to the four chemical bases that make up the structure of all genomes."

When the Spacers stared at him as though he were speaking in tongues, Eric sighed. "Something tells me I've lost you," he said. "Well, now you know how I feel at most of your brainstorming sessions. Okay, I'll try again. Halley is showing us a series of letters that it's translating from the hex code being dumped into our detection devices, right?"

"Right," Greg volunteered for the group, supported by grunts and nods all around.

"Okay," said Eric. "Just in case you didn't know, the four chemical bases that make up all genetic structures are adenine, cytosine, thymine, and guanine, which are identified by the letters A, C, T, and G, and each combination of these four bases is called a DNA codon. With me so far?"

Again, nods all around.

"So what letters are you seeing on Halley's data dump?" he asked.

"Mostly your four base letters," said Greg, still not convinced but definitely interested. "But there are other symbols mixed in with the letters too. What do those mean?"

"Lets start with the letters, or combinations of them," said Eric.

"Like I said, each DNA digit has four components, four letters, that describe a particular gene. For now, if we take the translation four letters at a time, we can use the DNA codon tables in Halley's memory banks to build the genetic structure that's being described."

"Build it how?" asked Ben, picking up the challenge. "Do you have simulation software that can take this data and draw us a 3D model?"

"Of course," said Eric. "We've had it for years. But we haven't had the technology to use those pictures to actually build the structures they describe until now! That is, until Zach figured out how to use his kitchen-table CRISPR methods to cut and paste existing DNA pieces to build the genetic structures we want."

"Eric, are you telling us that you and Zach Rojas could make a 3D rendering of the genetic information in this message and then built us a real-world sample of it?" asked Tess.

"Yep," Eric assured her. "It's really pretty fantastic what Zach can do with a pipette, a microscope, and a few tissue samples."

"But what about the other stuff in the message? The symbols that we don't understand and are not apparently genetic code bits," Greg pressed. "What do we do about that?"

Ben Fischer sat down beside Greg to study the repeating message again.

"Greg, it's standard practice to include a set of symbols in most programs to tell the computer when an executable code starts and when it stops, right?" Ben asked, posing the question more to himself than his colleague. “Tell Halley to show us what those symbols look like in hexadecimal language,” he said.

When the hex symbols for “Start” and “Stop” flashed in front of the programmers, they both let out a yelp.

“There,” said Ben. “The symbols for ‘Stop.’ Those are the ones in the message. But stop what? What do they want us to stop?”

As all eyes turned to Eric, he answered quietly.

“Let’s make this gene they’re describing and find out.”

22

Gathering Storm

After the exciting discovery of a possible genetic message hidden in the latest wavefront encounter, the Spacers were reluctant to return to their carefully crafted cover lives to wait for the results of Eric and Zach's work. Being the first people to detect the possible existence of extraterrestrial life was one thing. That was something the guys at SETI had been trying to do for so long that it wasn't even news when they told the media they thought it was likely such life existed. But being the first to communicate with ETs was a whole different ballgame. If it panned out, they would either be rock stars of the scientific world or locked away in a looney bin for having a newly defined mental illness called something like "space-o-phrenia."

While the seemingly endless waiting for news from Eric and Zach went on week after week, Tess decided she had to get away for a while to sort things out, even for just a day or so.

One of the things Tess loved about living on the San Francisco Peninsula was that she was always within a half-hour's drive of a foggy ocean beach, a secluded forest trail, or a windswept hilltop overlooking the clusters of bustling communities that hugged the shores of the Bay. As she sat on a boulder on the top of one of her favorite hilltops to gaze at the world and feel the fresh breeze coming off the Pacific, she was once again assaulted by the feeling that they were all standing on the edge of a very exciting, very dangerous, cliff—one that could elevate, or possibly end, all their lives.

Alone with her thoughts, she tried once again to puzzle out all that had happened and all that could be waiting for her in the years ahead.

Before Eric had brought her the news that her unique DNA allowed her to see things differently, to know things differently, to envision how things could be, she'd been resigned to her place in the world as a perennial gadfly with the smarts to challenge things as they were, but without the power or resources to turn those challenges into meaningful change. Recently, though, she had begun to feel that her place in the universe was shifting. No longer ignored or brushed aside by people she respected or feared, Tess understood that she was fast approaching center stage in a drama she hadn't foreseen, a drama that was likely to redefine what remained of her life.

Now, suddenly, she had a loyal group of friends and colleagues who believed what she believed and had risked everything to follow her. What's more, she could soon have access to the kind of explosive information that might, just might, get the attention of an even larger group of people—people who did have the power and resources to change things. Whether they would use the information to support or oppose her vision of how things could be was unknown, but she knew, in the marrow of her bones, that they had to be given the choice to fight back against the threat the Spacers had discovered or to turn a blind eye and allow the current trends toward distrust and division to define humanity's existence for the foreseeable future.

Although Tess had never been one to back away from a fight, she paused now on the top of this hill to consider what the next fight might cost.

In the early days of their clandestine project, Tess had been grateful for the support of the Spacers and happy to be counted among those they called friends. After all they'd been through together, however, she had come to think of them more as an extended family and felt responsible for their continued welfare. As someone whose own family had never understood or accepted who she was, Tess valued her new family with a passion typically reserved for biological relatives or even lovers. And although she could readily accept whatever risks the path they were on held for her, she was tortured by the idea that she may be leading her new family into a situation that would further endanger them.

As she edged her way down the rock to begin her trek along the ridgeline trail, Tess let her mind float free, hoping that her IV gene would kick in to help her envision what might lay ahead.

Mile after mile, she trudged on, fighting to ignore the growing pain in her knees and hips, pain that always resurfaced with exercise. Letting the warming wind whip at her face and hair, Tess allowed her worries to fade into the background sound of her shoes crunching on pebble-strewn grassland and her breath matching the rhythm of her steps.

After a time, familiar flashes of possible futures took form in her mind. One vision held images of titanic battles between unnamed, entrenched factions; another showed history-making declarations in iconic courtroom contests. Another still resolved into a scene of gathering forces surging toward a blurred horizon.

When she halted her march along the grassy ridge, huffing,

sweating, and aching, she thought about what she had foreseen. It came to her, then, that she and her Spacers were facing a future that could include elements of all three visions—all-out war, titanic legal battles, or rising grassroots movements—and that it would be up to her to make sure they survived the gathering storm with as little cost to life, limb, and sanity as possible. How she was going to do that, though, was still a mystery.

***

Later that evening, after she had showered and recovered somewhat from the physical stress of her hike, Tess poured a fresh cup of coffee for herself and Richard as they sat together on the couch in her new townhouse. Although not luxurious by any means, the recently built, two-bedroom unit located in downtown San José was a definite step up from the cramped studio apartment in Mountain View where she'd been living for most of her adult life.

With an image of the coming events still fresh in her mind, Tess had reached out to Stonger to get his reaction to what she had seen as a possible future for them all.

"Tell me, Richard," she began. "Did you ever in your wildest dreams think we'd end up here?"

"Here, where?" asked the elder scientist with a twinkle in his eye. "In your new digs without a chaperone?"

"No, damn it," Tess replied, laughing at the implication that they might somehow be romantically connected. She did love him, but as a father or even a grandfather. "Here at the point of a double-edged sword, sitting on information that could save humanity while being hunted by the very people we're trying to save."

When Stonger didn't answer right away, Tess sighed, gazed into her coffee cup and went on.

"We're at that point, Richard, where we're going to have to fish or cut bait, as my Uncle Ralph used to say. If and when we decide to go forward with this thing, we're never going to be able to go back again."

"Back where?" asked Stonger, raising his eyebrows in an exaggerated attempt to appear naive.

"Back to our normal lives, as Anna puts it. Back to the safety of being ignored by everyone. Face it, Richard. There's a certain appeal to leaving the cares of the world behind and living out our lives as safely as possible. I know it appeals to me sometimes."

When Tess rose and walked toward the front window of the living room that looked out over the manicured landscaping in the courtyard of her gated complex, Stonger put his cup down on the low table in front of the sofa and stood up to follow her.

"What are you afraid of, kiddo?" he asked quietly. "Really, what's eating at you, besides the stuff we already know is nipping at our heels?"

Gazing out the window, she spoke aloud to herself and to her friend. "I don't think I ever really bargained for all this drama," she admitted. "Everyone looks at me like I have all the answers, like I should be leading the charge up the hill or something. Hell, Richard, when you think about it, I'm probably the least qualified of all of us to lead anyone anywhere. After all, I'm just a technical writer, not a scientist like you and Anna and Prasad, or an engineer like Greg and Ben and Chuck, or a biologist like Eric. I've never been in charge of a mission like Helen or Dick. And even Mike Murphy would be hard pressed to fix all the hardware I've managed to break in my lifetime."

Taking her gently by the shoulders to turn her around and face him, Stonger spoke directly to her fears. "It's your show, Tess. Your ideas. Your vision. People believe in you because you have that kind of vision—the kind that sees connections in things that other people can't or aren't willing to see. If it wasn't for you, the rest of us would still be laboring away in our own little cubicles wondering why we weren't getting anywhere and feeling lost. It takes someone who can pull all the pieces together and make sense of them to make any headway in the world, and that's what you do, isn't it? You make sense of everyone else's science and math and technology so people can use it to get stuff done. Isn't that what a technical writer does? A good one, I mean?"

Turning back to the view of the courtyard, Tess sighed. "I guess I'm afraid I'll let everyone down somehow, including myself," Tess replied. "Oh, I don't mean I'd ever sell out or go back on my word or anything like that. And we both know it's not in my nature to back away from a fight. But lately, I've felt like people must have felt on a beach after a big earthquake hits and just before the tsunami shows up. I know something huge is coming, Richard, and I know I'll try like hell to get us all through it, but I'm afraid I won't be able to get it done. I guess I'm just afraid."

"Welcome to the human race, Tess," Stonger chuckled. "We're all afraid, all the time. Of death. Of sickness. Of failure. If we weren't, we wouldn't bother to run away from predators or store food for hard times. Fear is natural, Tess. It's what we do with that fear that makes us more or less human. If we just lash out or hide, it seems to me we're less human—sort of like the cavemen. But if we think about it and figure out a way to overcome what we're afraid of without hurting each other or causing too much damage, we're more human—at least more of the kind of humans we could be. After all, isn't that what this whole thing is about? Fighting on the side of being more human against those who'd have us be less human?"

"But what if we fail, Richard? What if we fail because I screw things up somehow?" she wailed.

"Then we fail," Stonger replied with absolute surety. "But we fail working for something we all believe is worth the risk and in the company of people who live what they believe. The minute we launched those CubeSats, we all signed up to go the distance, Tess, and we signed up to go there together. From now on, whatever happens, happens. Yeah, we may get our brains beat out—or other parts of our anatomy zapped out like Prasad is always saying—but at least we'll know our time on Earth was worth something."

Tess smiled, feeling the warmth of her friend's support and approval. "Are you saying we've discovered the meaning of life, Richard?" she asked with a tired grin.

"No," Stonger replied in all seriousness. "I'm saying we've discovered the meaning one life can have. And in this case, it's yours."

23

Change

Tandor was changing. Not so that anyone living in respectable family pods would notice, but changing nonetheless. Slowly, quietly, Tandorans living on the fringes of society began to seek each other out to exchange thoughts and feelings about the state of their world and their place within it. Often led by those who called themselves the Awakened, these small gatherings took place in secret. Usually, one or two Drifters, or sometimes young members of a low-ranked pod would encounter each other working a haj field, exchange knowing glances, and describe a secluded area within a day's journey where a small communing could take place out of sight of elders or Keepers.

There, things would be spoken of that hadn't been openly discussed in living memory. Forbidden topics such as non-preselected reproduction, free choice of function within society, the value of supporting a Community of Keepers that contributed no labor to life on

Tandor other than ensuring their own place remained above all others, and the rightness or wrongness of the Plan were all explored.

Of course, all Tandorans knew that discussing such topics could bring an immediate sentence of nonexistence from the Community, but those who gathered had been told by the rest of society that their existences were of small value in the first place, so they felt there was little to lose if they were discovered. And the excitement they felt at the thought that they might someday be able to break out of their bleak life paths was nothing like they had ever experienced before.

After such gatherings, these typically subservient outliers held themselves a bit more erect, took orders from higher-ups with a new sense of resentment while observing in stark detail the differences between their lives and the lives enjoyed by respectable Tandorans who never seemed to question why things were the way they were.

As a growing number of Awakened Tandorans dreamt of a time when no citizen would suffer want or abuse or hardship, a kinship bond was formed that embraced each other's needs and pledged what support they could offer even as they thirsted for a way to bring their dreams into the light of the Tandoran sun.

~

In X's Domain, although shielded by rank upon rank of Bodywatchers and elder Keepers, the distant rumblings of this change could be felt. At first, X noticed what seemed to be a subsonic humming underlying the measured mental music coming from the Tandoran population. As the most powerful mind on the planet, X used its skills to reach out beyond the walls of the Domain to seek the source of the low-toned noise that was at first annoying but that was rapidly becoming a discordant distraction. When no single source could be identified, X pulled its mental probes back behind the safety of its insulated walls, hoping that the phenomenon was a temporary one, like a weather event that would eventually pass.

X was soon to discover, however, that its hopes for a return to the metered tranquility of a unified Tandor were not to be realized.

~

In an ironic twist of fate, it was Sern who announced the arrival of Delft and Mernd into the presence of X during the leader's semi-cyclical audience with well-respected pod leaders to consider supplications for more status for themselves or their families. Sern maintained the impassive stature required of a Bodywatcher while listening intently to the matter the two elders of its former pod brought before the assembled Keepers. Receiving no deference or acknowledgment from their former podmate, Delft turned away from Sern to address the massive form of the Tandoran leader.

"WHAT BRINGS YOU BEFORE US?" X bellowed with ritual intensity.

"Mighty and most respected X," Delft began, cringing and bowing. "Our family pod has suffered great loss and is no longer able serve the Plan as it once did."

"EXPLAIN."

"Since the time, many cycles past, when the Keepers brought one of our younger podmates into their Community, our family has known disappointment and discord. When we received the call, Mernd and I had great misgivings about Sern being allowed to join in the sacred merges used to spread the Plan throughout the universe, but of course we knew that your own wisdom and insight far exceeded our poor understanding, so we remained silent."

They weren't so silent to me, Sern thought. *All I heard from them was resentment and distrust.*

"After Sern was inducted into the Community, the time of Questioner arrived, followed by your cleansing Examinations. To our surprise, Sern was not only allowed to remain in the Community—something I admit we hoped would not happen—but was taken from us altogether to become a Bodywatcher."

"ALL BODYWATCHERS AND KEEPERS HAVE COME FROM SOME FAMILY POD TO SERVE THE GREATER GOOD OF BRINGING ABOUT THE TANDORAN PLAN FOR ORDER IN ALL THINGS—A SACRED DUTY AS YOU SHOULD WELL KNOW. YOUR POD GAINED STATUS WHEN ONE OF YOUR OWN ASCENDED TO SUCH A HIGH POSITION. THIS WAS NOT A LOSS; IT WAS A NOBLE SACRIFICE IN WHICH YOU AND YOUR PODMATES SHOULD TAKE PRIDE!"

But Delft was not to be dismissed. It had come too far to back down now, especially in the presence of Sern, who it believed was the source of all their troubles. "For a time, Great One, we did take pride in Sern's new position, as unexpected as it was. But then things began to change. While still with us to serve the needs of our family, Sern had gone out among the Drifters to provide them with surplus hajra we had stored, declaring that some forgotten, ancient texts made it our obligation to share with those in need. I have led my pod for many cycles, Lord, and have no knowledge of such texts," Delft declared with a self-righteous air. "Then, just as these questionable journeys became too frequent for Mernd and I to tolerate, Sern was called for Examination and never returned to answer for the damage it had caused."

"WHAT DAMAGE DID THIS CAUSE?"

"It broke our pod apart," Mernd wailed, no longer content to be a silent observer of the drama taking place. "Because of Sern, our young ones are gone, with none to take their place!"

"GONE WHERE?"

Delft moved forward to retake control of the exchange, giving Mernd a hard look. "When Sern left and was granted its newly exalted position, its agemates—Pert and Lelt—followed the example it had set, going out among the despised ones to offer help and comfort. It was disgraceful! When these journeys became more frequent, lasting longer and longer, Mernd and I had to put a stop to it altogether!"

"AS YOU SHOULD. AS POD ELDERS, IT IS YOUR DUTY TO MAINTAIN THE SAME TANDORAN ORDER AT HOME AS WE IN THE COMMUNITY STRIVE TO MAINTAIN ON OTHER WORLDS."

"But, Lord," Delft pressed, "that was when our pod broke apart. After we had forbidden the young ones to go out among the outcasts, they disappeared, taking all that they had and most of our stored hajra with them. We believe they actually chose to live among the rabble, but we do not understand why or how they could make such a choice, since choice was not something they were allowed in our pod. Both young ones were created for the roles they were to fill in our pod. Each was to be capable only of that intended role. That is how it has always been in family pods. For all the cycles Mernd and I can recall, no podmate has ever chosen to abandon its place in a family. Of course, some have been banished for sinful behavior or unlawful thinking, but no healthy, sane Tandoran that was supported in a family pod has ever simply left, abandoning everyone and everything for an unknowable existence among the rejected. This has broken our hearts as well as our pod and we are here today, Lord, to beg your help in retrieving our young ones and in finding out how this could have happened."

When Delft had finished, X beckoned to Sern to approach its platform. "WHAT DO YOU KNOW OF THESE EVENTS, SERN?"

"Master, I know nothing of what happened to my agemates as I have not returned to my family pod during all the cycles in which you have allowed me to serve your needs in the Domain."

"BUT YOU HAVE RECENTLY BEEN AMONG THE OUTCASTS, HAVE YOU NOT?"

"I have, my Lord, at your direction, to identify and return any who would oppose the Plan. This I have done, and more. I have brought failed Keepers back into the Community to be healed that they may serve the Plan with increased strength and dedication."

"WHEN YOU WERE AMONG THE RABBLE, DID YOU ENCOUNTER ANY WHO JOINED THEM BY CHOICE, ANY WHO WERE NOT FORCED TO LEAVE THEIR NATURAL HOMES?"

"No, Lord, I did not. But several cycles have passed since you sent me out," Sern replied with the innocent demeanor it had crafted to present to X during such interrogations. "Things may have changed."

"CHANGE IS A SIN ON TANDOR. IF THERE HAS BEEN CHANGE, THERE MUST BE SINNERS BRINGING IT ABOUT, SINNERS THAT MUST BE ELIMINATED!"

Turning its gaze on the two cringing elders awaiting a decision, X made its pronouncement.

"I WILL TAKE UP THIS PROBLEM OF YOUR FAMILY POD AND SEND YOU WORD WHEN IT IS RESOLVED. UNTIL THEN, RETURN TO YOUR HOME."

"But Great One," Delft protested. "We have no home to return to. Our pod is broken with no young ones to labor for our hajra. How will we exist until your word is received?"

"THAT IS NOT MY CONCERN. BE GRATEFUL YOUR PROBLEM WILL RECEIVE MY ATTENTION! NOW GO!" X boomed with absolute dismissal of the two elders who now rushed to take their leave of the assembled throng, but not before sending searing gazes at their former podmate who they still believed had been the cause of their distress.

"ONCE AGAIN, SERN, YOU WILL GO OUT AMONG THE DRIFTER ENCAMPMENTS TO BRING BACK WORD OF ANY

DISHARMONY YOU FIND THERE. BUT THIS TIME, YOU WILL TAKE MY BODYWATCHERS AND THE ENTIRE COMMUNITY OF KEEPERS WITH YOU TO ENSURE THAT ANY SINNERS FORMENTING DISHARMONY ARE ELIMINATED FROM EXISTENCE!"

"Master, it is the nature of Drifters to be in disharmony. If it were not, would they not reunite with their family pods in the settled communities of Tandor?" asked Sern, secretly rejoicing for the chance to reunite with its Awakened podmates but fearful of what may befall them should the forces of X come upon them unaware.

"NOT IF RESPECTABLE CITIZENS ARE CHOOSING THE SIN OF CHANGE AND DISHARMONY OVER LOYALTY TO THEIR PODS. IF THIS IS HAPPENING AS DELFT ATTESTS, IT IS A THREAT TO THE ORDER THAT DEFINES TANDORAN LIFE. A THREAT MORE DANGEROUS THAN THE QUESTIONER. A THREAT THAT MUST BE WIPED FROM THE PLANET WITH ALL SPEED," X declared, gathering its bulk to present its most imposing stature to the assembled Keepers. "HEAR ME! DISHARMONY AND CHANGE ARE THE ENEMIES OF ALL TANDORANS. WE SING TOGEGTHER WITH ONE MIND, ONE SONG, ONE PURPOSE, OR WE DO NOT SING AT ALL. THESE SINS MUST BE STAMPED OUT WHEREVER THEY ARE FOUND. PREPARE YOURSELVES FOR THAT ACT SHOULD IT BE REQUIRED OF YOU! THE VERY EXISTENCE OF THE TANDORAN PLAN FOR ORDER IN ALL THINGS HANGS IN THE BALANCE!

~

Pert and Lelt had grown since leaving the patterned life of their family pod. Facing hunger for the first time, they had learned to forage. Facing danger from life forms living in the wild, they had learned when to defend themselves and when to flee. Facing citizens from all levels of society, they had learned who to trust and who to shun.

Facing the life questions discussed among the Awakened and the growing number of young Drifters-By-Choice, they had learned of their capacity for seeing beyond the Plan to envision the possibilities that lay ahead for their world if others could also find the courage to question.

Now and again, Pert and Lelt would hear about the exploits of their famous podmate as they were being shared among the encampments, of its wisdom in forestalling movement against the Keepers until the Awakened had gathered enough strength to become a viable force, of its sacrifice and cunning in allying itself with the dreaded X so it could warn the Awakened of any danger headed their way. Although they were proud of Sern, Pert, and especially Lelt, missed their podmate terribly, had missed it since the awful time it left to be Examined. Fearing for Sern's life, they had pleaded with Delft for permission to accompany Sern to the Domain to offer what love and support they could. When Delft refused their entreaties, they realized that order was more important to their pod leader than the welfare of its family. When Sern was spared and then promoted to Bodywatcher, Delft's fury at Sern's good fortune helped them see that it was not just order, but personal power within that order, that was most important to their elder. It was then that the two young Tandorans began their own quest for truth within a world that forbade them to question the meaning of their lives.

Blinded by its corrosive resentment of Sern's success, Delft took little notice of how Pert and Lelt were managing the loss of Sern's presence in their family. When the young ones decided to follow Sern's lead and venture out among the Drifters to distribute hajra, Delft was annoyed, but not overly concerned as there was always a surplus in their storage rooms. By the time Delft and Mernd decided to ban them from further exposure to the unruly elements that drifted in and out of the haj fields, Pert and Lelt had succeeded in making contact with members of Sern's Awakened pod and had pledged to support whatever moves were made to oppose the Plan and the power of X's Domain. Their decision to leave behind their oppressive existence and enter a life of their own choosing, even if that life was to be hard and brief, was easy to have foreseen had Delft and Mernd ever looked beyond their rage at Sern to see the discord that was spreading all around them.

Then, while enjoying the refreshment of communing with the dispersed network of Awakened Tandorans, Lelt and Pert were jarred by the scream of a familiar mental voice. "Arise! Alert! They come to seek our annihilation!" screeched Sern inside the minds of all the Awakened who were listening.

"Sern?" Lelt sent back along the merge connection. "Is that you?"

"Lelt? Pert? Beware! Delft has sent the forces of X to hunt you down and all others who defy the Plan. It is a killing force meant to wipe us from existence!"

"What should we do?" asked Pert, echoing the question in the minds of all the Awakened.

"Fight," declared the disembodied voice of their leader. "The time has come to take our world back from X and its Plan."

Butlr, who had been leading the gentle communing before Sern's warning broke into their merge, sent the next questions that needed to be asked.

"Do we fight with our bodies or our minds, Sern?"

"Both," came the hardened response. "Make no mistake, this force is committed to taking our existences from us in any way that it can. To go on, we must oppose it with all the strength we can bring to bear."

Butlr then addressed the larger community listening to the fateful exchange.

"Gather at the base of the high country to prepare for the coming battle. Reach out to any you think might be willing to join us. Help them understand that we must prevail against the Keepers if our belief in a free Tandor is to survive. Tell them to come with the courage that Sern and those who sacrificed themselves on our behalf have shown. But above all, tell them to come!"

24

Discovery

When the waiting was finally over and they were summoned by Eric and Zach to assemble at their genetics lab, the Spacers were immediately assaulted by acrid smells coming from the rodent cages stacked against the walls and the open beakers of mysterious chemicals arrayed on every surface.

"Geez, Louise," protested Chuck Maddock. "If I'd wanted to breathe in a stench like this, I'd have offered to clean out my neighbor's cat box!"

When several others began sniffling and coughing, Zach flipped a wall switch to turn on a ventilation fan.

"Sorry about that, guys," said Rojas, edging his way between bodies to the center of the small room. "I guess Eric and I are so used to the smell, we don't notice it anymore."

"Well we notice it, Rojas. So before I have to go out and lose my lunch, what's going on? What have you found out about the gene in the message?" demanded Maddock, still suffering from the effects of the chemical-laced atmosphere.

"It's right here! Look for yourselves!" Zach responded, gesturing to the mouse-filled containers lining the walls of the lab with obvious pride.

"Look at what?" asked Tess, trying to be patient with the maverick scientist. "Please, Zach. I know it must be obvious to you and Eric, but the rest of us are in the dark here. What are your little pets trying to show us?"

"They're not pets, Bailey," said Zach, offended by the notion that he was engaged in anything but scientific research. "They're subjects in a groundbreaking genetics study, a study that will knock the socks off the entire bioengineering community!"

"Fine, Zach. So what do your study subjects tell us?" asked Tess, attempting to keep her exasperation at Zach's unwillingness to communicate out of her voice. After all, she'd known many smart people with the same problem over the course of her career.

"Let me take it from here, Zach," Eric offered.

"Yes, please," implored Helen Miranski. "And do cut to the chase, Eric, so we can get some fresh air!"

"Right," Eric answered. "I showed Zach a 3D map of the gene coded in our message from 'out there,' and like I told you, he was able to build a prototype with his CRISPR kit. But we still didn't know what the gene was for, what it did inside a living organism, so we bought a bunch of lab mice from a biotech supply outfit in South San Francisco and used a viral vector to get the gene into their DNA."

"Viral vector," said Tess. "Like the flu? You gave your mice the flu?"

"Yes and no," said Eric. "We took a flu-like virus and used Zach's technique, which we are patenting, by the way, to modify it by replacing the genetic material that causes illness with our mystery gene. Then, when we injected the mice with it, instead of getting a fever, they demonstrated behaviors we think our mystery gene causes. And before you ask, yes, we followed controlled, double blind test protocols, giving half the mice the unaltered virus and the other half our altered one. And yes, we documented every step of the experiment in lab notes and with time-stamped videos."

Now it was Stonger's turn to press the biotechnologists for answers. "So what did you observe, boys? What did the mice with the mystery gene do?" he asked.

"It was what they didn't do that caught our attention," said Zach, excited to finally getting some traction with his audience. "They didn't adapt."

"Adapt to what?" asked Stonger.

"To anything," Zach responded. "When we altered the feeding routine for both sets of mice, the unaltered ones responded to the change by approaching their food containers at the new times we established. In effect, after getting over the flu, they learned something new. The mystery mice, as Eric and I are calling them, never adapted to the change. In spite of there being no food in their dishes at the times they used to feed, they kept going back to those feeders at the same time every day. One particularly stubborn mouse even starved itself to death reacting to conditions that no longer existed. I guess you could say it was stuck in the past."

"That's a really sad story, Zach," said Anna Tran. "But it's hardly conclusive for a cause-and-effect of animal behaviors."

"True," Zach answered, "but that was just the first the effect we documented. After the feeding change, we exposed both groups of mice to a variety of new stimuli, like loud noises, flashing lights and so forth. Unaltered mice reacted the way you'd expect, fearful at first, followed by curiosity, and finally adaptation, resuming the behaviors vital to their survival, like eating and drinking and pooping. The mystery mice, on the other hand, reacted only with fear, cringing in their corners unable to alter their behavior to cope with the new conditions. Again, several stayed in that state long enough to perish. At the end of the experiment, while we still had enough mystery mice alive to test, we introduced a new male and female mouse into each cage."

"I'll bet that woke them up," snickered Mike Murphy. "Nothing like a little sexual competition to get the juices flowing!"

"That's what we thought too," said Eric. "But that's the part that convinced us about what the mystery gene was designed to do. In the unaltered, control mice, males competed with males to mate with females or, when two or more females were in the cage, the mice coexisted peacefully."

"Yep, just like in real life," quipped Helen, winking at Tess and Anna.

"But the mystery mice showed a pattern of behavior that we'd never seen before, outside of maximum-security prisons or maybe psych wards," Eric continued. "Male or female, gender made no difference, each and every mystery mouse attacked the new animals until they were either dead or totally submissive. No exceptions. Every single one of the mystery mice perceived this final, new condition to be an unqualified threat and moved with whatever strength it had left to eliminate it."

The stillness in the laboratory, broken only by the wheezing of the ventilation fan, settled onto the Spacers who were still struggling with the foul air.

"Sound familiar?" ask Stonger quietly.

"It sounds exactly like the combative behavior we saw take over the guys at Langley when the CubeSat alarms went off," said Tess. "Damn. I hate it when I'm right!"

After another somber silence, Prasad Shandra addressed the two biotechnologists. "Eric, Zach, are the genetic alterations you originally found in the DNA database at UCSF at all similar to this mystery gene?" he asked.

"No, Prasad," Eric replied. "Not similar. They're identical. Let me show you."

Reaching over to the laptop computer tucked into the corner of the lab, Eric brought up a 3D rendering of the originally detected genetic alterations from patients receiving services at UCSF. On a split screen, he displayed the gene map from which Zach's prototype was built. When he superimposed one image over the other, no differences remained.

"As you can see, this alteration has been messing with our best and brightest for at least a generation," Eric concluded.

"If that is true," pressed Shandra, "What can be done? Can any of these persons be 'unaltered'?""

When all eyes turned to Zach Rojas, he shook his head and answered sadly. "Right now, no. As far as we know, the alteration is irreversible. In the future, it may be possible to replace the altered gene with a more benign one, or maybe even the original one if we have that data, but there's currently no way of knowing what a replacement like that would do to the rest of the organism, what other biological processes it might affect. Even though the human genome has been mapped for decades, we still have limited knowledge of what most of our genes do. The only research going on in that field involves fatal genetic diseases like sickle cell, but progress had been slow and not exactly promising. If it weren't, big pharma companies would have been hawking genetic fixes by now and charging immoral sums of money for them, sort of like they did for hep C and AIDS. Like the guy said in that old movie about political scandals, 'follow the money, boys and you'll find out what's really going on'!"

Ben Fisher then brought up a point that some people had

apparently forgotten. “Eric, what about Tess’s IV gene, the one that’s kept her safe from the wavefronts? If we all had one of those in our genome, wouldn’t we be protected too?”

“Perhaps,” Eric replied, “but there would be some risk. Tess’s IV gene occupies the same position in the human genome that the gene targeted for alteration does, and although she appears to be immune from the effects of the ELF waves, she may be paying a price for it. Tess, why don’t you tell them how we met in the first place?”

Tess took a breath and coughed with the effort before relating the story. “For a long time, since I was a kid, I’ve had a lot of medical problems. It’s what brought me to UCSF in the first place. When none of their world-class doctors could figure out what was causing my symptoms, Eric stepped in to do some clandestine research on my DNA and was demoted for his trouble. Even though he couldn’t pin down a specific cause for my problems, he did isolate this IV gene of mine, something he said was unique in all the bioengineering research he’d done. At the time, we only knew the gene allowed my body to manufacture neurotransmitters in combinations and concentrations that weren’t supposed to be possible and that it most likely contributed to my ability to come up with ideas that saw connections in things most other people missed. And it’s been great, getting those ideas. But it’s also probably messed up my immune system so I get arthritis in places nobody should under seventy or eighty. I get tired a lot, things like that. So if you all were to substitute my immune-from-alterations IV gene for your vulnerable-to-wavefronts normal gene, you might be signing up for the same kind of health issues I’m dealing with. And I can tell you, it hasn’t been a lot of fun.”

Nodding his head with new understanding of the stakes involved, Ben asked the next question they were all contemplating. “But has it been worth it, Tess?” he asked. “Would you trade your IV gene for an easier life?”

"Not for a heartbeat," she responded quickly. "I figure something's going to afflict all of us at some time or other. If my particular affliction happens to be tied to the skills I've been granted to help us get a little better as a species, then so be it. But what I'm not willing to do, Ben, is make that choice for you or anyone else. So before you get Zach's genetic cart before your own personal horse, you need to consider what might be the outcome if you mess with your own DNA. If you haven't been altered—and Eric tells me he's got a quick test that can tell us if you have or not—replacing your native gene in that position with my IV gene may buy you physical problems you could regret in the future. And there's no guarantee it would make you any smarter or give you the kind of skill set I've developed over the years. The only promise being made here is that with my gene in your DNA, the ELF wavefronts will bounce right off you like you were a diatom in our CubeSats."

"That's good enough for me," declared Stonger. "I've already lived longer than I should have, longer than I planned on, and I do not want what's left of my life to be driven by fear of new things or the inability to adapt to what may come up tomorrow."

While some Spacers agreed with Stonger's pronouncement, others were more cautious about the risks and benefits of what they were now calling "the IV treatment."

"Before we get too far down this road, let's look at the bigger picture," Dick Rauch suggested. "Is there any way of knowing how widespread the mystery gene has become, now that we know it's been around for at least a generation? If it's become a common alteration, aren't we whistling against the wind here? Hasn't the human race already been irreversibly changed by this whether or not we bring evidence of the change out into the open, and won't that change be part of mankind's generational DNA for the foreseeable future?"

"Let's ask Halley," suggested Greg Banyon. "At the rate it runs queries, it can mine every DNA database in the world. All we have to do is tell it to find every occurrence of the mystery gene in the millions of genetic maps that already exist, identify the owners of the altered DNA, and give us the percentage of the population that's been altered. Shouldn't take more than a day. Maybe two."

"Actually," said Tess, "I was going to ask you to do just that, Greg, but for a different reason."

"What do you mean? What reason?"

"To buy ourselves some protection for when we reveal all this to the world. And yes, Dick, we're going to go public with it no matter how widespread the alteration has become because it's our scientific and moral obligation to share what we've learned so people can decide for themselves how they want to deal with it. But when we do, we're going to need some protection, not from the waves necessarily, but from anyone who's already been altered and who might want us and everything we've discovered to disappear."

"How would Halley's report protect us, Tess?" asked Anna, afraid that the conflict she'd been dreading might soon begin.

"We have to hold something over the heads of anyone who's been altered and feels they need to destroy us or drive us into submission, like the mystery rats in Zach and Eric's experiment. If Halley can identify the owners of the altered genomes, we can store that information in a secure place and install a dead man's switch to protect ourselves," said Tess.

"A dead man's switch!" replied Ben and Greg simultaneously. "Great idea, Tess."

"Okay, time out!" said Murphy. "What's a dead man's switch, and why do I get a bad feeling about having to set one up?"

"It's a way to safeguard a piece of information so that it's unattainable by anyone except the person or persons who own it. Usually that means storing the data on a bunch of different servers, distributed throughout the world. The data remains secure in its many incarnations until one of the servers misses reception of a code sent daily by the data owner. When that happens, all the servers simultaneously release the information to the internet, targeted media outlets, and every social media site on the planet. That way, what was once a well-guarded secret automatically becomes widely known if something happens to prevent the data owner from sending the code—like getting dead. So we IT guys call it a dead man's switch, no disrespect to the ladies," Greg quipped.

"But if we're going public with everything, what information do we need to hide?" asked Maddock.

"We won't go public with everything, Chuck," said Tess. "We'll hold back the names of people we know have been altered, but make it known that we have that information. After all, these people didn't ask to be altered so there's no reason they should suffer more abuse. Unless, of course, they behave like the mystery mice and come after us. When that happens, we'll either reveal their identities ourselves or let the dead man's switch do it for us. Either way, they'll be outed, and people will know who the enemy within really is."

"Okay," Dick agreed. "We'll agree to put in a dead man's switch as soon Halley tells us how many altered humans there are out there and who they are. Until then, let's get out of this rat incubator and head back to the Mothership!"

25

Life and Death

There had been no wars in the living memories of most Tandorans. For more than a thousand cycles, violence on Tandor had been confined to solitary acts of aggression between individuals, or more commonly, state-sanctioned executions by the Keepers. So when Butlr gathered the forces of the Awakened in the high country, it turned to the Tandorans living there who had successfully defended their isolation since the time before the Plan to help the Awakened learn how to survive in a battle against the superior force that was approaching.

Cerrg, leader of the isolationists, reluctantly agreed to address the growing throng.

"The most important thing to know about winning a fight is that you must be willing to lose, must see yourself as lost, before you begin," the elder Tandoran said. "That way, your fear of being defeated will not become a weapon your enemy can use against you."

When Cerrg sensed that this way of thinking was new to its audience, it tried to explain further. "If you fear hunger, your enemy will use that fear as a weapon, and the threat of depriving you of hajra will hold power over you. If you fear nonexistence, the threat of depriving you of that existence will hold power over you. So if you see yourself as already defeated, the threat that your enemy may defeat you with its superior strength will hold no power over you and you will be free to battle to your fullest."

A young Awakened known as Fan stood forth to press the concerns of its bondmates. "Respected Elder," the small Tandoran intoned, "how do we fight against Keepers who have more physical stature and greater mental power than we possess? Will they not simply destroy our bodies after they disable our minds?"

"So?" asked Cerrg. "If you see yourself as already disabled and destroyed, does that not free you to throw all that you have into the struggle? If the Keepers prevail, all they have won is what is expected of them. But if some of you prevail by throwing everything you have into the battle, what will become of the Keepers who are left? Will they not see themselves as less than they should be?"

While its audience considered what they had heard, Cerrg put a question to them. "Why do you think the Keepers have allowed us to stay apart in the high country for all the time they have dominated you from their Domain? This is because when they were still coming to power, we resisted them with enough force to place doubt in their minds about how completely they could extend their control over us. For all the intervening cycles, it has been that doubt that has kept them in their Domain and given us the power to keep ourselves apart."

"Were many lost?" asked Fan

"Many," Cerrg replied. "On both sides. But our fallen did not mean defeat for us because we had already seen ourselves as fallen. The

Keepers, though, saw themselves as invulnerable, so when some of their number fell, it was truly a defeat for them—a defeat the remaining Keepers did not wish to repeat. In the end, though we were fewer in number than when we began, we were able to stand our ground against the forces of X and its Community of Keepers—a ground they have not wanted to reenter since that long-ago time."

Butlr then addressed its followers.

"It is true that the Keepers have more strength and experience in imposing their will on others than we do. But as Cerrg tells us, they also have more to fear than we do. Each Keeper has accumulated great personal privilege and status over its lifetime. The threat of losing that privilege and status is what gives X power over them. They come to confront us because X is using the power of that threat to drive them. But those running from something are never as strong as those standing up for something. We are all standing up for the idea of a free Tandor, a Tandor where we can aspire to do or be anything we wish, where a privileged few no longer rule the lives and destinies of the many, and where each being owes its support to the continued existence of every other being."

"What should we do, Butlr?" asked Pert, who had gained a certain respect from the younger members of the Awakened for its willingness to question old beliefs and its former association with the revered Sern.

"When the Keepers come at us, half of our number should stand forth to engage them," the elder replied. "At first, they will be taken aback at the strength of our resolve, but they will gain courage to press forward when it appears they can overwhelm us. Then, when they commit the rest of their force to the business of our annihilation, the remaining Awakened will enter the field from all sides to surprise them again, this time with the power of our real numbers as well as our ferocity."

"That surprise will give you the advantage," Cerrg assured them. "For all the cycles they have held sway on Tandor, the Keepers have believed that nothing should or could change, so they will not know what to do when faced with the change your massed resistance represents."

"Won't they call for more forces from the Domain? Won't they cry for the power of X to aid them in defeating those of us who remain?" asked Fan.

"Perhaps," Butlr answered. "But remember that X has never had to deal with real change since it came to power. And we have one more weapon to call upon, should the battle hang in the balance."

In chorus, together, the massed army of the Awakened chanted the name of their leader who remained hidden with its volunteers among the forces of those coming to destroy them.

As echoes of "Sern, Sern, Sern, Sern, Sern" rang and then faded between the crests of the Tandoran high country, followers of the original Questioner divided themselves into the battle groups that would soon confront the approaching menace of the Community of Keepers.

~

The overwhelming sense of righteous anger feeding the Keeper army's killing lust could be felt by all Tandorans as X's force made its way to the high country where X was certain the sinners would seek refuge. Too massive in bulk to make such a journey itself, X had sent its entire cadre of Bodywatchers and Keepers to meet the threat of sinful changers while maintaining mental contact to oversee the action.

As Sern and its undercover supporters marched along with the Bodywatchers, they took special note of those intent on gaining stature by demonstrating particular brutality in the coming conflict. Grendi, the senior Keeper Sern had replaced in the mind of X, along with its henchmen Jakkl and Stang, broadcast visions of the mayhem they planned to visit on sinners to everyone in X's mental merge.

When the peaks of the high country came into view at last, Sern sent a final message of warning to its Awakened network, hoping they had been given enough time to make what preparations they could to survive the coming onslaught.

"ATTACK!" demanded X through the merge. "THEY ARE FEWER THAN YOU AND WEAKER! THEY WILL FLEE BEFORE YOU IN FEAR! TAKE THEIR EXISTENCES FROM THEM! DO IT NOW!"

But as the Keepers surged forward to engage the group of Tandorans facing them on the rise of the first plateau, they saw that the sinners were not taking flight as X had predicted. Instead, they linked themselves together in body and mind to form a wall of resistance the Keepers had not anticipated. When a song of defiance arose from that wall to push back against the scream of rage emanating from the massed Keepers, the attacking force stalled in confusion, unsure of how to proceed when faced with the defiance of those who had always quailed before them in the past.

"FORWARD!" X ordered. "THROW YOURSELVES AGAINST THEM! I WILL KNOW WHO HESITATES AND WHO FIGHTS FOR THE DOMAIN!"

Sensing an opportunity to regain X's favor, Grendi, Jakkl, and Stang raised their voices above the mental chaos to take command. "Follow us!" they cried as the main force began to slow. "We will silence their foul noise when they see that we will not stop or show them mercy!"

As the three Keepers rushed to the forefront of their army, others fell in behind them to resume the attack. When the two sides finally joined in battle, the force of the impact could be felt throughout the planet. Young Tandorans were awakened from sleep by the mental screams of agemates in the death grip of a Keeper. Older citizens gathered their pods together to protect them from the seismic pounding coming from the body clashes in the high country. Before long, all Tandor knew that the fate of the planet hung on the outcome of a battle being waged between the forces of X and those who would oppose the Tandoran Plan for Order in All Things.

Though they had not been called to throw themselves into the fight, many Tandorans sent their mental support to one side or another. As expected, the planet's elders urged the forces of X to crush the bringers of change, while most young ones and nearly all Drifters harmonized with the struggling Awakened.

Pushed by X and pulled by Grendi, Jakkl, and Stang, the Keepers mounted an all-out assault on the front ranks of the Awakened standing on the plateau, ranks that included Pert and Lelt.

At first, the young Awakened Ones absorbed the blows from Grendi and its henchmen, struggling against their pain to stand fast for their beliefs as Butlr had urged them to do. But when the bruising clashes were followed by mental assaults that slashed through their linked consciousness to attack the essence of their beings, the young leaders could no longer sustain their bond and fell beneath the attack of the Keepers. With vicious intensity, Keepers drove their young victims into the soil and air of Tandor, snuffing out their existences as their death cries echoed throughout the high country.

Emboldened by the fall of the first rank of rebels beneath the fury of the attackers, those in the rear of X's army rushed forward to join in the slaughter and prove their worth to their all-seeing master. When the entire Domain force was committed, Sern and its undercover allies slipped out of the melee to conceal themselves behind a nearby hill. Hoping that Butlr would be able to unleash the Awakened forces in waiting before all was lost on the plateau, Sern watched in agony as it witnessed Pert and Lelt fall under the killing blows of Grendi and Jakkl, sending what comfort it could to ease their final moments.

Just as it appeared that Domain fighters would conquer the remaining Awakened, a subsonic humming crept into the consciousness of every Tandoran—the low-toned hum that X had hoped would pass when it was first perceived at the beginning of the cycle. As the annoying sound grew in intensity, it became clear that it was coming from the mental bonds of more discordant Tandorans than X and its supporters had ever imagined could exist. Instead of a temporary phenomenon as X had once thought, the hum now overpowered all mental music on the planet, disrupting merges and drowning out private communication, including X's!

With no ability to seek guidance from their commander, the Keepers paused their slaughter long enough to see a new army approaching their position from all sides. The newly arrived Awakened again linked bodies and minds with each other and those left alive on the plateau to completely surround the Keeper force. Once again, their song of defiance filled the air and the minds of everyone on the killing field. At a signal from Butlr, the joined Awakened surged forward to close the circle, eliciting strangled cries from Keepers on the edges of their compacting force as the physical blows and mental assaults from the rebels began to reduce their numbers.

When a small number of Keepers taking refuge from the battle in the center of their forces saw several Bodywatchers standing on a hill behind the lines of the encroaching force, they cried out to the one being they believed could save them, the one X had always trusted. "Sern, help us! Do not let the sinners take our existences from us!"

At the sound of their true leader's designation, the Awakened fighters paused in their determined drive to end the existences of all Keepers and turned, in unison, to the figures perched on the hill.

As the cacophony of the battle sounds subsided, Sern's mental and physical voice could be heard echoing throughout the high country. “Keepers! Surrender yourselves. No harm will come to you if you threaten no further harm to others.”

From the Awakened, poised to deliver the final blows to their enemies, a chorus of *No!* and *Kill them all!* and *We finally have them!* arose.

Using all the strength of will it possessed, Sern leaned into a final, all-out mental merge with its followers to deliver its final message. “If we do to them what they have done to us and those we cherish, what will we then stand for? Will we not become just the next group of tyrants? Have we not sacrificed our bodies and our podmates to release our world from tyrants so that all Tandorans might live without fear of domination by X or its Plan or any who would decide our lives for us?”

When it was certain the Awakened had heard and understood its message, Sern declared that the surviving Keepers should be taken to various locations in the high country to live out their existences with those who had learned to be free by knowing what they stood for.

“Now,” Sern commanded. “It is time for all who remain to return to X!”

26

Revelation

It was a press conference unlike any that had been seen before.

As a veteran of NASA press events, Tess knew that she would have to have scientific experts on the stage to lend credibility to the information being announced. Thus, sitting at a table equipped with an array of microphones were the Spacers, every one of whom had volunteered to come forward with Tess to break the news. Only Greg Banyon and Ben Fischer were missing. After weeks of planning and discussion, it had been decided that their continued anonymity may be vital if the dead man's switch ever needed to be pulled.

Due to the unorthodox nature of the announcement and not knowing how long she would be able to stay on the air once people like Ormage at the NNSA got wind of what was happening, Tess had arranged to pipe the event simultaneously to the internet, network news outlets, cable TV, public broadcasting media, and throughout the social media universe. No one on the planet who was in any way connected would be able to avoid hearing at least part of what was about to be revealed, whether they wanted to or not.

When the ambient noise subsided in the large auditorium the Spacers had rented from the Tech Museum in downtown San José, Tess stepped to the podium at the side of the stage to introduce her colleagues and address the audience members who were there in person and those listening around the world.

"Good afternoon. It's fitting that this announcement comes to you from the heart of the Silicon Valley, which many believe to be the birthplace of the innovations that have shaped our modern world. It's fitting because the news we bring today concerns what we believe to be the most ominous threat to that kind of innovation that mankind has ever known."

When her microphone emitted an ear-piercing whine indicating that someone in the AV booth had tried to increase the volume, Tess stepped back, waited for the feedback to stop, then continued, but this time with the rapt attention of the entire audience. "On the stage behind me are specialists in the fields of aerospace, materials science, physics, engineering, and biotechnology who are here to answer any questions you may have about what we're announcing today." Pausing a moment to make eye contact with the science writers and national reporters she had personally invited to the event, Tess took a deep breath and cut to the heart of the matter. "Over the past two years, proof has been found of an ongoing attempt from beyond our planet to fundamentally alter the human genome in a way that would change the very nature of our species."

When the initial silence following that statement gave way to a tidal wave of questions washing over the room, Tess held up her hand to quiet the room again. "Before we take questions, let me give you a few facts that may provide the answers you're after. First, the digital data on which we base this statement is being made available to everyone as we speak. It includes specifications for the cube satellite network launched last year that detected the low-frequency electromagnetic waves periodically engulfing our world, 3D renderings of the before-and-after effects these waves have on the human genome, statistical proof that these effects have been occurring for at least the past several decades, and experimental proof of the behavior changes likely to show up in those with altered genes, the most alarming of which is a sudden inability to cope with or adapt to new conditions. Instead of the curiosity and willingness to cooperate that helped mankind emerge from caves, individuals with altered genomes may manifest behavior that reacts primarily with fear—fear of change, fear of new ideas, and most of all, fear of each other. It is our contention that this kind of fear may be causing the unusually aggressive behaviors we've all seen become more common lately. From personal violence to religious conflicts to resurgence in the need to dominate neighboring countries and cultures, we believe those leading these movements and perpetuating these actions have been so affected by the alteration in their DNA that they are no longer able to see value in the collaborative efforts humans once employed to overcome challenges to our survival.

"Next, let me assure all of you in the audience, and everyone listening throughout the world, that even though the team that made this discovery is based here in the United States and has had ties to NASA, it is not associated with any government or government agency in this or any other country. We are an independent group of science professionals who believe we've found what may be the cause of recent social and cultural catastrophic events and hope to enlist the help of anyone who finds value in our discovery to reverse the trends we believe make the future of mankind problematic at best, and a dead end at worst.

"Finally, although we have succeeded in identifying most of the individuals who have suffered from these externally imposed genetic alterations through extensive data mining, you will not find their names in the information we are releasing. This is for their protection and for our own. While the altered behavior of these individuals may be contributing to the trends we want to reverse, they did not ask for this alteration to be visited upon them and identifying them to the world could increase the overwhelming sense of fear that may drive them. However, understanding the possible cause of their behavioral tendencies could give them an incentive to overcome their genetic drivers. As sentient beings, we all have the ability to resist reactive behavior in favor of cognitive choices, and we're hoping these altered individuals will choose to do just that. But if they don't, we recognize that our announcement today will be seen by them as a monumental threat that must be eliminated at all costs. Accordingly, our team has stashed the identities of these individuals throughout the digital world and set a dead man's switch on their release. If any members of the team go missing or our data packets become corrupted somehow, the switch will be thrown and everyone, everywhere will know who the culprits might be. All right. Now the team and I will take your questions."

Amid the sea of hands that shot up, Tess pointed to a science reporter she'd known while publishing papers for NASA. She rose and introduced herself. "Connie Swisher from *Scientific American*. If you won't tell us who these altered people are, can you tell us how many of them are out there and if they can pass on these alien genes to their offspring?"

"So there's good news and bad news about that," Tess replied. "From what we can tell through an incredibly robust data analysis, about five percent of the population whose DNA profiles exist in the digital world have been altered. Of course, less than half of the people on the planet have recorded such profiles and most of those live in what we call the industrialized world. That's the good news, I suppose. That unaltered folks still outnumber the altered population many times over. The bad news is that once your DNA is altered, you can pass that genome on to your children. We don't yet know if the altered gene is dominant or recessive. If it's found to be dominant, all children of altered individuals will manifest the traits driven by the gene. If it's recessive, two persons with an altered genome would have to mate for their children to be affected. It's a study that still needs to be made and one we hope we can get funding to conduct. Next question."

A man Tess recognized as Bob Dorner, head of SETI, the group looking for proof of intelligent life in the universe, shouted a question above the rising noise level in the room. "Who does your team think sent the invasion waves in the first place?"

"We don't know, Bob," Tess replied. "All we know for sure is that the waves originated from outside of our planetary atmosphere. As you'll see in your data packets, the waves appear to be sent for two purposes. First, to create the alterations in individual genomes that make it more difficult for those persons to adapt to change. Then, most recently, to alert us to the molecular specifics of the alterations being made. There has been speculation within our team that two different sources using the same wavefront conduit may be involved in these events, but of course, until actual contact is made, the who, what, and why questions surrounding these phenomena will remain unanswered. This is another field of inquiry that we hope will be undertaken by the aerospace community in the months and years ahead."

"Follow up question," pressed the man from SETI. "Granted that you don't know for sure, but where does your team think all this may be coming from? Pure speculation!"

"I'm going to ask Prasad Shandra, our aerospace specialist, take that one. Prasad?"

Leaning into the microphone closest to him, Prasad spoke with the assurance the Spacers had come to expect from anything he said. "We think there may be a possibility of interaction with an overlaying quantum universe. But as you say, it is pure speculation on our part."

Over the next several hours, as an unending stream of questions came in from the audience and the digital world, Tess felt the mood in the room change from shock and rampant skepticism to anxiety, and then to curiosity, a transition she was hoping to see.

When those attending the press conference in person appeared to be tiring, Tess closed the event with a final plea. "By now, you've all had a chance to look at some of our data and begin to think about what it all might mean. We know it will take some time to understand and even more time accept. But we urge you, every one of you, to open your minds to the possibilities of what may lie ahead. If we can regain the will and ability to look beyond our fears to develop the kind of technologies that will not only meet our current needs but help us grow beyond our earthbound existence, then we should look at this invasion as a wake-up call to get us back to the business of human progress. Thank you all or your time and attention."

As the Spacers exited the stage and the press began to pack up their equipment, Tess told everyone to meet back at her apartment to assess how their performance went over and speculate what the most likely reaction to their revelations might be.

27

Redemption

Xfrenda lumbered about its Domain, knocking over furnishings and crashing into walls as it screamed its outrage into the empty rooms. When the subsonic hum of the Awakened overwhelmed its connection with the Keeper army, X had been rendered mentally blind, a condition that first confused and then terrified the Tandoran leader. For the first time since it emerged from the generation tanks, X was alone. No mental music from podmates, agemates, bondmates, or followers hung in the silence around its form. No Bodywatchers or Keepers rushed to support its bulk. The crushing force of the mental and physical vacuum surrounding its existence weighed upon the tyrant as nothing ever had before, pushing it down to the floor where it remained, unable to maneuver.

After half a cycle, X detected a new timbre in the disrupting hum. Higher and louder, the source of the sound seemed to be getting closer to the fallen despot, something X hoped it was imagining in its pain and despair.

~

From the fields of the fallen on the great plain of the high country, Sern and the surviving Awakened began their slow journey toward the Domain. Joined by fellow Tandorans who had sent their songs to aid in the struggle for freedom, the moving mass soon covered the landscape from horizon to horizon.

When the throng flowed past the village where Sern's family pod was located, Delft and Mernd came out to confront their former podmate.

"What have you done, Sern?" Delft demanded, charging at the leader of the revolt. "Where are Pert and Lelt? Where are the Keepers? What has happened?"

Sern stopped its forward progress to meet the onslaught of the elders who embodied everything the Awakened had fought to defeat. Backed by the songs of its followers, Sern easily deflected Delft's physical and mental challenge. Soberly, Sern faced the two remaining members of its original family pod. "Pert and Lelt no longer exist. The Keepers you set upon them ended them, brutally," Sern said with a tang of bitterness in its tone. "Pert and Lelt, along with many, many others, sacrificed themselves to bring about a new Tandor where all may question and find their own way without the subjugation that you, and others like you, impose on family pods throughout the world."

"How dare you?" screamed Delft, demonstrating the contempt with which it had always held the young Keeper. "What do you think you are? You and your rabble are throwaways, the leftovers of a decent society. You will all soon find that X will not tolerate the

Tandor you describe, unruly and unruled. You shall see! X believes in us, not you!"

"Yes, we will see," Sern agreed, turning away from the sputtering elders, "and very soon. Farewell. May you both exist long enough to appreciate what our young ones have brought about."

~

The music emanating from the approaching mass of Tandorans was new to X, unfamiliar in its cadence and harmony. To this most aged of all Tandorans, the sound felt strangely discordant, almost chaotic compared with the orderly tempo and measured tones of traditional Keeper songs. But strange though it was, the music of the Awakened held a power that could not be denied or resisted. It was the song of the planet itself.

When Sern broached the entry hall with Butlr and Cerrg at its side, they encountered X's large moaning mass crouching on the floor, folded over on itself.

"TRAITOR!" shouted X when it recognized Sern at the head of the delegation. "YOU WERE SENT TO CRUSH THE SINNERS, NOT TO JOIN THEM!"

"I have not joined them, Lord," replied Sern with surprising gentleness. "I created them."

"IMPOSSIBLE. I EXAMINED YOU. YOU ARE MY BODY-WATCHER. YOU CANNOT TURN AGAINST ME."

"In all truth," Sern responded, slowly flowing toward the fallen form of its former master, "I have never been with you. I am the Questioner, the Keeper who first asked, 'Why'?"

"LIES! ALL LIES! I WOULD HAVE KNOWN IF YOU WERE THE QUESTIONER. YOU ARE JUST A TOOL WHOSE ANGER I FOUND USEFUL TO PUNISH THE DISLOYAL AND WEAK MINDED. YOU

ARE NOTHING!"

"And yet I stand before you at the head of an army of those you and your Keepers have abused and discarded over the millennia. I may be nothing, but they are not! They are the Awakened of Tandor."

"AWAKENED TO WHAT? THAT THEY ARE UNWORTHY OF MY NOTICE? THAT THEY ARE BENEATH THE KEEPERS IN ALL THINGS? IT IS KNOWN BY ALL DECENT TANDORANS WHO REVERE THE PLAN AND NAME ME AS THE ONE TO ENFORCE ITS SACRED TENETS. YOU STAND AT THE HEAD OF AN ARMY OF OUTCASTS WHO MY KEEPERS WILL SOON ANNIHILATE!"

"You have no Keepers left to command, X," replied Cerrg, moving toward the quivering bulk on the floor of the Great Hall. "Those spared from the battle are defeated and scattered among my villages, living apart in the high country."

"WHO DARES ADDRESS ME AS X? WHO DARES ENTER MY DOMAIN WITHOUT PERMISSION?"

"We all dare, X. All the Awakened," answered Butlr, moving to Cerrg's side. "We are here to take our world back from you and your Plan and any who act on your behalf."

"YOU CANNOT," X declared with absolute conviction. "MY POWERS ARE SO MUCH GREATER THAN YOUR PITIFUL MEWLINGS THAT I COULD DESTROY YOU WITH A THOUGHT!"

"Perhaps," Sern responded. "And we are prepared to give up our existences if we must to secure freedom for Tandor. But as powerful as you may be, X, you are now alone. Standing together, we Awakened and the uncounted number who are lending their voices to our song cannot be destroyed. As we proved in the high country, when one falls, another comes forward to take its place. Then another and another and another until those who oppose us spend their strength in futile struggle against the changes we seek. Your time is over, X. You cannot prevail. You may yet inflict pain and damage, but it will bring you no closer to victory."

A growl of rage arose from the massive form once so feared by all Tandorans.

"SO NOW YOU BELIEVE YOU WILL TAKE MY PLACE AND RULE OVER TANDOR?"

"No," replied Sern quietly. "We will merely prevent you or any of your remaining followers from retaking control of our lives and our planet. You will be confined to your Domain and forbidden to sing outside these walls for as long as you choose to exist. If you do not agree to these terms, the Awakened will join together to sing your existence to an end."

"NEVER!" X screamed.

Gathering itself into a frightening spectacle of mass and power, Xfrenda shot fiery bolts into the bodies and minds of the delegation of Awakened in its Great Hall. Reaching out to gather the songs of all "decent" Tandorans, X demanded an immediate merge to silence the music of the sinners and drive them from existence. But as the measured music of its supporters flowed in to help X restore order to the planet, its merge was met note for note with a rising volume of Awakened song that soon swamped the tyrant's combined force, leaving nothing to be heard or felt in its wake.

Sern, Butlr, and Cerrg slowly rose from the floor in front of the quivering mass of X. Damaged but not destroyed, the three leaders of the joined Awakened aimed a note of nonexistence toward their attacker, followed it with a chord of oblivion, and finished with a symphony of cleansing and infinity.

~

Outside, Sern addressed the throng of Tandorans who had massed at the walls of the Domain, the once-feared symbol of X's power and its

Plan for Order in All Things.

"Facing the power of our merged voices, X and its allies have been defeated," Sern announced. "X is no more."

Cheers went up from the crowd, with cries of "Sern, Sern, Sern Sern" echoing among the assembled.

"What now?" asked a voice from the center of the throng. "Will you lead us, Sern?"

"Not now, not ever," Sern replied. "From this time forward, you must lead yourselves and be responsible for the choices you make. My Awakened podmates will always be there to advise and guide any who have questions about what we fought for, but we must all now turn to the work of remaking Tandor into the hopeful place in the universe that it once was, so many cycles past."

28

The Shape of Things to Come

When the Spacers exited their press conference at the Tech Museum, heading for Tess's apartment, they entered a world suddenly suffering from the spasms of shifting beliefs and power structures.

With their revelation of a possibly extraterrestrial cause for the recently escalating conflicts between people and nations, they had offered a scientific basis for questioning the motives of any who promoted such conflicts. Further, the Spacers had suggested that those who impeded the spread of new technologies promising human progress might be doing so under the influence of an alien race.

As might be expected, the reaction to this news in the halls of power was immediate. As the press conference ended, the president of the United States, Jeremiah Walford, called in James Powell, the newly appointed head of NASA, to address an emergency meeting of the Cabinet. In all the years following the cancellation of the space shuttle program, no NASA chief had ever been called to the White House. As the increasingly conservative Congress slashed the Agency's budget year after year in favor of the defense spending needed to support escalating foreign wars, NASA's political importance had faded into the background until many Americans no longer knew what the Agency did or why it was given any budget at all.

Now, suddenly, the defense of the nation, if not the world, was back on NASA's plate as it had been during Space Race in the 20th Century.

"Jim, how the hell did this happen without your people giving us a heads-up?" demanded President Walford, obviously shaken by the Spacers' revelations. "How could a bunch of retirees and minor scientists nobody ever heard of beat us to the punch like this?"

"Sir," Powell replied. "NASA has not been given the funds or authorization to conduct space-based research for thirty years. Most of our top people have left in the face of government downsizing and mandatory retirements to work in the private sector, if they could find jobs, or sit on their porches and watch other countries overtake us in the sciences and space exploration. I guess these particular retirees got tired of waiting for the US to wake up to the fact that securing the safety of our nation includes securing the safety of the space around our planet."

"Spare us the lecture, Jim," said Walford, who was more used to controlling press events than being blindsided by them. "You know how it works in Washington. Whoever's got the biggest bat gets to the plate first. Since 9/11, that bat's been in the hands of the military and the intelligence community, for all the good it's done us. Now we find that defending the nation from enemies both foreign and domestic suddenly means adding space aliens to the list! My God, man! Are we convinced these people know what they're talking about? And if they do, what should we be doing about it?"

With that, Ryan Godfrey, head of the Department of Energy, spoke up. "Actually, sir, we may have had some warning that this was going to break. About a year ago, Taylor Ormage from the NNSA met with two of the people holding that press conference about a paper they wanted to present on those CubeSat findings of theirs at a NASA Space Weather Conference. At Goddard, I think. Naturally, he dismissed their claims of alien wavefronts as nonsense and warned them to drop the matter. Apparently, they didn't take his advice to heart."

"That's just great," said the commander in chief with all the sarcasm he could muster. "Ryan, I want to know why Ormage wrote them off when we still had the chance to bring all this in-house before the whole world got wind of it. Bring him in for a heart-to-heart right now and tell me if we need to find a new boss for the NNSA."

"Yes, sir," said Godfrey, turning from the conference table to speak quietly into his cell phone.

"Jim," the president continued, "you are now the head of the most important Agency in the government. I'm signing an emergency funding order to give your people whatever resources they need to get to the bottom of this whole thing and come up with a plan to protect our people from these alien waves, or whatever they are. You have one week to figure it out and report back to me."

Seeing a nod from the head of NASA, President Walford turned next to Nancy Arlington, secretary of Health and Human Services. "Nancy, I want you to get the head of the CDC in here to brief us on this genetic alteration business. Make sure that briefing includes this CRISPR technology they were going on about. Maybe we can come up with some kind of vaccine to prevent the spread of these genetic changes so I can reassure the nation that their children won't be the next incarnation of the walking dead!"

Facing the two eight-hundred-pound elephants in the room in

the persons of Brigadier General Elias Brinkley from the Department of Defense and Dr. William Mathews of the CIA, President Jeremiah Walford issued a final Executive Order. "Gentlemen, I want unmarked cars sent to find these people—all of them—to tell them they will be meeting with me at the White House tomorrow. I'll have my press secretary announce that they are being received to honor their accomplishments and to further instruct our science, health, and space communities about the ramifications of their discoveries, which is actually the truth. Above all," he emphasized with slow, deliberate speech, "do not threaten them in any way or imply that there is any need to pull that damn switch of theirs."

Mathews and Brinkley looked at each other for a moment before responding to the president's directive.

"Sir, what if they resist? If they refuse to come to the White House? What should we do then? Let them just walk away?" asked Brinkley.

"Yes, General, that's precisely what you should do. If they won't agree to come voluntarily, we'll sic the press on them to ask why they don't want to help defend the nation from this alien invasion of theirs. If the pressure to cooperate doesn't come from anyone inside the government, we can't be accused of strong-arm tactics. Don't worry, gentlemen. In the end, they'll come. I have some experience with what the press can do if they're properly motivated and see an exclusive at the end of their camera lens. In the meantime, I want you both to mount a thorough investigation of their backgrounds—each and every one. I want to know who the hell they are, who they're working for, and what kind of threat they pose if a hostile force gets hold of them. And have the NSA check out that dead man's switch to find a way to disarm it. As of right now, ladies and gentlemen, the United States Government is taking control of this situation so that we are never playing catch up again, at least not on my watch!"

***

In government centers around the world, similar meetings were taking place between heads of state and their scientific and military staffs as every world power with an active space program began to see an opportunity to displace the US from the position of prominence in space it had held since the moon landing in 1969.

In Beijing, orders were issued to acquire specifics about the configuration of the diatoms that had apparently deflected the ELF wavefronts so that similar materials could be incorporated into every spacecraft currently under construction and overlaid on the several small space stations China had installed in low Earth orbit to support their moon colony program. In the Kremlin, intense discussions were taking place between the head of Russia's resurgent military and the CEO of the Roscosmos State Corporation, the entity created to bring the financially failing space industry back under tight state control. Plans were made to build and launch a system of ELF-proof, military satellites equipped with the laser weaponry needed to disable space-based assets from other countries should Russia feel threatened by the West or any other alien civilization. In Delhi, state funds were immediately transferred into the coffers of educational institutions specializing in aerospace engineering—programs that had seen record numbers of graduates emerge in recent years to put the country on the forefront of space exploration and that had put such pressures on expats like Prasad Shandra to return to India to help their mother country. In Paris and Tokyo, the heads of the European Space Agency and the Japanese Space Agency put in urgent calls to Dr. James Powell to find out what NASA's intentions were before going to their own governments with action plans.

All at once, it seemed, the planet that had questioned the value of putting resources toward space exploration for so long was taken over by a space fever that promised to grow with every passing news cycle.

***

In the halls of a very different kind of power, meetings were also taking place. By secure telecom, Zoom, and webcam, by invitation only, CEOs of international consortiums supplying the tools of war to conflicts around the world understood how the Spacer's revelations might threaten their business models.

When the news broke that people promoting the very conflicts that kept them in business might be genetically flawed or under the influence of alien beings, a need for swift action to counter that notion was recognized by everyone engaged in the business of war. War was, after all, the biggest business on the planet. Untold monies had been funneled into the prosecution of wars, all wars. As a result, new technologies allowed to get into production had been generally focused on the development and refinement of advances that would make slaughtering the inhabitants of war zones more efficient. The war business, therefore, had become a technology-driven industry with an unlimited customer base, no price caps, and no regulatory oversight enabling international arms dealers and defense contractors of all stripes to accumulate a level of wealth that set them apart from the rest of humanity.

The possibility that some obscure scientists might put all that at risk was a turn of events that could not be tolerated. Something must be done.

"How about we make them all disappear?" asked Gerald French, CEO of a company supplying a variety of high-tech armaments to governments in Africa and the Middle East. "A car accident perhaps?"

"Tempting," responded Sheik Ali Karami, one of French's best customers and a prominent stockholder in many of the oil companies supplying fuel to military aviation interests. "But until we know more about their ability to release the names of the 'altered', as they call them, I fear we must be cautious. If the world comes to believe only the altered want to fight wars, many of our best customers will sue for peace, just to prove they've not been contaminated. For now, our goal must be to keep all this in the realm of conjecture and ensure that no names are released."

"Agreed," said a shadowy figure over the telecom connection who'd been invited to the conference but who declined to be identified by name. Fellow conspirators only knew him as Prelate, indicating, some thought, a relationship with some kind of church, but nobody knew for sure. What they knew was that Prelate always made good on his commitments to ensure that targeted governments felt the need to go to war and that the warring governments would turn to the arms dealers for supplies. "I'll approach my contacts in cyberwarfare to assist us in this matter. Until then, I suggest we remain off the public stage even more than we are now. If we are able to remove their fail-safe device, we can begin a campaign to discredit their findings. If they can be branded as charlatans, world attention will turn away from them, and we can use our ground-based assets to deal with the threat."

***

"Here they come," announced Stonger as he peered through the vertical blinds occluding Tess's front room. "Same stupid cars, as if they think everyone doesn't know who drives those black SUVs!"

The Spacers had spent the past few hours in front of Tess's TV, cycling through the news channels and sharing pizza. Although they had all agreed that the course of action they'd taken that day was the only one open to them with any significant chance that they could get their message out into the world and survive the effort, they all knew that whatever came next would probably determine the survival part. And what came next was apparently the men in black suits Tess and Richard had met at NASA Goddard, and later at Langley.

Taking a deep breath to steady her nerves, Tess answered the inevitable knock on her door. "Hi guys," she quipped, hoping to show a brave front. "Long time, no see—at least that I know about."

"Ms. Bailey, ladies and gentlemen, the president of the United States sends his greetings and congratulations on your amazing scientific achievement," intoned the tall, black-suited man sporting an obviously digital device behind his left ear and a suspicious bulge under the lapel of his jacket.

"Yeah, I'll just bet he does," called Stonger from across the room. "Okay, son, you've delivered your message, now beat it! Tess and I had enough of your company at Langley!"

Unfazed by the hostility in Stonger's tone, the black-suited man pasted a wide grin on his face in an attempt to reassure his audience that he represented no threat to them, and then proceeded to step across the threshold of Tess's apartment without waiting to be invited in. "President Walford, along with the rest of the nation, was impressed with your announcement today and would like to invite you all to the White House for a private briefing," the agent continued.

Tess and Richard looked at each other for a moment, then turned back to address their visitor.

"Is that an order? Or do we have a choice in the matter?" Stonger asked.

"Let's say it's a sincere request on behalf of the leader of the free world to enlist your help in defending our nation against the threats you have so ably identified today. We've already announced your invitation to the national press, so it will be a high-profile visit. And because it will be so high profile, the president wanted us to ensure your safety from this moment forward. If you choose not to accept his invitation, we at the Secret Service are still tasked with ensuring your safety, so we will have to establish a perimeter for your team to be maintained until further notice. If you do accept his invitation, however, we only need to accompany you until you meet with him. But it's entirely your decision."

As this was a turn of events Tess and Richard had not anticipated, they turned to confer with their friends, bunched together at the opposite end of the room.

"Wow," said Tess. "I think we've just bought ourselves some upscale protective custody, at least until we accept their 'offer' to meet with President Walford."

"Meet with the president!" exclaimed Chuck Maddock. "Really?"

"Wow!" said Anna Tran. "I never thought I'd get to do something like that!"

"Does he want to see all of us," asked Eric Chow, "or just you space jockeys? I'm just a lab rat. It's Zach who's the genius here."

"No such thing," Rojas declared. "If it hadn't been for your detection of the alterations, none of this would have happened."

"Please," said Helen. "Let stop the back-slapping for a moment and consider the question, and the risk, before us. If we're all 'invited,' and we all go, can we still use the threat of the dead man's switch to make sure they let us go home again?"

"Absolutely," Tess assured her. "Our IT team is standing by to transmit the code tonight and every night until we all feel the danger of 'disappearing' is past, if it ever is. Besides, if the world press has already been told we've been invited to brief the president of the United States, it'll be a lot harder for anyone to ignore our findings. And if we gain a bit of temporary celebrity, the glare of the spotlight may dissuade any frontal attacks being planned."

"Well I for one don't care about frontal attacks or disappearing anymore," declared Mike Murphy. "I agreed to the risks when we decided to go public with this stuff. Right now, I just want to walk into the White House with my head held high and be treated like somebody important."

"I'm pretty sure that's how they'll treat us as long as we hold those identity files over their heads," said Tess. "Prasad, what's your take on this?"

"I do not see that we have much of a choice," responded the aerospace expert. "I think I would rather have the United States government asking us polite questions than being spirited away by some other government to answer the same questions under some form of duress I do not wish to contemplate. As a naturalized citizen, I will give it a chance to earn my trust."

"Then it's decided?" asked Dick Rauch. "We're going?"

"Looks that way," said Tess. "But I get dibs on the Lincoln bedroom if we have to stay overnight!"

***

They did stay overnight, and the next three days and nights as well. After their initial photo op with Walford in the Oval Office and a quick recap of what had been announced at the press conference, the Spacers were ushered into meeting after meeting with government experts in all the scientific areas their findings touched—bioscience, physics, aerospace, mechanical engineering, communications, and computer science. At every meeting, the experts appeared to be impressed with the Spacers' personal knowledge in their fields and their ability to work together to push beyond current thinking.

The final meeting with the president on the last day of their "visit" included NASA's James Powell, Nancy Arlington from HHS, Brent Ranger from the CDC, and General Elias Brinkley representing the DOD. No press was invited.

"Ms. Bailey, Dr. Stonger, ladies and gentlemen," Walford began when everyone was seated on the sofas and chairs furnishing the Oval Office, "I want to personally thank you for giving us your time and insight over these past few days so that we might better understand what has happened, and what may lie ahead. As most of you are, or have been, connected to NASA, I'll let Dr. Powell fill you in on what is now being proposed. Jim?"

"Thank you, Mr. President," said the NASA Director, turning to face the Spacers who were loosely grouped together in the room. "First, let me ask you all something. If you were running NASA right now, and had all the budget you needed, what would you do to respond to the information you've presented?"

Glancing at her team, Tess cleared her throat and took the lead in answering Powell's question.

"With all due respect, sir, the first thing I'd do is replace everyone in NASA Legal with attorneys who have been proven to be genetically unaltered, something that can be determined quite easily with Zach and Eric's new DNA test," she said with the intensity of someone who was finally allowed to say out loud what had been eating at her for more years than she wanted to count.

When Powell expressed surprise at this statement, Tess rushed to explain.

"Look. NASA used to employ the smartest, most capable people in the world. In many Centers, it still does. Every single day, those people come up with ideas that could revolutionize their fields. And every single day, at every Center, those ideas are dismissed or shelved as soon as they get to NASA Legal. It's widely known in the private sector that there's no point in trying to license or buy any of these discoveries because someone in NASA Legal will make sure the market window will close long before any progress can be made in acquiring rights. At Ames, I have personally seen so many great concepts die like this that I often wonder why some of the remaining scientists keep trying. It's not only disheartening, it's intellectually toxic. My only conclusion as to why this situation persists is that someone, or everyone, in Legal has been so altered by the ELF waves that the mere idea of allowing something new to emerge terrifies them. But if that roadblock were removed, I think you'd see an explosion of inventions and technologies that could do great things for us, like find ways to adapt to climate change, overcome pandemics, develop new sustainable energy sources, and so on. We might even be able to find a way to defend the planet against further wavefront invasions!" she said, relieved at sharing her concerns with someone who might be able to act on them.

Then Stonger took over.

"The next thing I'd do, son, is reestablish the manned space flight program as a national priority!" To Richard Stonger, anyone under the age of seventy was liable to be called "son." "Probes and satellites are fine, but in the end, they're bloodless mechanical substitutes for the human heroes that used to turn our eyes toward the stars in the hope we could someday get to those stars."

Clearing her throat to get Director Powell's attention again, Tess summed up.

"Again, with all due respect, sir, if we can get NASA back to the inspirational track it started on, we could redirect the energy now being used to kill each other and our planet toward progressing as a species. It seems that whoever or whatever sent those destructive ELF waves our way was trying to prevent us from doing that, and frankly, sir, I'd like NASA to take the lead in defeating them!"

"Defeating them," echoed General Brinkley. "Now that's an idea I can get behind. And I think the Congress will, too, Mr. President."

"But what about the damage that's already been done?" asked

Arlington. "What would you propose we do about that?"

"Eric, Zach, you're up," Tess replied.

Zach nodded at Eric to respond to Arlington's question.

"We've just started to understand the human genome and how it works," Eric replied. "Zach and his friends in the biohacking world jumped ahead a bit, but only enough to see that alterations have happened, not nearly far enough to figure out how to fix them. We've got an idea about what may be needed to prevent it from continuing, but we don't yet have the means or the manpower to pursue those ideas, and nobody in the private sector has been anxious to fund us because as yet, there doesn't seem to be any easy or quick money in it. What we'd like to see happen is for the US government to launch a Manhattan style project in biotechnology that would have the goal of discovering what each gene in our DNA does so we can use CRISPR to 'unalter' the 'altered' without causing other problems and in the process, get a handle on eliminating some of the genetic diseases that big pharma is just starting to target!"

When none of the meeting attendees voiced any more questions or objections, Director Powell took the floor again.

"Mr. President," he said, looking directly at the leader of the free world, "in light of what we've just heard and after verifying their information with my people—at least those I still trust—I'd like to propose that Ms. Bailey be appointed to the position of Deputy Director at NASA in charge of Agency reorganization. Further, I'd like to enlist her assistance and that of Dr. Stonger and his colleagues in redrafting the NASA Mission Statement to get us back to the point where manned spacecraft can once again 'point us to the stars' as they so ably put it."

President Walford immediately cut off Tess's stunned protest with a firm, "Done. What else?"

The CDC's Brent Ranger was next to chime in.

"Sir, in the same vein, after a thorough vetting process is conducted to identify any altered employees who may have escaped detection of an overt no-can-do attitude, I propose Dr. Chow and Dr. Rojas be appointed to head a new Division of Genetic Studies under the auspices of my Agency to pursue the goals they've outlined here today. Of course, that would mean access to an open checkbook from Congress, but if the alternative to funding such studies is that a similar vetting process be required of all our elected representatives, I have a feeling most senators and congressmen will go along with the proposal."

Again, Walford affirmed the suggestion with a quick "Done." When the Spacers had time to digest what had just happened, Walford concluded the meeting with a final request.

"Gentlemen, ladies, the one area of your findings we have not addressed is the computer science you've utilized for Dr. Shandra to suggest that influence from a parallel quantum universe may be involved. And given that he is primarily an aeroscience engineer and not a computer scientist, why don't you tell us who is missing from your group and where they happen to be at the moment?"

"We can't do that, Mr. President," Tess responded firmly. "Even though we are all thrilled with your offers to make the changes we believe are needed, our only real assurance that those offers will materialize lies in the fact that the identities and locations of our IT team remain unknown so they can keep their fingers on our dead man's switch. Until we believe we no longer face being dismissed as crackpots or made to go away by whatever means are available, we're going to keep that little insurance policy in place. Now if that means you need to rescind your offers, then we'll walk out through the front door and tell the world press how hospitable and welcoming you and your administration have been and ask if anyone else out there is interested in pursuing our ideas."

As Walford scanned the faces of the Spacers in his office, he saw that they were of one mind on this point and decided not to risk letting a foreign power benefit from what these people could offer.

“Agreed, Ms. Bailey. We’ll leave it there for now. Our previous offers stand and will be announced to the White House press corps within the hour. But when the time comes that you no longer feel threatened, I’ll expect you to bring your computer team in from the cold.”

29

Contact

Greg Banyon and Ben Fischer watched the press conference from their workstations in the basement of the Mothership with a mixture of pride and dread. When Tess got to the part about having a computer-based means of disclosing the personal identities of altered individuals, Greg turned to Ben and winked.

"Watch! I'll bet you a case of anything you're drinking that hack attacks will be coming in faster than the ELF waves ever did," he said, not entirely sure he was joking.

Within an hour of the conclusion of the press event, Greg's prediction was proven correct. Although nobody was told of the Spacers' connection to the iconic computer company employing Greg's team, nothing remained a secret in the age of the internet for long. The digital record of gate entries over the past several months would ultimately tell a dedicated search algorithm how many times individual

Spacers had visited a "friend" in the company's quantum computing division, when that friend had been hired away from his previous position at NASA Ames, and where he most likely was located on the campus.

But knowing who and where did not give digital snoopers a way to access the what that was being protected by Halley's sophisticated data structures.

"So now it's a race," Ben surmised. "Can they get to us before we out them? What do you think is happening to Tess and the others? They haven't called in since the cameras were turned off."

"I guess we'll find out tonight when they either check in with the 'hold fast' code or they don't," said Greg, turning back to his screen. "And if they don't, you and I and our families and anyone we care about will have to use our exit plan after we pull the trigger and hope for the best. Personally, spending the rest of our days in that tropical paradise off the grid is starting to sound pretty good to me!"

"No, Greg. I know you," said Ben, picking up his data tablet. "You couldn't sit on a beach without access to your Halley for very long before you started barking at the coconuts or scrambling around like the crabs! I know that because I feel the same way."

"Yeah, I guess you're right. But until we have to run for the exits, let's make sure these cyber attackers can't get into Halley's memory core. As good as they are, I don't think anyone else on the planet has gotten as far into quantum computing as we have, at least not yet."

When Tess and Richard called in that night to send the hold fast code and let the two computer scientists know what had happened at her apartment, Greg and Ben were relieved, but still on alert.

It wasn't until several days later when the White House press corps announced the appointments of individual Spacers to new high-level government positions that they began to relax and return to the fascinating pursuit of building the first, fully functional quantum-based computer on the planet. As the months went by and the daily hold fast code continued to come in like clockwork, the sense of threat and urgency that had kept them hunkered down in the lab began to ease. To the delight of Greg's department manager, who still had no idea he was protecting the most highly sought-after secret in the digital universe, the two computer engineers began to make some real progress with Halley's functionality.

Cyberattacks in the form of sophisticated code worms and Trojan horse programs continued to batter at Halley's I/O ports, but after a while even that form of threat appeared to subside when no chinks were found in the Spacers' IT armor. From their secure location, Greg and Ben watched with satisfaction as Tess and the Spacers slowly implemented the changes at NASA they had all agreed were vital if the US were ever to retake the lead in space exploration. When the budgetary restraints were removed from previously hobbled research initiatives at NASA Centers throughout the country, an explosion of new technologies emerged in the public and private sectors. The unprecedented number of new patents and product licenses injected a level of venture capital into the world economy that had not been seen since the end of the Great Recession in 2012.

By that time, everyone had relaxed into what they believed to be the beginning of a scientific renaissance, so when their SpacerNet alarm alerted them all once again that something astonishing was happening, they reluctantly made their way back to the Mothership to see what new challenge they had to face and overcome.

~

Sernl was leading a semicyclical merge with its growing family of Awakened podmates when their soothing, reassuring song took on a new, vibrant tone.

For all the cycles that had passed since the demise of X and the restructuring of Tandoran society, Sern, who had aged enough to earn the longer designation of Sernl, had labored to refocus the talents and strengths of its kin into the healing of wounded souls once known as Drifters and the reeducation of those who clung to the tenets of the now-repudiated Plan. It had been an arduous task, but one that Sernl found fulfilling when it realized that most citizens had finally given up their need to control others in favor of improving themselves.

Toward that end, Sernl had offered instruction to its podmates on how to meld their music into the kind of merge that could see beyond Tandor to observe the wonders of other times and places, the purpose of these excursions being to experience the joy of creation instead of attempting to restrain it.

When Sernl's merge came upon the sentient beings that had first fired its need to question the Plan, its podmates sensed their leader's excitement and changed the tone of their merge to match it.

"Long ago, in the time of X, we once tried to prevent these beings from learning of us and of the glory of life," Sernl sung within the mixed mind of the merge. *"When we began our quest to restore honor to Tandor, we sent a message of warning to this species in the hope they would receive it and find a way to throw off the effects of X's invasion into their timeline. From that time to this, we have not returned to see if our message was received, but it appears they are once again making the progress that will put them back on the common evolutionary path of all sentient species."*

"Shall we send another message, Sernl?" hummed the mind of the many. *"Shall we tell them of our new purpose?"*

"No more messages," Sernl sang in counterpoint. *"Let us simply open our minds to their universe to find if they can hear us yet."*

And as they sang in multimodal harmonies, an alignment between the two realities was created, an alignment that was detected by something or someone designated as "Halley."

***

"Well congratulations, fellas," said Stonger as the entire group of Spacers assembled in Greg's lab. "You've succeeded in blowing your cover by bringing us all here. You know we're under constant watch by the FBI, CIA, and NNSA. I'm fairly certain the Secret Service follows every move we make and investigates everyone we meet. What the hell is so important that you'd want to put yourselves and all of us in the line of fire?"

When Ben and Greg just smiled back at the agitated group for a moment, Prasad picked up on their excitement and leaped to a conclusion that took even him aback.

"You've done it, haven't you?" he asked. "You've achieved discoherence!"

"Disco-what?" asked Maddock. "Speak English, please."

"Discoherence," Ben replied with an ecstatic grin on his face. "The place where two quantum states share the same environment for enough time that direct, linear communication is theoretically possible. The math will break your brain, and the theory has been unprovable because, until now, the common environment required for discoherence to exist is near absolute zero, Kelvin."

"That's cold, right?" asked Murphy. "Really cold?"

"You could say that," replied Stonger. "It's only been achieved in the laboratory under extraordinary conditions. Basically, it's the background temperature of outer space."

"Fine, fine," said Maddock. "You've gotten it really cold in here. So what?"

"So," said Greg looking at Ben with a smile of delight that could light up the room, "when we got it 'really cold' in here, Halley got a real-time communication from another quantum state, another quantum universe, if you will."

"What kind of communication," Tess demanded. "What was communicated?"

"From what we could tell, someone or something said 'Greetings. We come in peace.'"

TANDORAN LEXICON

PLACES

The Domain - massive complex built to house the Founders and the Keeper Community

High Country - mountainous, rocky areas that border the plains

The Plains - fertile, planet-circling grasslands farmed by family groups known as pods for crops that sustain the population of Tandor

INHABITANTS

Founders - ancient Tandorans that created the Tandoran Plan for Order in All Things

Keepers - High status Tandorans with exceptional mental skills that enforce the harsh rules of the Plan on Tandorans and other sentient beings in the multiverse

Drifters - Damaged or disgraced Keepers that wander the planet as itinerant workers

Awakened - Tandorans that reject the dictates of the Plan to pursue their own life paths

Isolationists - Tandorans that have refused to follow to the Plan and have chosen to live apart in the planet's high country to remain safe from the Keepers

INDIVIDUALS

X - the last surviving Founder, Xfrenda - reverently known as X - that possesses the most powerful mental abilities on the planet and that rules over the Keepers

Grendi - X's second-in-command

Sern - young Keeper that secretly questions the value of the Plan and becomes the leader of the Awakened

Lelt and **Pert** - Sern's empathetic young agemates in its family pod

Delft and **Mernd** - stern elder leaders of Sern's family pod

Butlr - Sern's Awakened second-in-command

Cerrg - leader of the Isolationists

ACKNOWLEDGMENTS

The greatest gift anyone can give an author is reading what they write, especially in the beginning. Although many friends and colleagues were consulted during the writing of this novel, three individuals were there for the entire journey.

My husband, Michael Mangini, who not only encouraged me to begin but required me to finish, no matter the outcome.

Margaret Marshall, who read each chapter as it was formed, begging for more to see "what happens next" even before I'd figured it out.

Marla Arcadi, who delighted in my writing a fictional story about the time we shared as office mates at NASA Ames.

To these, and any other readers who sometimes wonder what their lives could possibly mean in the long run, I give my thanks for going on the journey with me to discover an answer that they, too, might share.